"Action, intrigue, and high stakes drama — just what you want from a thriller. Toss in a little lust and greed, and it's the perfect mix for a classic, on-the-run adventure."
- Steve Berry, *New York Times* and #1 Internationally Bestselling Author

"Landon Beach is the real deal. And *The Sail* is a top-notch thriller with suspense to burn!"
- Ted Bell, Author, *NY Times* Bestselling Alex Hawke Series

"Hoist *The Sail* for an enrapturing voyage across Lake Superior that thrills, enlightens, and keeps the pages flying to the very end."
- Dirk Cussler, *New York Times* Bestselling Author

"*The Sail* is a fast-paced thriller with plenty of action and some welcome wisdom too. Read it."
- Thomas Perry, *New York Times* Bestselling Author

"This book has it all. Landon Beach combines the emotional and heartwarming journey between father and son with a taut, tense thriller set in the hauntingly beautiful waters of Lake Superior. Just when you thought it was safe to get back in the water..."
- Robin Burcell, *New York Times* Bestselling Author

"*The Sail* is exactly the kind of adrenaline-fueled page-turning fun that you'd expect from an author named Landon Beach. This book earns my highest compliment... I wish I'd written it."
- Jeff Edwards, bestselling author of *Steel Wind* and *The Damocles Agenda*

"*The Sail* is both touching, poignant and suspenseful. Not everyone can touch your heart and also keep it beating like a drum…The end is a great surprise, and beyond moving—I was a bit overwhelmed, and that is really what I expect from a novel. Thrilling, chilling and rewarding."

- Peter Greene, award-winning author of The Adventures of Jonathan Moore series.

"Having read Landon's first book, *The Wreck*, I had to read this new one. The author develops both characters and plot in a way that systematically unfolds and draws the reader in. Most of what I read is set in tropical climes, so reading a sailing adventure set in the Great Lakes was new for me. I thoroughly enjoyed this book!"

- Wayne Stinnett, Author of the Jesse McDermitt Caribbean Adventure Series

THE SAIL

Landon Beach

Landon Beach
Visit my website at landonbeachbooks.com

Printed in the United States of America

First Printing: February 2019
Landon Beach Books

ISBN-13 978-1-7322578-1-8

For Becca, Paige, and my students. The greatest gift of being a father and a teacher is the time I have spent with you—and what I have learned from you. I love you all.

THE SAIL

PROLOGUE

NOVEMBER 10, 1975 - 7:00 P.M.

The seaplane was off course. Twenty minutes ago the navigation systems had failed, and now Captain J. W. Wilson was piloting a descent through a storm. He should radio for help, but no one was supposed to know that they were up here tonight. Nothing was visible: his backup option was pissing away with the barrage of raindrops obscuring the windows and trailing off into the wind. If he could only see a strip of water where they could land, anchor the seaplane, and ride out the storm on the beach.

A bolt of lightning lit up the sky outside the co-pilot's window. Thunder boomed as loud as if it were fed into the earphones the men were wearing. The plane banked to the left as Wilson jerked the controls—eyes wide open—and then eased them back to level the plane.

"Sweet Jesus that was close, pally," said the co-pilot Jimmy Morris.

"Almost too close," Wilson said taking a sip from a flask. The liquid burned on the way down. A little Jacky Dee to calm the nerves.

He screwed the top back on and then placed the flask inside his flight jacket. Well, flight jacket was generous. It was a dirty parka with *J. W.* stitched on the breast and *Captain* stitched underneath. They had been advised to fly without any identification in case they were searched. But Captain J. W. Wilson didn't give a shit. No jacket, no flight. No wallet, no flight. No flask, no flight. Why not? He was down to a pint a day.

"We should start seeing water soon," Morris said, peering out the window. "There's no way we could still be over land."

And how would you know that, Jimmy boy? We haven't known where we were for the past twenty minutes. Wilson jerked his thumb toward the aft of the plane. "Bring the bags forward and have them ready in case we've gotta ditch. I'm not showing up with nothing."

Morris looked back at the black bags heaped on each other behind the back bench, then his eyes met Wilson's. "Ditch? Man, you think it'll come to that?"

Wilson brought the bill of his tattered Boston Red Sox baseball cap—he'd never seen a Red Sox game—down close to his eyebrows and then focused on the descent again. "Just get them."

Morris unbuckled his safety harness and moved out of the cockpit. Lightning flashed again and the plane dipped to the right this time, enough for Morris to lose his balance and hit his head on the cargo door. "For Chrissakes, keep her level, pally. I just about left the building."

Wilson ignored him and continued to ease the controls forward. The rain stopped. There seemed to be an opening in the clouds below and he flew toward it. As they descended, it began to snow.

Morris got his footing and then knelt on the back bench. He grabbed the two bags and placed them on the seat next to him. Sweat beaded on his forehead, slid down his nose, and dripped onto the bench as he turned around and sat down. He started to unzip one of the bags.

"Keep it closed," Wilson ordered from the cockpit.

"Aw, c'mon, man. Don't you want to know what we've been carrying for the past six months? Especially now, since we might pay the piper."

"You know the contract," Wilson said. "Besides," he paused, "you don't want to end up like Wilford, do you?"

They both thought back to June.

Five Months Earlier

The plane glided to a stop on the moonlit surface of the water. Wilson shut down the engine and Morris moved aft to open the cargo door. Water lapped against the seaplane's pontoons, and a stiff summer breeze blew into the plane. Wilson joined him and together they positioned the two bags on the back bench. Once this was done, Morris jumped down onto one of the pontoons. Wilson passed him a pair of binoculars.

Morris scanned the horizon. "We radio them, right?"

"We maintain radio silence, Jimmy."

Morris dropped the binoculars around his neck. "Oh, right," he said.

Wilson could see that Morris was nervous. Couldn't blame him, though. Wilson had been scared out of his crow his first time. "Don't be asking any questions when they show up. Just pass the bags to the boat crew *very* carefully," said Wilson. "Then we get right back in the plane and head home."

"Do we ever find out what's in the bags?" The binoculars were up again as Morris scanned for the boat.

"Don't you listen?" Wilson said. "It's all part of the deal. The bags take off from Vancouver by truck, travel through Winnipeg, and end up at our seaplane dock in Lake of the Woods where we load the bags and lake hop until we touch down here in Lake Superior. We deliver the bags, don't say no fuckin' word to nobody, and then head back and wait until we're needed again."

"Okay, okay, pally. Lighten up," Morris said. "Where do the bags go after we transfer them?"

"No clue," said Wilson, "and I don't wanna know."

"What happened to your last co-pilot?"

The motor of a powerboat in the distance could be heard. Wilson looked at his watch: 1:25 a.m. "It's them. Get ready."

Morris scanned left and saw nothing. Holding on to the wing with one hand, he leaned out over the water. Farther to the right he thought he could see the outline of a boat approaching them with no running lights on. "I think I've got 'em."

"Remember, not a word," said Wilson.

"Aye, aye, sir," Morris saluted with a shaky grin.

Wilson didn't hear him as he ducked back in the plane. He moved to the cockpit and retrieved a revolver from under his seat. If they thought of pulling anything tonight, he'd be ready. No way would he be taken as easily as Wilford had been. Dumb. So dumb. Why did Wilford have to look in the bags? Why did he have to ask the men on the boat about the contents? Stupid. Captain J. W. Wilson had been sober for three years, but when they took Wilford away that night, he'd broken at the first waypoint home. The metallic scraping sound of the lid being unscrewed. The aroma from the first whiff as he put his nose over the bottle. The watering of his mouth. The sweat on his neck. The feel of the smooth bottle in his weathered hands. The slow deep breaths and the thump of his heart as he raised the bottle to his mouth. And, finally, the first warm spirits hitting the back of his throat as he sucked on the bottle and gulped. Liberation. Heaven. The dulling of pain.

The memory of Wilford's screams lanced through his mind, and he had to shake his head to snap out of it. He slid the gun in between his belt and trousers and then untucked his shirt to cover it.

The boat approached, and two men in dark t-shirts and blue jeans—one he'd dubbed "Tall" and the other "Gun"—walked to the stern of the cabin cruiser. Tall picked up a line as the third man—the helmsman—backed down the boat and then cut the engine. Tall threw the line to Morris. His hands were sweaty, and he almost dropped it but got a grip and secured it to the pontoon.

Tall and Gun pulled on the line until the starboard gunwale was a foot or two away from the pontoon and then tied the line off to a pair of cleats.

Wilson tapped Morris's shoulder, and Morris looked back and then took the bag Wilson was holding out. He transferred it to Gun, and Gun passed it to the helmsman who stowed it below.

When Morris passed the second bag over the gunwale, Tall spoke to him.

"Come aboard. We've got something to show you," Tall said.

Morris snapped his head around to Wilson and looked at him as if asking: *what do I do?*

Wilson just nodded.

The helmsman took the second bag below as Tall and Gun helped Morris board. Wilson began to slide his hand under his shirt but stopped when the helmsman reappeared. Tall uncleated the line and threw it to Wilson.

"We'll be back in ten minutes," said the helmsman.

Wilson gave a thumbs up sign and began coiling the line. Fifty-fifty chance he'd never see Morris again.

The helmsman turned on the engine and drove the boat away. Three minutes later, he shut off the engine and Tall went below and returned with a weight belt, mask, and dive light. "Strip down to your skivvies, Jimmy," Tall ordered.

"What the—"

Gun cut Morris off. "Are you supposed to be talking?"

Morris shook his head and began removing his clothes.

Tall motioned to the water off the stern. "We need a little help tonight. There's some...some *thing* down there that we need to make sure is staying put." Tall bent down over the transom and dipped his hand in Lake Superior. "Water's not too bad tonight, but I advise that you make it quick."

Morris was in his underwear now, ghost white legs and sunken chest with small patches of hair exposed to the night air. He shivered as Tall passed him the equipment.

"It's about fifteen feet straight down, toothpick. We'll wait for you up here," Tall said.

Morris sat on the deck and swung his feet over the stern. The water rose up past his ankles. His rear began to feel cold as the water on the deck soaked his underwear. He turned on his light and jumped in.

The shock of the cold water made him shake, and he almost dropped the light. The weight belt did its job: he continued to sink. Once he made it to the bottom he would look for this thing and then get the hell out of there. Yes, he was freezing, but this should be easy.

It came out of the dark as his feet hit the lake floor and he swung his light around. A human body with no arms, one eyeball missing, and small bites taken out of its face and legs. The legs. The legs were anchored to the lake bottom by heavy duty rope and two cinder blocks. Morris went to scream, but then he saw a silver chain around the neck. He reached for it. At the end of the loop was a flattened rectangle of silver. Holding the rectangle in his hand, he aimed the light down and read the inscription: "Fast" Eddie Wilford. Now he screamed, sending a stream of bubbles up.

The sound of the motor starting above made Morris drop the chain, release the weight belt, and he kicked upward.

His head broke the surface of the water, and he looked up into the eyes of Tall, peering down at him over the transom. "Don't ever look in the bags or talk about your job," Tall said. Morris nodded. Then, Tall turned around, and the boat sped away.

Fifteen minutes later, the seaplane was taxiing toward Morris.

Wilson steered the plane through the snowy gap in the clouds, and he could finally see below. "Water, Jimmy."

Morris rejoined him in the cockpit and strapped back in. The plane continued to angle down, and the storm began to let up. Morris looked at the water. "I told you we had to be over water, J. W. Now, we just gotta find a place to let her down near shore."

7:10 p.m.

Enormous waves crashed over the "Pride of the American Flag" *Edmund Fitzgerald*'s deck. Loaded with 26,116 long tons of taconite pellets from Burlington Northern Railroad Dock at Superior, Wisconsin, the 729-foot ore carrier pitched and heaved in the churning water, trying to find a magic line through the eighteen-foot seas. Water crested over the port side, spread across the deck and over the hatch covers, and then slid over the starboard side back into the lake. At the dock in Wisconsin, deckhands had secured the 21 hatch covers—each hatch needing 68 clamps manually fastened. Thankfully they hadn't broken this routine or they might have sunk hours ago.

Captain Earnest McSorley stood in the pilothouse clinging to a radar console that was bolted to the deck—and inoperable. The bow rose as the *Fitz* climbed a wave. McSorley lunged for the radio console and held tight as the ship dipped and screamed into the trough. Fresh vomit from the quartermaster slid on the deck toward McSorley's feet and then slid back as the bow began to rise again. The veteran captain grabbed the radio's microphone. In 44 years he had never been in conditions like this, and for the first time he felt fear—not for himself, but for the twenty-eight other men onboard that were his responsibility.

His ship had been traveling with the *Arthur M. Anderson*, a freighter also carrying taconite pellets, since yesterday. The *Anderson* was presently aiding the *Fitz* in navigation; McSorley had radioed *Anderson*'s captain, Jessie B. Cooper, two hours earlier to explain that *Fitz* had a bad list, had lost both radars, and was taking heavy seas over the deck. Additionally, the *Fitzgerald* carried no fathometer or depth gauge. To measure the depth of the water, the *Fitz* still used a hand lead. A crew member would stand at the bow and drop a line with a weight attached to the end overboard. When the weight hit the bottom, the crew member would report the depth. Sending a man out to do that now would be sending the man to his grave.

"*Fitzgerald* to *Anderson*, over," McSorley said into the microphone.

Another wave: McSorley lost his grip on the radio console and the sixty-two-year-old fell to the deck and slid away, arms grasping for anything to hold on to.

"This is *Anderson*, over," a weathered voice answered over the speaker.

McSorley's right hand found a fire extinguisher bolted to a bulkhead, and he held on as the next wave began to lift the *Fitzgerald*. When the ship began to level out, McSorley pulled his way back to the radio console.

He keyed the microphone. "Read you loud and clear, Cap. How is our heading and position?"

"Caribou Island and Six Fathom Shoal are well behind us. There's a line of ships nine miles ahead that will pass you to the west," the first mate on the *Anderson* answered. "How is *Fitzgerald* handling?"

McSorley looked out the pilothouse windows at the snow falling down and limiting visibility to no further than just beyond the bow: they were blind. He looked up at the anemometer. *65 knot winds.* He was about to speak into the microphone when waves crashed over the pilothouse sending a wall of water over the deck. The seas had increased to twenty-five feet. One cargo hold hatch had failed...maybe more. *We may not make it. My crew is sick, beaten up, and this witch of a November gale is wearing down the old girl.* He keyed the mic. "We are holding our own."

"Look at that sonofabitch twist and turn," Morris said. He was looking out the seaplane's window at a huge cargo ship being tossed by the gigantic slate colored seas below.

J. W. Wilson swiveled his head and took a quick peek out Morris's window. "I'm glad we're up here, Jimmy," said Wilson. He tried the radio switch. Dead.

"Please don't try and land us down there," said Morris. "Those waves would bend this plane into a pretzel."

"I don't plan on it," said Wilson. Then, he motioned down to the ship. "She must be headed for the safety of a harbor or bay. We might be close to land." Wilson steered the plane to the right.

"Hey! I can't see her anymore," Morris said.

"I'm going to try and parallel her course," said Wilson, "it's our best chance of surviving this thing with our radio and nav equipment fried." Wilson began to steady up on a course. Then, he looked out his window. "Okay, Jimmy. You can sneak a peek of her—oh my God!"

Morris almost joined Wilson in the captain's seat as both men looked below.

The giant ship had nearly folded into a 'V'. A few mangled lifeboats floated away in the huge seas as the water lifted the ship—flattening it out for a moment—and then snapped it in two.

"She's goin' down!" Morris shouted in terror.

First the fore, then the aft section slid below into the deep. For a few seconds nothing remained on the surface. Then, the Great Lake seemed to burp, and a few pieces of flotsam came up, including what looked like an inflatable life raft.

"Gone," Wilson said.

Morris sat back in his seat and, for some reason, began to cry. Wilson circled the spot where the ship had been. He saw no one in the water. "Gone."

Wilson pulled out his flask and took a healthy pull. Morris was sniffling and looking out the window at the snow. The winds had shifted. There was nothing they could do about the ship. How many had gone down with her? Wilson screwed the cap back on the flask, leveled the plane out, and steadied onto the course that the ship had been steering.

* * *

Wilson's hands began to feel cold. He looked down at the heater. The familiar hum from the vents had disappeared. All he heard now was the steady sound of the propellers, engine, and Morris's snoring. Shit. What else is going to break? The cold moved to his neck. He shivered and slapped both of his cheeks. How much time had passed? A half-hour? An hour? Fifteen minutes? The blank stare syndrome reserved for monotonous spaces of time had taken hold of him. Wilson could see himself loafing around the mall, high, listening to Milt Jackson or in his senior year algebra class hearing the bell ring, the teacher starting to talk about something he had no interest in, staring at the wall—zoning now—noises dissipating, a white blur, other thoughts that refused to become clear, and...the bell announcing the end of class. Another forty-five minutes lost to the ages. Same deal for driving on a long boring interstate: jolting upright in one's seat—*where in the fuck am I?*

Wilson pulled on a pair of gloves and woke Morris.

"Heater's gone, Jimmy boy," said Wilson, "better put on your jacket."

Morris squinted and then rubbed his eyes. "Where are we?"

The snow was gone and the plane seemed to be descending.

"See that?" Wilson pointed out the window.

On the horizon was land.

Morris sat up. "Yee haw, bubba! We're gonna make it out of this mess after all."

"Just in time," Wilson said. "If the heater's gone, I don't wanna find out what's next."

"I'm gonna get me a paper tomorrow and see about that ship we saw go down. We'll be celebrities being the only ones who know how she sank."

Wilson pulled on Morris's collar and brought the co-pilot's face to within six inches of his own. He stared into Morris's eyes. "We're not talking to anyone," he ordered. "Have you forgotten what we're carrying back there?"

Morris broke eye contact and looked toward the back bench. Then, at Wilson.

"Uh huh," Wilson said. "We've gotta figure a way to get that delivered before we say a word about the ship." He released Morris's collar. "Understood?"

Morris sat back. "Yeah."

Wilson began to focus on flying again. Suddenly, the plane dropped. "What the—"

"Look!" Morris said.

The right propeller began to slow down...then, it stopped. For a moment, both men just stared at the motionless blades. They both shot their eyes to the left propeller and watched it slow down, sputter, and then stop...

Scrambling in the cockpit: Morris in the backseat reaching for the bags, Captain J. W. Wilson fighting with the controls.

The plane diving toward the water.

Screaming...

...Impact.

Explosion in the fuselage—one man burning. More screaming. One man trying to exit the plane, but pinned.

Water flooding the cockpit and fuselage.

Fire on the water.

The wreckage sank below the surface, putting out the fire, leaving only the moon's reflection on the black water.

Landon Beach

PART I

Preparations

1

LAKE HURON

OFFSHORE HAMPSTEAD, MICHIGAN, JUNE 1995

The bow flattened the waves and the wake gurgled as the thirty-six-foot sailboat came about.

"Trist, get ready to tighten her up," Robin Norris shouted over the wind to his son as the boom swung overhead and snapped to a halt.

Tristian Norris pulled on the mainsheet, and the sail became pregnant with air. *Levity* heeled to starboard, and the smooth wooden hull began to slice through Lake Huron.

Robin looked up at the tattletales on the mainsail; both were streaming taut, parallel to the boom. "Cleat her," he said and sat down behind the wheel. Trist did and sat back down on the starboard cockpit bench.

"She looks seaworthy to me," Trist said.

It was the final trial run—an overnighter—before they left for their summer sail, *the* summer sail that Robin had promised Trist since they had purchased the boat three years ago. The previous day had been filled with practicing procedures they would carry out in emergency situations: man overboard, collision, fire, abandon ship, loss of equipment, foul weather, and any medical situations that arose. When they had bought the rotting, abused, and broken boat from marina owner Ralph Shelby for practically nothing—Shelby said it would never float again and just wanted to get it off his hands—Robin had set the bar at not only getting the yacht to sail again but to circumnavigate Lake Superior the summer before Tristian's senior year in high school.

Last night, they had anchored, tested the new grill Robin had mounted on the aft rail, and slept under the stars. There were always *problems* with a boat, but it appeared that there was nothing to stop them now from attempting the voyage.

"A few days to load supplies, get this beast on a trailer, and take her up," Robin said. "Tomorrow's your last day at the hardware store, right?"

"What's mom going to do with us gone all summer?"

Robin watched as Trist's black hair blew across his forehead. His hair was smooth and longer like his mother's and behind Trist's Ray-Ban sunglasses were the same brown eyes as hers too. Trist's skin was a blend of Robin's Caucasian and Levana's Chippewa heritage—closer to Levana's in the summer, Robin's in the winter. Why was he noticing these things at this moment? He knew. Since the diagnosis, he had been in a hyper-sensitive state of observation. Familiar things: the amount of air in the tires on the car, exactly how much toilet paper was left on the roll in each bathroom, how many beers were on the top shelf of the refrigerator, the bottom shelf. Weird things: a detailed inspection of how much dirt was on his socks before putting them in the hamper, how much dust was on top of the fridge, how many napkins were in the holder on the kitchen counter. Even sentimental items: what earrings Levana had on (he'd never taken time to notice before), the family photographs in the hallway, and now his son's skin color, which he'd known from the moment Trist had come out of the womb and Robin had picked the doctor up, thrown him over his shoulder, and—he still didn't know why—spanked the doctor's bottom in celebration.

"Dad?" Trist said.

Robin's head jerked. "Yeah, bud?"

"You're zoning out again. I just asked what you thought mom would do while we're gone."

Was he being too selfish? Should they not go? Christ, after the past year, did Trist even want to go anymore? Should Levana come with them? No, she had made that clear. This was his time to make things right with his son.

"Probably relax without us bothering her," Robin said. A safe and weak answer. "What time does Uncle Tyee want you in tomorrow?"

"Same as always, seven." Trist looked at the shoreline in the distance. "Yeah, mom deserves some alone time."

He might have had most of his mother's looks, but his frame was a carbon copy of Robin's, only—and Robin hated to concede the point, though couldn't tell you why he struggled to—Trist was actually two inches taller than his 6'1". *Enjoy the 170 pounds at 17, kid. The question is: could you keep it under the 200-pound line for 20 more years like your old man had?* Robin paused, letting the question ruminate. Another small battle lost in the fight to not ask himself questions that he would not be around to answer. *Well, Levana will see if he can do it. Maybe next month's test results will bring the unreliable and unrealistic word of 'hope' out of the graveyard.* He was glad that Tristian didn't know about *that* yet.

How many times had he wanted to bring it up as an eye-opener, a bargaining chip? But he had resisted. Pity was not the way to curtail adolescent behavior. And *that* was *not* the way to let a child know that his father was on borrowed time. Parents are the bones that children sharpen their teeth on. And as much as Trist's teenage years had gnawed away at Robin's skeleton, and as many nights as he had wanted them to be over, now, he wished they would go on.

"Dad?" Trist said.

Sweat beaded on Robin's forehead, and he ran a hand over his closely cropped hair. His stomach felt queasy. Water was building behind his eyes, and his sunglasses were on the verge of becoming blurry. He gripped the steering wheel harder. He would not lose it here.

"Dad." Trist said louder.

Robin turned his head toward Trist. "What's up?" he mumbled.

Trist pointed up at the main sail. "We're luffing."

Thank God. Something else to concentrate on. "Good call. We fell off a bit."

"*You* fell off a bit."

Robin ignored the critique. Don't fire back at him when he challenges you, Levana had said. Robin turned the wheel, and as the boat changed course, the sails became full again. "Ready to head in and start our preps?"

"I guess so," Trist said. "Need me up here right now?"

It had been like this since they had left yesterday morning. When he wasn't needed, Trist wanted to be as far away from Robin as possible—down in the cabin getting lost in a movie or book, or napping. At least they didn't have enough money for one of those ridiculous sat phones, or cell phones, or whatever the hell they were. What a waste of time and money that would be. However, he could see the day coming, and Robin Norris detested it.

"Trist—" Now was not the moment to fight him about time spent together. "I—"

Trist exhaled.

Maybe it was. "Well, you know we're going to be spending a lot of time together over the next 3 months."

"Yeah, I know. What's your point?"

"What I mean is that we can't spend the whole time just sailing and when the work is done go off into our respective caves."

18

"Do we have to talk about this now?"

Yes! He wanted to spend every waking minute he had left with him. "No, but I want you to think about it."

Trist rose and headed for the hatch leading down into the boat's cabin.

"Trist?"

Trist paused at the top step. "Call me when we get close to the marina," he said and then disappeared below.

2

R obin secured the last of *Levity*'s lines to the dock, and the boat rested in her berth at Shelby's Marina. A cooler and two duffle bags sat on the dock next to his right foot.

"She's on her way," Trist said as he walked across the dirt parking lot, returning to the boat.

"Help me with this stuff," Robin said.

They began to lift the cooler when a black pick-up truck with oversized wheels and gold-plated wheel covers sped through the marina gate. The parking lot became a haze of dust. Loud music blared out of the windows as the truck did a donut and then pulled up to the marina office. The driver shut the engine off and climbed out.

With greasy black hair and a gut already forming from weekends of beer that weren't supposed to happen until college, Kevin Shelby hopped out of his truck and spotted Robin and Trist.

"Yo, Trist!" Kevin shouted.

They set the cooler down.

Trist waved back.

"Hey, Mr. N," Kevin said to Robin.

Robin stared at him for a moment and then gave a short wave.

"Trist, man. You comin' out to Johnny's tonight? It's gonna be legend."

Out of the corner of his eye, Trist saw Robin glaring at him. "Not sure. Might be busy. Let you know later."

Kevin gave a nod then raised his right hand to his ear gesturing Trist to call him.

Robin wondered if Trist was seeing Rachel again.

The door to the marina office opened, and marina owner Ralph Shelby walked out.

"Get the fuck in here, useless," he said to Kevin.

The Norrises turned away. Ralph Shelby latched on to Kevin's arm, opened the door to the office, and pulled Kevin inside. Muffled shouting could be heard for a few moments, then a door slamming, then silence.

"I don't want you hanging out with that kid," Robin said.

"His old man's a jerk," Trist said, "and a drunk. The inside of that office smelled like a brewery when I was making the call to mom."

"That may be true, but I still feel the same."

Trist picked up a stone and then watched it sink into the water after he let it go next to the dock. "Kevin never really had a chance."

Robin thought for a moment. "Not much of one. Maybe he'll figure it out one day."

Trist puffed.

"What?" Robin asked.

"You know that's not going to happen, Dad. He's already gotten a DUI. His old man thinks that he just drinks." Trist paused. "But he's already moved on to harder stuff."

"Like what? Pot?" Robin said.

"Mostly. He sells it by the tennis courts in the park."

"So that's why I see his Camaro parked there."

"Yep."

"You seeing Rachel again?"

"Wha—What? Where did that come from?"

Robin looked down at the cooler and duffel bags still on the dock. "Let's get these up to the parking lot. Mom should be here any minute."

After they moved the gear, Robin locked the boat and joined Trist in the parking lot.

"Trist," he looked at Kevin's truck and then back at Trist, "you don't do any of that stuff do you?"

A forest green suburban drove through the gate.

"There's mom," Trist said, and he grabbed a bag and started walking toward the SUV.

Darwinger's Gas Station was the Norris's routine stop traveling north on US-23 out of Hampstead en route to their house. Two pumps and you paid inside the general store. Propane gas refills were half-off. The general store had four booths where locals congregated every morning for coffee and gossip under the auspices of Lloyd Darwinger Jr. and his wife, Jessie. 'Little Lloyd' had inherited the business when Lloyd Sr. had packed it in twenty years ago. Little Lloyd was fifty-two now and Lloyd Darwinger III—'Baby Lloyd'—was slated to take over in ten years.

The Suburban followed the road around a bend, and the woods opened up on the right to show the water. The wind had died, leaving the water a calm flat sheet of blue. On the left-hand side of the road the familiar ugly rectangular sign painted in bright orange with green letters spelling *Darwinger's*—which the locals complained about but would be even more upset if the coloring ever changed—came into sight. Twenty yards up the highway from the sign were two thirty-foot Native American Totem Poles side-by-side. Various faces and shapes were carved into them, and the poles were freshly painted in red, blue, purple, gold, and white. A North American Indian artifacts store had once stood next to Darwinger's but had been leveled by a tornado five years ago. When the owner decided not to rebuild, he left the Totem Poles and told Little Lloyd that he could do with them as he wished. The poles remained, and select members from the battalion of Darwinger nephews painted them each May before the summer season.

Across the road from the gas station was a boat launch and a rickety dock also owned by the Darwingers. Little Lloyd had offered Robin the opportunity to keep his boat there, but Robin had declined, as he couldn't be sure from day to day if the dock would still be there.

Levana slowed the Suburban and turned in. Despite being almost 40, Robin thought—half proud and half jealous—she refused to age. When asked to describe her looks, Robin answered, "Just imagine someone reaching into the movie screen and pulling the gorgeous woman 'George' out of the arms of Clint Eastwood in *The Eiger Sanction* and placing her into mine."

The Darwingers had never paved, and gravel popped under the tires as she swung the vehicle next to a pump.

Trist stretched in the back. "Mom, can you get me a Vernors when you go in to pay?"

"Dad's going in, Tristian," Levana said.

"Oh," Trist said.

"You want a Vernors or not, Trist?" Robin said opening his door.

"Yeah."

Robin turned to Levana. "You want anything, baby?"

"No, thank you."

"Be right back," Robin said.

As he walked around the side of the Suburban, he could hear a fan blowing through the open door of the gas station and the murmur of voices. He inserted the nozzle and began filling up. There was no one else outside the station. US-23 was dead. A pick-up parked by the Totem Poles was empty but still running. Quiet day, quiet town. He never regretted living in Hampstead. No worries about people stealing your truck while you dashed in to get a six-pack.

Robin removed his Detroit Tigers baseball cap and wiped the sweat from his forehead with the sleeve of his T-shirt. A cold glass of lemonade would hit the spot. He put his cap back on and watched an old man and a boy make their way out to the end of the Darwinger's dock. The man was carrying a fishing rod and a five-gallon bucket; the boy was wearing a yellow life jacket and had a Fisher-Price rod in one hand and a bright red lunch box in the other. A memory of going fishing with Trist began to emerge, but he grabbed it and shoved it far enough back to where he could not see it.

The pump clicked off. After glancing at the damage on the screen, he put the nozzle back and screwed on the gas cap. The sound of abruptly raised voices pulled his attention to the open doorway. The townies that were piled into the booths drinking coffee were all putting their heads down on the table. Robin saw a man, whose head was almost level with the doorway, holding a burlap sack and pointing a gun at Little Lloyd Darwinger—backing him toward the cash register. Robin sprinted toward the building.

3

He stopped and hugged the wall next to the open door. From this position, he could see Jessie behind the counter pushing buttons on the cash register. The gun was now aimed at her. Little Lloyd was out of view.

"Shit!" she said, slapping the side of the register.

"What?" the man holding the gun said in a hoarse voice.

"I hit the wrong button," Jessie said.

"Well, hurry up and fix it, bitch."

Little Lloyd came into view from behind Jessie and took a step toward the man. "Listen, asshole. She's doing her best."

"Stay right there, pops," the man said, swiveling his gun at Little Lloyd. The robber wore cowboy boots, denim overalls with a red cut-off T-shirt underneath exposing tan muscular arms, and an oily John Deere hat. He towered over the wiry gas station owner. Little Lloyd stepped back. "Yeah, that's what I thought."

Jessie hit a series of buttons, and the register drawer slid open. The man tossed the burlap sack to Little Lloyd and watched as Jessie began emptying cash into it.

Would he come out this way? Robin eyed the truck that was running. Must be his. He scanned over to the Suburban. Levana motioned as if to say, "What are you doing?" Trist lowered his window and looked at him. Robin gestured for them to stay put. He peeked back inside the store.

Little Lloyd handed the bag over the counter, and the large man snatched it. Robin moved back from the doorway as he heard footsteps approaching. His muscles tensed and his heart felt like it was going to bust through his shirt. He had an advantage because if the running truck was the robber's, then he would be heading away from Robin when he came out of the doorway.

The man stopped right before the opening and dipped his hat, "Thank ye." Then he bolted toward the truck, kicking up dust with each heavy impact of his cowboy boots.

It took Robin a few strides to close the gap; he rammed his head into the middle of the robber's back and wrapped his arms around his waist, squeezing as if to force his guts up through the robber's mouth. The man's hat flew off as he lost his balance and was driven to the ground.

The man tried to turn over in an effort to aim his gun, but Robin was too quick. He took a handful of slimy hair and slammed the man's face into the gravel. The man let go of his gun and tried to push himself up, but was soon flattened as two more bodies jumped on top of Robin. One was Little Lloyd Darwinger, and the other was Trist. The robber struggled against the three, but after his face was smashed into the ground one more time by Robin, he gave in. They stood him up and Little Lloyd belted the giant in the face, chest, and then the face once more. Levana was out of the Suburban and running toward them when Jessie came out of the station with a roll of binder twine followed by the remaining customers. Within minutes, the man was tied up to one of the Totem Poles and police sirens could be heard approaching.

After being interviewed by the police, getting a courtesy fill up of their vehicle, a free propane tank, a 12-pack of Vernors, and a case of Budweiser from Little Lloyd, the Norrises were on the road again.

"What was that?" Levana said.

"I don't like people who steal," Robin said.

"I watched the whole thing," she said. "I've never seen you like that before. It was scary."

Robin had never wrestled or played football, but he had taken karate during his freshman year at Central Michigan. The instructor, well past his prime, taught each class from a stool and began every class by saying, "Boys, nothin' fortifies a man more than gettin' kicked in the face and dropped to the pavement. The question is: Will you get back up?"

"I wanted to help," Robin said.

"Did you think about what could have happened?"

He hadn't. "It happened fast," he said and looked through the rearview mirror at Trist. "I had some pretty good help though."

Trist broke his first smile of the day.

"What if he shot one of you?"

"Bullet would have bounced off." The cool air felt good again as it flowed over his hands on the hot steering wheel. The adrenaline rush had made him want to drive home—to be in control.

"Don't make a joke of it, Robin. You and our son just tackled a felon."

"You're saying we should have let him go?"

"Yes. It's not your place to play sheriff, Indy."

And that was how she described him to her friends. 'Oh, you didn't know Harrison Ford worked at Hampstead Hospital? Yeah, he moved, and I married him.' Some people looked twice when they saw him in person, and the whispers grew—how long was he visiting from California? Fuck California.

"I thought we did well," Trist said.

Levana turned around. "Don't start with me, Tristian."

Robin thought about pushing it further, but backed down. Besides, he had done it. "Okay. No more sheriff."

She smiled at them both, "It was impressive, though," she started to grin, "kinda like..."

Robin and Trist said together, "Indy."

Levana did a dance in her seat, "You got it!"

"Thank ye," Robin said, dipping his baseball cap.

She rolled her eyes and laughed, "Okay, where did that line come from?"

"The robber."

"Oh dear God," Levana said.

A few minutes later the Suburban broke the crest of another rise in US-23 and below them lay the last winding mile until the turn-off to Haven Point and home.

Levana's brother, Tyee Beecher, ran the family hardware store in Hampstead. After passing away twelve summers ago, their father had left the store and waterfront lot it stood on to Tyee and left a separate lakefront lot and exactly two-hundred thousand dollars to Robin and Levana, a godsend to two young parents with an almost zeroed-out checking account. Tyee, Robin, and long-time friend and local bait store owner Mickey Leif had built the Norris family home on that lakefront land: a three-story log fortress. It was testament to his character that Tyee was not bitter about what was left to his older sister; the spacious waterfront lot plus the hardware store's value was close to half-a-million dollars then, nearer to a million now.

The house was five miles north of Hampstead, but a welcome five miles. It was quiet, they had decent neighbors who were seen rather than heard, and it provided the opportunity for the Norrises to live life their way. There were no computers in the house and only one television and one phone unplugged every night at 6:00 p.m. However, there was a state-of-the art workout room; a two-story library; a theater room with a stage where Robin, Levana, and Tristian would recite Baldwin, Ginsberg, Frost, Bishop, Rich, Miller, and Williams; a music room with surround sound and a collection of records that put the local music store to shame; a wine cellar; a sewing room; and a meditation room with floor-to-ceiling windows that looked out over Lake Huron.

In terms of solitude, Robin was a reincarnation of the scholarly Trappist monk Thomas Merton, but with a short fuse that he had failed to lengthen. If Merton's famous book, *The Seven Story Mountain*, was the tale of an older, wiser Thomas Merton looking back and critiquing a younger, uneducated Thomas Merton, then Robin's book would record a futile attempt at helping Trist avoid the sins of his father.

The furniture in the house was hand-made by Robin and Tyee. When they had started, his brother-in-law had said, "What in the hell does a Hampstead Hospital nurse like you know about carpentry?" After he corrected one of Tyee's miscalculations on the angle of cut for a chair back, Robin had replied, "Apparently, enough."

To one side of the house was a fruit and vegetable garden, and to the other side, a gigantic pole barn where Robin and Trist had restored *Levity*. Levana claimed that they were never moving again—she would die in this house. It had always been a joke between them, but now it was *he* who would die in it.

Robin saw a sign on the side of the road and slowed the Suburban.

"What are you doing?" Levana said. "We're almost home."

"I'm going to check out this garage sale real quick for some odds-and-ends we might need for the trip."

Robin pulled off on the shoulder and turned the vehicle off. The best deals on "stuff" were not at Wal-Mart, but rather at summer garage sales on US-23. However, he'd never stopped at a sale on this stretch of highway before and didn't know the owners of this particular house—another idiosyncrasy for the lakefront property on either side of Hampstead: the owners could be residents of the town or they could simply be well-off visitors who summered in Hampstead.

"Can you make it quick?" Levana said.

"Be back in a jiffy." He looked in the back seat at Trist. "You wanna look around?"

"No thanks," said Trist.

Robin gave Levana a quick peck and then began walking up the driveway. The sun was hidden behind a wall of clouds and through the trees behind the garage Robin could see the navy-colored lake water.

He entered the garage. A stack of plastic water jugs—who in the hell would buy any of those—forced him to maneuver to the center aisle formed by two large metal tables. His arm brushed a jug. It fell, and he sliced his thumb on the corner of one of the tables as he tried to catch it. A quarter-inch red line split his thumbprint. Great. He looked for something to wipe the blood on but found nothing—at least nothing he was willing to buy in order to apply pressure to the cut.

He walked out of the garage, put his thumb in his mouth, and then sucked up as much of the blood as he could; he spat in the grass—an old trick he had learned from his grandfather. He examined his thumb—still bleeding. Funny. The bleeding had always stopped when his grandfather had done the trick, but then again Robin had been young and maybe his grandfather's thumb had kept bleeding too. Come to think of it, his father had done the same thing whenever he had cut himself.

He re-entered the garage, too cluttered for anyone to notice that he had left, and located stacks of books on a corner table—wouldn't hurt just to see what's here real quick.

The first stack: cheesy romances with worn covers, a *Reader's Digest* collection of condensed novels, and a paperback dictionary. He moved to another stack. Half-a-dozen mammoth paperbacks by James A. Michener. He had read two of the books, *Space* and *Centennial*, so he picked up the other four: *Texas*, *Hawaii*, *The Source*, and *Alaska*. Wait. Would he be able to finish all four before...well, maybe Trist would enjoy them one day.

Baby clothes on this table, tools on that table, was that a diaper pail with a $5.00 sticker on it? There seemed to be nothing he and Trist could use. Then, he saw something that couldn't be for sale.

He moved past the table overflowing with baby clothes and stood in front of a brand new Desco Light Duty Diving Outfit. Robin searched for a sticker and couldn't find one.

"Stupidest impulse buy I ever made," said a voice behind him.

Robin turned to see an older gentleman wearing a Detroit Lions t-shirt.

"And I'm not talkin' about the *t-shirt* I have on." The man pointed a thumb at his shirt. "A gift. I wouldn't give this team a dime. When Barry Sanders retires, we're through. But you know what the biggest problem is?"

"Not a clue."

"We've *never* had a quarterback."

"Not much of a football guy," admitted Robin.

The man took a measure of him. "Not much of a football guy, huh? Well, at least one of us is smart. Should've given up watching the game years ago." He gritted his teeth. "William Clay Ford Senior...ah, whatever."

"If you want to talk hoops, though," Robin said, "Then I'm your guy."

"You play?"

"Played," Robin said. "Just high school, but my younger brother walked on at CMU."

"No kidding?"

"Well, he never saw much of the floor. Got dunked on by Majerle during his first practice, and I don't think he ever recovered."

The old man hooted, "Who didn't get dunked on by Thunder Dan?"

"Good point," Robin said.

The old man rubbed his white beard. "You much of a divin' guy?"

Robin put his hand on the stacked air tanks connected to the compressor. "Actually, I've been pricing these lately. My son and I are taking a sail around Lake Superior this summer, and I wanted something we could dive with to clean the hull or recover a lost item if we're shallow enough—without having to rig up a tank." He searched around the table. "I don't see a mask or air hose."

The owner bent down and pulled up a box from underneath the table. "Here's the rest of it: one commercial free flow mask, one-hundred and fifty feet of three-eighths inch floating air breathing hose, and a scuba style weight belt with a quick release buckle, four vinyl coated three-pound weights, plus one two-pound bullet weight with a brass snap and umbilical clamp."

"This all looks brand new," Robin said. "Have you ever used it?"

"Once. Works like a charm. The two-horsepower oil-less electric compressor is everything it's billed to be and more."

"Why are you getting rid of it?"

The old man smirked. "Can't use it anymore." He leaned up against the wall and settled in to his story. "I retired a year ago and had some extra cash from my buyout, right? I'm thinkin' about diving off my boat and don't want to invest in the whole nine yards of equipment. Just something nice and easy. So, I drive two hours to a dive shop, and in the store is mister compressor. My eyes get big, and, within twenty minutes, the guy's got me convinced that I'm Jacques flipping Cousteau. I get home with it and the next day set out for my dive. Now, the specs say that the working depth limit for this set is between thirty and fifty feet. But I figure I've got one-hundred and fifty feet of hose, right? So, I decide to push it a little and...boom!" The man clapped his hands together. "I put a hole in my right eardrum. Stupid. Have you ever dived before?"

"Many times," Robin said.

The man looked embarrassed. "Well, you won't have any trouble with it then. What's your offer?"

Every compressor unit that he had researched was between three and four thousand dollars. He had been hoping to go used, but only used once? He doubted the man would come down much. "How much were you thinking?"

A short woman roughly the same age as the man entered the garage from the house, and when she saw what Robin and the owner were discussing she rolled her eyes, chuckled, and said, "Oh, Adam. You and your senseless ideas." She pointed toward the compressor. "That one may take the cake as the worst of all." She continued to look at the table where the diving gear was set out. "Where's your fins?"

"I'm not selling the fins, all right?"

She put her hands on her hips. "You told me you were selling the fins too."

"Hush, dear. I'm trying to sell the stupid thing," the man said to his wife.

She shook her head and began straightening some of the baby clothes.

"I don't think she liked my diving experiment," Adam said, watching her organize a stack of bibs. "My daughter came and dropped off a bunch of stuff. Her babies aren't babies anymore."

"I understand," said Robin. "My baby is seventeen."

Adam continued to watch his wife but nodded. Then, he turned back toward Robin. "Where were we? Oh, the price, right." He studied Robin.

Trist appeared at the edge of the garage. "Dad, mom wants you to hurry up."

Adam motioned toward Trist. "They grow up fast don't they?"

"They do," Robin said.

Trist turned and went back to the Suburban.

Adam put a hand on Robin's shoulder. "I'll tell you what. I didn't want to lose too much on this, but I think the old lady wants to see it disappear today.

So, if we were to go by the garage sale bartering rules, I'd probably say something like two grand. And you'd say one grand. And we'd settle on fifteen hundred. Let's bypass the song and dance. Fifteen hundred."

"Sold," Robin said.

"Oh, almost forgot," Adam said, reaching down under the table again. He stood up and in his hand was a dive knife that also looked like it hadn't been used. "Take this," he said. "Your feet are much bigger than mine, or else I'd give you the damn fins too."

"You sure?" Robin said.

Adam winked to Robin, "Dads should impress their kids." He shook Robin's hand and then joined his wife to continue their cheerful bickering.

Robin headed for the car to get Trist to help him load up the compressor...and to get the checkbook from Levana.

5

A cool evening breeze blew through the screen of the open sliding glass door that led from the third-floor master bedroom to the large widow's walk. The wind opened Levana's robe exposing a cream-colored silk nightie as she pulled the screen door handle. Robin was seated on a built-in bench with an adjustable reclining back, facing the lake and reading a handwritten list with a flashlight. It was 11 p.m., and the moon's light formed a glimmering sliver of white on the otherwise ebony surface of the lake.

Levana closed the screen door behind her and stepped onto the walk with two glasses of cabernet.

"List complete yet?" she said, handing him a glass.

It was as ready as it was going to be. Even as he studied it again, uneasiness crept into his stomach. He was sure that he had missed something.

Every chart of Lake Superior was rolled, corrected, and stowed below the navigation table in the cabin of the boat. He had a handheld GPS for back-up, and the motor had been overhauled during the winter. The water capacity was fifty gallons, but he had an extra thirty gallons in the two beer kegs strapped against the bulkhead in the v-berth, which he had transformed into a supply depot and sail locker. On the opposite bulkhead, he had mounted two Coleman steel-belted coolers which kept ice frozen in one-hundred-degree weather for three days. He had an emergency handheld VHF radio, first aid kit, and an inflatable life raft. Levana had packed Trist's passport along with his. He had made sure that his watch had a new battery and had brought extra batteries for every item that required them on the boat. Each piece of equipment's technical manual had been stowed on a shelf made of mahogany, hand-rubbed alive through multiple coats of varnish in the boat's salon.

Levana had worried about them getting lost and starving to death so she had Tyee rent a refrigerated truck to transport the food and drinks to the Upper Peninsula where they were putting the boat in. She had ordered steaks, fresh cartons of eggs, meatballs, spaghetti, bacon, sausages, crescent rolls, cans of beef stew, cans of tomato soup, a case of beer, three 24-packs of coke, five gallons of fruit juice, half-a-dozen boxes of breakfast cereal, cheese blocks, Bisquick, Saltines, granola bars, cold-cuts, and canned fruit. The longest they would go without making a port call would be four or five days. Then, they could re-supply as necessary.

After a night shift last week, he had *borrowed* a duffel bag full of supplies from the hospital. First, he had replenished his "home supply" of 2 liters and a line. The first—and possibly only—thing he had learned from his mentor years ago was that doctors and nurses always kept their own supply of saline bags suffused with electrolytes, B-12, and B-complex at home to cure a hangover.

Next, he had packed the narcotics. Morphine as the primary—the gold standard in pain management; his back-up was Demerol. Both were injected with a syringe—he preferred using carpujects—so he had packed a dozen. Both Morphine and Demerol made a person drowsy and constipated; he had thrown in a box of suppositories. He had loaded a bottle of Dramamine for motion sickness if they faced heavy seas, and a bottle of Phenergan for nausea to be taken three to four times a day. Even though his "home supply" was replenished, he was taking no chances of either he or Trist becoming dehydrated at sea. Therefore, he had filled the rest of the bag with materials for an IV: alcohol swabs, a rubber band for a tourniquet, tubing, bags of saline, and a variety of needles—the bigger the needle, the smaller the gauge. The bags would have to be kept at room temperature. If it got too hot, he could place them in the boat's refrigerator, but he would need to warm them up so that they wouldn't hurt either he or Trist. He had read that in World War II, medics tucked bags inside their shirts to keep them warm.

Tomorrow, he would stow the new compressor and two complete sets of dive gear—fins, mask, snorkel, wetsuit, weightbelt, BCD, regulator, and dive knife—in the dive equipment cabinet he had built with Tyee in the v-berth. When he dropped Trist off for work, he would go behind the hardware store and use his brother-in-law's compressor to fill up the four scuba tanks. He had also ordered brand new West Marine oilskins and rubber boots for them in case of foul weather. They had arrived at the store yesterday, and Tyee had the box waiting for them.

Robin aimed his flashlight at the bottom of the page and ran his finger down the last items on his list. Tennis racquets and balls, basketball, camera, binoculars, air pump, tent, sleeping bags, hiking boots, stove, two propane bottles, backpack, six bottles of Deep Woods Off, three tubes of sunscreen, two fishing poles, tackle box, bait, a dozen bars of soap, lantern, and—he looked at the flashlight in his hand—the rest of the page was blank. He switched the flashlight to his left hand and wrote FLASHLIGHT and BATTERIES underneath LANTERN. He switched off the light and took the glass of wine from Levana. He had been advised not to drink—the hell with that.

"I think we're ready," he said.

She sat between his legs and leaned her back against his chest. They each took a drink of wine—the only sound in the night air was of waves hitting their beach.

"I scheduled the truck to be at the hardware store at seven a.m. the day after tomorrow to load up the food and supplies."

"Thank you, darling," Robin said. "I'll have the boat out of the water and on the trailer by eight. After that, we'll wait for you and Tyee to show up in the truck. Then, it's on to the U.P."

"So," she said, and took another sip. "How did it go?"

"We'll be all right," Robin said. He took a sip now. "In fact, sometimes, I think he knows more about sailing than I do."

"That's not what I'm asking."

He knew it too. She wanted to know how he and Trist were getting along. "We had our moments," he said.

"What does that mean?"

Here goes. "He still doesn't respect the fact that I know what's best for him, even if it means telling him something that he doesn't want to hear."

"With that line of thinking starting last summer, right?" Levana said.

"Yes. Ever since I came home from my shift because I got sick that night and found his bare ass moving up and down on our couch over his girlfriend, he thinks that every talk we have is a lecture." Robin swirled the wine in his glass and tipped it back. "He wasn't even wearing a rubber for Christ's sake. I know he thinks I embarrassed him when I asked them to get dressed and then made Rachel leave, but he's gonna mess up his life if he gets some girl pregnant right now." He could feel his temper rising. "I don't want him to corner himself as a teenager. Do you realize how hard it would be to make it now being eighteen with a baby?"

"Are you lecturing *me* now?" Levana said.

Robin exhaled—damn it—another trait Trist had picked up from him. "I'm sorry." He rubbed her left shoulder with his free hand. They listened to the waves once again.

"You can't control every move he makes, Robin."

"I know. It's just that I keep thinking back to my old man. I told myself time and time again I would never be that kind of father to Trist and Jon—." He still couldn't say his name. He stared at the water, gathered himself, then continued. "Do you know the only thing I remember from my college psychology class is the day my professor walked in and said, 'For those of you wanting to treat your kids differently than you were treated, I've got some news for you: unless you make a conscious effort to treat them differently, you will end up treating them how you were treated whether you like it or not.'"

"You've never told me that before," she said.

"Do you want to know where I'm really at?"

She lifted her head off his chest and nodded.

"I know that I don't have much time left with him," he paused, trying to stay calm. "I'm in a tough spot. At some point during every day the past few months I've thought of something that I should pass on to Trist. Some pearl of wisdom," he paused, "no, that's a stupid saying. Some lesson learned where I messed up and don't want him to. And I feel the need to tell him, because soon I won't be able to."

Levana raised her hand to her face and began wiping her cheeks.

"For sixteen years, I have been a different father than my own and been proud of that. But now I'm frustrated because for the past year I'm sure that I have been like a monkey that won't get off his back. He's confused because I'm not like that. And now I've got him thinking that he has to prove his manhood to me. And that's not what I want at all. I already respect him, but I'm struggling with knowing that I have less time than I ever imagined to pass on what I've learned. Not only am I getting cheated out of getting to see my son become a man, I feel he's getting cheated by not having me there to lean on after he graduates from this hormonal overload."

Robin's eyes filled. "I wanted to help him buy his first car," he said while raising his wineglass and his other hand at the same time in protest. "I wanted

40

to be there when he bought his first house and help him fix it up. I wanted to be there when he brought home the woman he was going to marry, and have the right to say something stupid and inappropriate like, 'When do you guys think you'll start trying to have kids?'."

Levana kept wiping her eyes.

"I wanted all of that," he said and wrapped his arms around her.

She hugged him back and then turned around and faced him. "I don't know how much longer I can go not telling him what you have."

"It's not the right time yet," Robin said.

Levana cried, "When *will* it be?"

Robin stood up and walked to the railing overlooking the water. "I plan on telling him on the sail," he said.

"How?"

"I don't know yet. But I promise I will."

She joined him. "I have a suggestion to help you with your lectures."

He turned to her. "Anything. My method is ripping me apart."

"I want you to buy a journal tomorrow after you drop Trist off at the hardware store. You can pick one up at Lily's. It will be behind the art pencils before you get to the books."

"I'm not a writer, Levana."

"It doesn't matter. You don't have to sound writerly and call it a journal; call it a notebook."

"What's it for?"

"Whenever a lesson or piece of advice comes to mind, I want you to write it down," she said. She gathered herself. "I will make sure he gets it."

He considered her suggestion while watching the wind blow her hair away from her face, exposing her high cheekbones and dark complexion. "I have to ask this. Do you still want us to go?"

She didn't hesitate. "Yes. And now I have to ask you something."

"Anything," he said.

"Are you so hard on him about his future because at one time you thought *he* was a mistake?"

"We did what we had to do."

"Answer me."

He pulled her against his chest and looked over her head at the water. The moon had slid behind a group of clouds, and the entire lake looked like a black bedsheet with someone moving their hands underneath it. "No. He was never a mistake," he said. "And neither were you."

When Robin Thomas Norris was eighteen, he registered for the core freshman course load at Central Michigan University. He told his parents before leaving that in four years he would have an undergraduate degree in Sports Medicine with a minor in English and would be on his way to being a trainer for an NBA team. The perfect life awaited: he'd help keep athletes on the floor during the season, get to travel the world, and read everything he could get his hands on while doing it. His mother believed in him; his father thought he was wasting his life.

Robin's entire childhood had comprised of reading about injuries, studying their cause, getting injured—then studying himself and going to seminars once a month at St. Luke's Hospital on the newest treatments for tennis elbow and shin splints. Going to Central to study his passion was a no-brainer in his estimation; he didn't care what anyone else thought.

The first semester passed without incident. He secured a job as a student trainer for the men's basketball team, and when he wasn't doing that, he worked at the university library where on off hours he had access to books, magazines, and video documentaries about sports psychology, athletic training, and famous sports stars and their injuries—most of which ended their careers. He abused authority by sending official notices to students who had material checked out that he wanted, requiring them to bring it in.

There had been the usual partying and socialization, but when one finds the keys to his uncle's liquor cabinet at fourteen, there is little left to the imagination by eighteen. He was not as prone to make drinking a central focus in his life as other freshman who were experiencing the juice of love for the first time. As for women, Robin had ended a high school relationship early in the semester and other than an occasional kiss or even inebriated consummation, he wasn't interested in the long term—until February.

On his way to class, and running late, he watched a girl slip on a patch of ice right in front of the academic building they were about to enter. Helping her pick up her books and get to her feet, Robin got caught in her dark brown eyes. Black hair fell to her shoulders, and her cheeks were red due to the chill. Their breaths created a small cloud between them. After an eternity—one moment—she said "Thank you." Before Robin could say anything, she had turned and entered the building.

For two weeks he thought of nothing but her. He searched by bike and on foot, checked the university registrar, asked around, and crashed parties he wasn't invited to. About to declare defeat on a Friday night while filling in at the library for a student who had called in sick—probably to party—Robin saw her. He approached. After botching his opening, he recovered with concern about how she was doing after her fall. She asked what his name was. When he said, "Robin," she replied, "Named after our state's bird, huh?" In fact, he *had* been, but he lied and said, "No." Then, he faltered again showing his age through nervous attempts at small talk and humor. With nowhere left to go, he helped her locate two books for a paper she was writing on the status of Michigan's High Schools. Attempting to prolong their time, Robin told her that he was getting off work in a half hour and asked if she'd like to get some coffee—which he didn't drink. She accepted.

Levana Ogin Beecher was a junior, pursuing a teaching degree in secondary Mathematics. Her father had wanted her to study business so she could take over his hardware store one day, but she had other plans. Her goal was to get out of Michigan as soon as possible and teach someplace—anyplace—that didn't have snow.

Robin had shared her sentiment and explained his plans to travel the country with a professional team. The mutual interest catapulted the conversation into the wee hours and led to a repeat the following night.

A month later, they were dating and—against her better judgment—sleeping together every chance they had. Robin was keeping his grades up, and they planned to see each other over the summer. He'd still be helping with the team and working summer camps. She was heading home to some place called Hampstead. They would make it work.

As a source of pride, he reported the success of his first year to his father, hoping for a glimmer of approval. His father replied, "Life happens when you're making other plans." On the Thursday before Memorial Day weekend, Levana found out she was pregnant. Robin had asked, "Is it mine?" and was slapped across the face.

The marriage took place in July, and, with no other option that made fiscal sense, they moved into the basement of her parents' house after their weekend honeymoon to a Michigan State Park where Robin drank for three days and Levana threw up for three days. Feeling the responsibility of bringing in some form of income, Robin dropped out of school and got a full-time job working as an orderly at the Hampstead Hospital. He was mopping floors when Levana went into labor, and on December 3, 1978 Tristian Dichali (meaning "speaks a lot") Norris was born.

The following fall, her mother agreed to take care of the baby during the day while Levana resumed her college classes. After receiving her teaching license in the spring, she started interviewing for teaching positions. On the third interview, she ran out of the room and vomited all over the hallway floor—she was pregnant again. They hadn't planned for the second baby—or the first—but in a way, Levana felt relieved. She hoped that by getting pregnant again so soon, she could prove her relationship to Robin was strong and that her parents would accept them as a family and not as two kids who forever altered their lives in a dorm room bed. Levana's mother professed a love for their family; Levana's father hovered in the background, waiting for Robin to prove him right: to fuck up beyond belief and be dismissed for good.

The exact opposite had occurred. With another child in the wings, Robin attended community college at night in addition to working at the hospital during the day. He received a nursing degree, and when their second child Jonathan turned two, he delivered the proud news to Levana: they had saved enough money to move out of the basement.

Movers had been hired, an apartment picked out, and a plan made that would get them out of Hampstead in five years. On the afternoon of the move, Levana's mother loaded the boys into the family station wagon to take them to lunch, Jonathan sitting behind Levana's mother.

Right before the turn-in, a concrete mixer truck traveling in the opposite direction blew a tire and swerved into their lane. Levana's mother and Jonathan were dead before the ambulance could be heard. Tristian entered the hospital in a coma, but would come out of it a month later just in time to see his grandfather laid to rest after suffering a massive heart attack.

The Norrises never left Hampstead.

7

Beecher Hardware shared a parking lot with the Hawthorne Fish House. There were sixteen parking spaces with fresh yellow lines painted over smooth blacktop that had been finished two weeks before. Business had suffered a little while the lot was being redone, but it had been way past due. Now, the customer flow was back to normal.

The sun cast a warm glow above Lake Huron as Robin pulled the Suburban in next to Tyee's pick-up. Levana was still sleeping back at home, and in the passenger seat Tristian had the blank red-eyed stare of a person who had not had much sleep the night before. Robin was holding back his checklist of questions to determine just what in the hell his son's night had entailed.

He shut off the engine. "Ready?" he said to Trist.

Trist nodded then rubbed his eyes.

They exited the SUV and started walking toward the front of the store. From across the parking lot, the owners of the Hawthorne Fish House, Gary and Lucille Hawthorne, walked out the front door of their building. Robin hadn't seen them since the parking lot had been finished.

"Mornin', gents," Gary said.

"Hi Robin. Hi Tristian," Lucille said and waved.

They stopped, and Trist gave a half-hearted wave. Robin said, "Parking lot looks good."

"Took long enough for them to finish," Gary said. "You guys are headin' out this week, right?"

"Tomorrow morning," Robin said.

"What an experience," Lucille said, smiling as if fighting back pain and tears.

She knows. Robin looked into Gary's eyes; he does too.

"I better head in and see what Uncle Tyee needs me to do," Trist said and then waved goodbye to the Hawthornes while heading toward the door.

"Tell him I'll be right there," Robin said.

"Okay," Trist said over his shoulder. He reached the door and it opened with the familiar chime.

"He's turning into a nice young man," Lucille said.

"Got a ways to go," Robin said reflexively. *Don't be a jerk.* "But we're proud of him."

"Got your fishin' poles ready?" Gary asked. "I hear the whitefish are almost jumping out of the water and into boats up there."

"Got 'em packed," Robin said. "I'm heading over to Mickey's for bait later this morning."

"He's doing pretty well for himself," Gary said rubbing his chest. "But that bait store that just opened up near Shelby's Marina is startin' to burn my ass."

"Why?" Robin asked.

"Because he keeps spreadin' lies about Mickey just to get more business. Well, he hasn't been around this town long enough to know how things work. If he keeps it up, I'll submarine him and his business because I know all the fishermen."

Robin smiled. Gary Hawthorne was not a man you made angry.

"Where are you two headed this morning?" Robin asked.

"Bringing Mickey some coffee and then out to the bight to see how the construction is going on our new place," Lucille said.

"Looking forward to moving in?"

Gary rubbed his chest again. "It'll be hard leaving our old house. We raised our kids there. Lots of memories."

"Your chest all right?" Robin said.

Gary looked at Lucille and then back to Robin. "Pain comes and goes. I probably keep sleepin' on it funny." He jerked his thumb at Lucille. "She keeps naggin' me to go in and have it checked out."

"Couldn't hurt," Robin said.

"That's right," Lucille agreed.

Robin put a hand on Gary's shoulder. "When I get back, if he hasn't gone in yet, I'll carry him there myself."

They laughed and Gary looked at his watch. "We won't keep you any longer, Robin." He put out his hand and Robin shook it. "Want to hear all about it when you get back. Maybe we'll have everybody over for dinner."

Lucille surprised Robin with a hug. As they parted she said, "You boys be careful out on that water."

"We will," Robin said, and they walked off in separate directions.

The front door chimed as he entered, and he smelled coffee, lumber, and sawdust. The sound of a power-drill came up from the basement. No one was behind the counter, and the aisles were empty.

"Anybody home?" Robin shouted.

The drill stopped, and from the basement came a deep hard voice, "Comin' right up."

Heavy steps could be heard on the stairs, and soon his six-foot-five-inch brother-in-law came into view. Tyee was thirty-six, with black hair parted to the right, green eyes, and a body that might have been built in a laboratory. His back, chest, and arms were enormous strings of muscles pulled down to a thirty-four-inch waist. His leg muscles looked like they should be casted and put on display in some physiology hall of fame. And he held the distinction of being the only person in Hampstead who was just as fit as Robin. They had felt themselves going soft in their late twenties and made an agreement to work out together five times a week in Robin's home gym. Until this past year, they hadn't missed a workout.

"He's down there," Tyee pointed to the steps and then gave Robin a manly hug.

At some point over the past decade, Tyee had gone beyond being his brother-in-law and had become his closest friend.

"How's the renovation going?" Robin said as they parted.

"Slower than I want, but soon I'll have a place to sit down and have coffee. Never needed a break room before, because I didn't need breaks. But we're not twenty-three anymore are we?"

"No, we're not," Robin said.

"Got your box for you."

"Thanks."

"And somethin' else," Tyee said.

"What?"

"Follow me."

Tyee led them behind the counter and into the back room. In the far corner was a make-shift cabinet made out of plywood secured with a master lock. Tyee pulled out a ring crammed with keys and flipped to the key that unlocked the cabinet.

He swung the door open. Inside was a gun safe. Another key, another lock, and Tyee pulled the safe door open. The interior held two 12-gauge shotguns. Boxes of ammo were on the top shelf, all facing the same direction and equidistant apart.

"And here I always thought you only kept your wallet locked up because you hate to have it in your pocket," Robin said.

Tyee gave a grunt as he bent down and pulled open a drawer below the shelf that the shotgun butts were resting on. Inside the drawer was a black wallet sitting on a pile of loose change. Tyee gave a devious smile and then closed the drawer.

"Why the guns?" Robin said.

"In case I need more firepower than the revolver I keep behind the counter. If I make it back here during a robbery and get my hands on one of these," he patted the shotgun closest to him, "I'll come out and blast the bastards. So far, nobody's been stupid enough to try."

"Hampstead has to have the lowest crime rate in the entire state, Tyee."

"I know, but people are still people the last time I checked. There'll always be shit goin' on that we don't see," he said. "Call it over preparedness or, hell, even overly cautious," he shrugged. "That's how I operate."

Tyee picked up one of the shotguns, unloaded it, and passed it to Robin along with two boxes of ammo. "Take this with you on your trip. I wish I could say the Great Lakes are safe from yo-yos, but we have had nice people on nice yachts taking nice trips who have never come back." Tyee closed the safe, then the cabinet, and padlocked the door. "You never know who you might run into up there."

Robin took the gun and ammo. "I've got a Saturday night special at home—"

Tyee cut him off. "Where you're headin' ain't home. With this, you don't have to be as accurate. Plus, people respect the sight of the double barrel."

Tyee led him out of the back room.

Trist came up the stairs and saw his dad with the shotgun. "Where are you heading with that, Dad?"

"Uncle Tyee thinks it would be a good idea to have it with us on the boat."

"It would be," Trist said.

Had they been talking about it? "Good. Take it out to the Suburban," Robin said passing the gun and ammo to Trist.

"You done sanding down there?" Tyee asked Tristian.

"Almost."

"Chop, chop, Trist. I want to be varnishing this afternoon."

They watched Trist leave the store.

"He still givin' you lip?" Tyee said.

Tyee was his closest friend, but this had been one area Robin had never discussed with him. *Levana.*

As if he knew what Robin was thinking, Tyee said, "Yeah. My sister can't keep her mouth shut." He grinned. "I still can't believe that Trist doesn't know about your condition."

"I'm having to rush my fatherly advice to him, and it's not going well."

"Don't worry about it. My father waited until my mom and your other boy died to tell me anything. Trist will be fine."

Robin was silent.

"You bring your tanks?" Tyee said.

"Out in the SUV."

"Let's fill 'em out back, and then I'll give you the box with the foul weather gear you ordered." Tyee paused, his eyes glancing across his store aisle by aisle. "You know, I ought to expand what I carry in the store. Nobody else in this town carries any boating gear that's worth a damn."

"Do it," Robin said.

Trist propped open the front door and then brought in the four scuba tanks.

"Now look at this guy," said Tyee. "You're startin' to anticipate, aren't you? That's another step toward becoming a man: thinking about what needs to be done and doing it before you're asked to do it."

Robin walked toward the door and grabbed two tanks. "Thanks, Trist."

"No problem," Trist said bringing in the other two tanks.

Tyee had started toward the hallway that led to the back door. "Hey, Uncle Tyee. Two guys stopped me in the parking lot and asked if you carried bait."

Tyee stopped and turned. "You send them to Mickey's?"

"Yeah, I did and gave them directions," said Trist.

Tyee nodded. "Good boy. We've gotta help Mickey get through this rough patch with that sonofabitch out by Shelby's."

"Gary and Lucille told me about that in the parking lot before I came in this morning," Robin said.

"The idiot's days are numbered now that he made an enemy of Gary," Tyee smirked.

"Speaking of Gary, have you noticed him rubbing his chest?"

"He did it twice in front of me, and I called him on it yesterday," said Tyee.

"Stay on him about it," Robin said.

"I plan to."

They exited out the back door and walked down a long dock to a shed that Robin had helped Tyee build. Tied up to the end of the dock was Tyee's boat *Magnum*.

"When are you going to paint the shed?" Trist asked.

Tyee laughed. "You mean when are *you* going to paint that shed?" He looked back at Trist. "Probably when you get back."

Tyee opened the shed and started the compressor. Robin and Trist set their tanks down, and Trist headed back to the store.

Tyee motioned for a tank, and Robin brought one inside and handed it to him. Then, Robin unfolded two chairs and placed them across from each other. Tyee hooked up the tank and sat down. The back door to the hardware store closed and the steady chug of the compressor was the only sound as the first tank filled up. Robin sat down.

When Tyee disconnected the first tank and waved for the second, Robin signaled for him to shut the compressor off.

Tyee did. "What's up?"

Robin took a deep breath. He'd rehearsed and rehearsed, but that was all out the window now. "Tyee, when I'm gone, I want you to look after Levana and Trist."

The men held each other's stare.

Tyee's voice shook. "Why you askin' me this now?"

"Because little by little, I'm getting weaker. I've lost ten pounds that I can't get back on. It's the start." He took a breath. Tyee remained motionless. "But I still feel like a man. I don't want to ask when that part of me has been taken away and I'm lying in some hospital bed asking. I've seen it in my line of work, and it's not pretty."

Tyee stood up and turned away. His hands rose to his face and stayed there for a long time. Robin closed his eyes and the memories began to appear: Tyee at Robin and Levana's rushed wedding, staring at Robin, then getting drunk at the reception and taking a swing at him for knocking up his sister; A few years later, sitting on this very dock fishing together, Tyee reaching his hand out to apologize; The unexpected hug at the joint funeral of his son and Tyee's mother; Then, a series of moments from Robin's gym, the sweat, the grunts, the encouragement to pump out one more rep. When he opened his eyes, Tyee had turned around and sat down. His eyes were dry but red.

"I got it covered," Tyee said.

Robin reached out his hand, and they shook as men do who know enough to be quiet at that moment.

8

VANCOUVER, B.C., CANADA, JUNE 1995

Fresh mulch crunched underneath Grant Livingston's boots on the six-foot wide path through towering Douglas firs. The trail left from the estate's north lawn and ran a quarter of a mile into the woods before making a 'T' where one could walk in either direction and circle the estate, ending back at the 'T' two and a half miles later. Livingston ran the trail at six every morning and then walked it before dinner every night.

The target appearance to maintain now was age forty. Everything that went into his body and every liter of sweat he produced trimming and shaping it was aimed at that target. The only area he would concede to his fifty-three years was hair color. Too much of a pain to dye it, the wrinkles on his forehead and around the eyes had finally convinced him that he couldn't get away with it anymore—it looked out of place, and his stylist had done wonders cutting and snipping, combing and gelling, modeling his black and gray hair into the coveted category of distinguished. A wrong part here, or a bit long there, and it dwindled down to: old.

Livingston looked behind him. Trailing him by twenty yards—as always—was his bodyguard, Eric. Dressed in denim slacks with a black cotton turtleneck, Eric Bannon was a chiseled copy of Livingston's own physique twenty years ago but taller and a much better marksman with a 9mm and a throwing knife. And...he was bedding Livingston's wife. The conquests were recorded by the estate's video surveillance system: on the wicker couch in the greenhouse, standing in the shallow end of the Olympic indoor pool, on an ottoman in the library, and in one of the guest suite showers.

Eric gave him the okay sign. Livingston signaled back and then continued, picking up his pace. If it had been his first or second wife, it might have mattered. But this was his third. She was three years younger than Eric, the owner of a magic ass, breasts that no sweatshirt could shelter from inspection, and a face that made anyone forget her lack of substance in the cranial region. She was seen with him, tended him, even humored him, but the truth was clear: she was uninterested in him. His one and only visit to a marriage counselor with his second wife had given words to her main complaints: he was a misogynistic, narcissistic bastard who was unwilling to change. Wifey number two had clapped from the therapist's couch when the therapist doled out the diagnosis. Livingston had smirked, and then shut down. The therapist was now married to ex-wife number two.

After the session, alone in his study, a repressed memory had assaulted his conscience while he sipped a scotch by the fire. He was eight years old and his father walked him across the backyard where his mother painted in the afternoons. Arriving at the easel, his father made him drop his pants and then piss all over his mother's finished painting—a work that had taken over a month. After destroying the painting, he began to cry as he zipped up his pants. It was then that his father had latched on to his neck and dragged him into the garage. Bending him over the workbench, his father had removed his own leather belt—and begun to swing. He didn't know which was louder, his screams of agony or the sound of the belt whiffing through air and smacking on his buttocks and back. When his father had finished, he said to Livingston, "Now you've got something to cry about."

His mind had started to access other sessions that had occurred from then until he was around fourteen, but his anger had taken over at that point, and he had left the study and worked out for two hours in his estate's gym. This was one way he dealt with the past. There was also another way.

Livingston looked at his watch. His guest should be arriving for cocktails now. Another half-hour to finish the walk, another half-hour to shave, shower, and dress for dinner. Then, business.

Livingston remembered the first time he saw him. November, 1975 in this house. The blessing of Korean descent made the man's age ambiguous, and the small figure approached Livingston in the same manner as he had used to approach his father: slow gait, eyes fixed on his, the mouth in something short of a smile, and the timed extension of his smooth hand.

"Mr. Sanders," Livingston said, shaking the man's hand.

Dai Sanders said nothing, but shook hard.

Sanders was a chain smoker, and cancer waited in the old man's lungs like a vulture sitting on a wounded animal's chest, peering into the eyes, waiting for death. Seventy-seven. Maybe less than a year left. No wife. A mistress. No children—that were known of. A multi-millionaire, by virtue of the work for Livingston's father, and now Livingston. Sanders was here to discuss his replacement.

The men sat down at the end of a long mahogany dining room table, and a servant uncorked a thirty-year old bottle of wine. After pouring the men's glasses, he disappeared into the pantry.

Sanders took a drink and then nodded his approval. He had the look of a man who had lived with a secret too long.

Livingston took a drink and watched Sanders light a cigarette—might as well go down swinging.

Sanders's performance in the company had been superior in every way for forty-one years, even strong enough to survive that one blemish. The board had been split as whether to execute Sanders when the hiccup occurred; the elder Livingston's vote to keep Sanders had broken the tie, but the old man had now passed away and Livingston was in control. Half the board members said that it was Sanders's fault: he was in charge of the seaplane's maintenance, and it was assumed that the plane had gone down. The other half said that it had been the pilot's fault for trying to rush the shipment in bad weather. The board let Sanders live but only on the condition that someone had to go. One cold Friday night in January 1976, Sanders's assistant—and part-time lover—left for a weekend getaway and never returned.

Livingston remembered thinking that something must be very wrong for him to be summoned back to Vancouver on the first available flight from New York—the destination of the goods his father shipped—that November morning in '75. He knew that the situation would not be discussed over the phone—business was *only* discussed in person. On the flight, he had read about an iron-ore carrier that had been lost in Lake Superior due to a huge storm. When he had arrived in Vancouver, he discovered that the ship was not the only thing the storm had claimed: the largest shipment his father's company had ever attempted had been lost. Over twenty million dollars in jewels.

The legitimate side of the family business was trucking in the U.S. and Canada and shipping on the Great Lakes Waterway and the Atlantic, and it had made the Livingston family millionaires many times over. As for the jewel smuggling, Livingston's father had been skeptical of adding another wing to his business. The jewels were stolen: either robbing couriers and retailers or through simple smash and grab operations by a large number of replaceable street thieves looking to make a quick buck, with enough cut outs between them and the boss that it didn't matter if a few got caught. It wasn't the stealing that his father had worried about, it was the transportation method. Speed was the name of the game; trucks were too slow for the entire trip, and the jewels had to be transported and sold off in a hurry. The sellers in New York had been bought off to not ask where the gems were coming from, but if the efficiency of the exchange dropped, then it put the operation at risk. Livingston's father hadn't trusted aircraft—never flew—and there wasn't enough of a profit margin for assuming the risk on his own. But, as a professional courtesy for another partner in a drug distribution machine, his father had agreed to transport the jewels from Vancouver to New York for a year—Vancouver to Lake of the Woods by truck, Lake of the Woods to Lake Superior by air, and the rest of the way by truck. When the mega-shipment disappeared, he had arranged to pay some of the money back, but avoided paying back the majority due to the fact that the business partner had hired the pilot and co-pilot.

The illegitimate side of the family business also allowed drugs to be smuggled aboard a small percentage of their vessels. In the early days, it was Livingston's father's trucks that did the main distribution. The product would travel the classic route from Colombia to Tijuana to Los Angeles and straight up the west coast to Vancouver. Here, his father's trucking business would swing into motion and take it wherever in Canada that the cartel wanted. However, the Royal Canadian Mounted Police in conjunction with the U.S. Drug Enforcement Administration started cracking down, and Vancouver soon lost all of its attraction as a distribution center. His father cut a deal with the cartel to remove the product from his company vehicles on the Canadian side of the border, and Livingston Trucking continued to operate as if nothing had ever happened.

The operation shifted to the Midwestern corridor: Colombia to Laredo to Houston to Dallas to Chicago to Minneapolis. From there, the product would be driven to Duluth and loaded onto Livingston's merchant vessels, which would travel across Lake Superior, drop off some of the product at Livingston's main house on the eastern shore of Lake Superior, which was still in Canada, where it was then distributed all over Ontario. The rest of the shipment traveled through the Great Lakes Waterway: Superior to Huron to Erie to Ontario and finally to the Atlantic Ocean via the St. Lawrence Seaway. In the beginning, it was easy. The DEA and Feds were always looking for ships coming up the east coast of the United States from the *south*. Livingston's ships always dropped off shipments to Boston and New York from the *north* and went unnoticed. Then, the agencies started figuring out that fighting the war on drugs was akin to plugging one hole in a sinking ship, thinking they had saved the ship, only to find out there were other holes where water was rushing in.

However, more and more holes were now starting to be plugged. For the past five years, Livingston had had to alter the route again to avoid suspicion. Small cabin cruisers rendezvoused with the merchants just north of Oswego, New York—Buffalo and Rochester were too closely watched. After picking up their shipments, the cabin cruisers would pull up to the dock, get loaded onto boat trailers, and then get driven to a warehouse where the product would be loaded onto harmless moving trucks and then down to Syracuse, over to Albany, and then south to New York City.

The traditional route south through the Atlantic Ocean only made one stop nowadays: a luxury yacht from one of the Hamptons' estates would travel offshore and meet up with one of Livingston's merchants once a month, which would keep the rich and famous hopped up in between shipments. Money was never an issue, for it oozed out of the city and danced all the way to Montauk.

If there was ever an emergency, then Livingston's main house on Lake Superior had enough personnel to offload and distribute the entire product—it would just take longer to get south.

"How are things at the house?" Livingston said.

Sanders took a drag on his cigarette and then exhaled. "The renovation was completed three weeks ago. The communication room is completely secure, the passage from the basement to the cave has been updated with a stainless-steel staircase, and a false back has been installed to disguise the sea cave, which can now hold the two cabin cruisers, the jet skis, and the new slip can accommodate a yacht up to one hundred feet if we need to keep an unwanted visitor's boat out of sight. It's more like a hanger now." Sanders took another drag, and then went into a coughing fit for almost a minute. He sucked down his entire glass of water, and then continued...after lighting up another cigarette. "The master bedroom now has an additional two hundred square feet, and the elevator in the master closet now stops at the sea cave. And," Sanders paused, "an extra guest suite has been built in the cave for security and your...your hobby."

Finally, the relevant part. "Is the room secure?" Livingston asked.

"Completely soundproof." He looked Livingston in the eyes. "No one can leave."

Livingston twirled the stem of his wineglass, watching the dark red liquid circle around the bowl. "Good," he said. "I had heard, though, that there were problems with the hydraulics that raise and lower the false back of the cave."

"Who told you that?" Sanders said.

Still so nervous. "No one important," Livingston said.

Sanders inhaled. "The hydraulics are fine. The false back raises and lowers in less than a minute."

"Excellent. And it lowers all the way to the lake bottom, correct?"

"On the sides, yes. But there is about two feet of clearance underneath the middle—a section of only about ten yards."

Livingston raised his eyebrows.

Sanders spoke reassuringly. "What you have to remember though is that it is thirty feet deep at that point."

Livingston relaxed. "Still, I want the area outside the cave patrolled."

"We have been and will continue to," Sanders said.

A buzzer rang next to his chair, and Livingston pressed a black button on a console underneath the table.

The door to the dining room opened and the waiter brought in two plates of roasted duck, sautéed vegetables, and another bottle of wine.

The waiter left the room again, and the men started their dinners. Sanders picked at his food.

"Something wrong?" Livingston said. "I'm okay with the cave door."

Sanders set his fork down. "It still bothers me."

Something else...the room—or twenty years ago? "What?" Livingston said. Another coughing fit.

"I'm going to die soon. We both know that," Sanders said. "And I can't forget that we never found the cargo, and we never found those two employees."

"It wasn't because we didn't search."

"Do you know how many times I've sat looking at a map of the northern United States and Canada trying to deduce where they could have gone? There is still a part of me that thinks they are on some Caribbean island kicking back and laughing."

"Not much of a chance. We'd have known if they'd tried to pawn off the goods. They're at the bottom of one of Canada's three million lakes—and we're never going to find them or the shipment."

"We should have never hired them," Sanders said.

Still hanging on to the pilot fault theory. Probably the only way he lives with himself. Livingston adjusted his tie, and then leaned forward. "*We* didn't hire them, remember?" Livingston sat back. "Dai, you recovered from it. We've made millions since then." He took a sip of wine. "And my father and I never thought you were to blame."

They were seated in the den smoking Cuban cigars from a box that had arrived last week. Livingston opened an eighty-year-old bottle of scotch and poured two glasses. Sanders did not take his eyes off the bottle as Livingston smelled the cork top before putting it back on. Sanders licked his lips as he accepted the glass.

"I've decided on your replacement," Livingston said.

"Keach?" Sanders said.

"No," Livingston said. "Bannon."

Sanders looked puzzled, and he took his first glorious sip of the aged single malt. "But, he's your—"

"Yes. He's my bodyguard. But I need someone I can trust at that position." Livingston took a sip of scotch, let the flavors roll over his tongue, and then swallowed. "And, you know how often I visit."

"He doesn't have much experience. Keach knows the merchant captains, and that's a must." Sanders lowered his voice to a whisper. *Christ, does he think the house is bugged?* "Plus, he's also been in the room the few times we've had to meet face to face with the folks from down south."

"All true. But I've made up my mind. You and Keach will bring him up to speed."

Sanders tapped his fingers on the table. "That could take some time."

"Nonsense," Livingston said.

Sanders began to cough again. "When do I start my turnover?"

"I'll notify Eric tonight. He'll fly out with us tomorrow."

"When will *I* move out?"

"We have a shipment coming in next week, right?"

Sanders nodded, still hacking.

"I think that should be sufficient to show Eric what you do. Then, you may move to the house we have set up." It was a one-story stucco on the beach in Boca Raton that Livingston planned on leveling and then building something bigger after Sanders passed away.

Sanders crossed his legs and relaxed. "It will be nice to leave Lake Superior."

"Tired of freezing from December to March?"

"I was a moderate drinker until I got put in charge of the main house and cave." Sanders raised his glass. "The past forty winters have turned me into a certified alcoholic."

Livingston looked at his glass of scotch. What does someone say to that? "Is there anything else to discuss?"

Sanders drained his glass. "No." He stood. "I think I'll turn in."

They shook hands, and Sanders left. Livingston punched a button on his intercom. Eric Bannon's voice answered, "Yes, sir?"

"I need to see you in the den," Livingston said.

"On my way."

9

LAKE SUPERIOR, AUGUST 1985

Richard and Evangeline Bertram made sweaty love in the salon of their brand new forty-six-foot custom made sailboat. It was taking time—it always took time when Bertram loved Jim Beam as much as her.

He lay on top of her pounding away like the waves on the hull, moaning, and disregarding her. *He's worse than usual tonight.* She brought her legs up and tried to fake the sounds that announced she was in ecstasy. Now he noticed her, and things soon began to happen. Thank. God.

Bertram rolled off and gasped for breath. The cushions were soaked beneath her and she could taste his sweat on her lips.

"Want a drink?" he said.

Those were his first words? No post-coital cuddling or chat to make up for the performance? Of course not, it was back to the bottle. "I'll pass," Evangeline said. "Someone's got to steer the boat tonight."

"We've got autopilot, kiddo," said Bertram, rubbing her inner thighs.

"We *had* autopilot," she said. "Have you forgotten already?"

The automatic steering mechanism had failed two days ago, almost running them into a moored Bayliner while they were at it in the master stateroom.

Since then, they had been alternating shifts at night, midnight to six a.m., while the other one slept. If it became too much—or they were going to have sex—they would anchor; the incident two days prior had scared her. She imagined the boat hitting something, poking a hole in the hull, and she and Richard scrambling naked to get into the lifeboat.

Bertram had offered to anchor every night, but she had insisted that they circumnavigate Lake Superior as quickly as possible. Why they had started the voyage on the western side of the lake made no sense to her, but they were now off the eastern shore and headed north. She liked the new boat, but she liked getting rich more. And the sooner Bertram returned to his millionaire client in the multi-million-dollar case against a Detroit auto company, the better. She was thirty, he was north of fifty. How many more suits like this would there be to cash in on? Not enough.

"All right," Bertram said. "I'm gonna have one more, help you get the anchor up, and then hit the sack."

She watched as he stood and then swayed toward the galley, grabbing the shelves on the port bulkhead to steady himself.

He was clumsy even without the help of Mr. Beam, but somehow he was still loveable. Despite being a terrible lay.

It was nearing two a.m. and Evangeline stood in the cockpit to check her course. The sky was a mesh of clouds that hid the moon, making the water even darker. Her face glowed above the amber light of the binnacle. N/NE. Good. Bring it a bit closer to shore. The wind had almost died to the point where she would have to motor, which might wake him. Even though the master stateroom was forward, he was a light sleeper, even laced with booze.

She looked up at the mainsail. Just before midnight, she had reefed it because the winds were too much for her to handle. Now, if the wind didn't pick up, she would take it down. She decided to go below and plot her two a.m. fix early and lay out her next Dead Reckoning plot. She did a 360-degree survey of the horizon with the binoculars like he had told her to do any time she left the cockpit—to make sure they wouldn't hit anything. They were less than two miles offshore and she could see lights dotting the coast. There were no navigation lights off the bow, to port, aft, or to starboard. Taking the two pieces of line he had rigged when the autopilot broke, she secured the helm on its current course. She hung the binoculars around the binnacle and then descended the steps into the salon.

The smell of wood was pleasant to her now that the boat's cabin had cooled from a flow of night air through the open hatch. During the day, it smelled like a hot, wet, pile of lumber and was too much. She had tried squirting some perfume here and there, but it had made it worse.

Taking a seat behind the mahogany desk, she took a drink from her coffee mug and then turned the knob on the Loran. A soft green glow lit the workspace—destroying her night vision—and she took a pencil and entered the boat's latitude and longitude into their log book. Then, she took a pair of dividers and marked off their position. The fix was right on top of her last DR. And he had said that this would never happen. She'd show him in the morning. With no adjustment to their course needed, the new plot would be easy. Using a parallel ruler, she walked their course over from the compass on the chart and extended a line from their position. She looked at their speed, and after adjusting her dividers swung an arc fifteen minutes out and then another fifteen minutes past that. She turned the VHF volume up, listened for their agreed time of one minute, and after hearing nothing turned the volume back down.

"Nothing happens up here in the summer, kiddo," he had said.

She had replied with, "But what if someone needs our help?"

"Fuck 'em. We're on vacation, remember?" The conversation had ended there.

Satisfied that she had met the requirements of her half-hour routine, she turned the knob on the Loran and the green glow vanished. She allowed her eyes to regain their night vision and decided to make a head call before going up.

The toilet seat was cold on her bare bottom, and she had to spread her legs to support herself as the boat rocked with the waves. She couldn't flush because that would wake him. She watched as her urine sloshed back and forth and she lowered the lid back down with care. He had it easy—could just pull it out and pee over the side on his watch. As she left the head, the boat heeled to starboard. If she had not been holding on to the hatch handle, she would have fallen over. Did they hit something? Should she wake him? She stood motionless for a moment and nothing more happened. Just confused seas, or maybe one of the lines she had secured to the helm had slipped off. Before getting him up, she would check to see if this was the case. Embarrassment at two in the morning was not something she needed. Plus, he was an asshole in the middle of the night after drinking. She headed toward the hatch.

As she emerged from the cockpit a hand went over her mouth and she was picked up off the deck. Her eyes went wide and she struggled to break free. It was no use. She was about to scream when another figure stepped in front of her and put a knife to her throat. The man was huge, at least six inches taller than Richard and outweighing him by fifty pounds.

"How many else onboard?" the man whispered.

She stood motionless.

He took the knife and pushed the point into her neck, just breaking the skin.

She winced in pain, and then held up one finger.

"Man or a woman?" the man said.

All that could be heard from behind the hand over her mouth was "Mmmmm."

"Just like we thought." The large man looked her up and down. "She's even better up close than what we saw of her through the binoculars today." The man reached out his hand and rubbed Evangeline's breasts in slow circles, looking into her eyes. "Now listen, you cunt. You're going to sit in the cockpit and call your man up here. If you even look like you're going to warn him, we'll kill both of you. Nod if you understand?"

Evangeline started to tear up.

He motioned to the man holding her, and the man tightened his grip.

"I said *nod* if you understand."

She nodded.

They positioned her behind the wheel and then headed forward of the hatch.

On her fourth call, there was movement in the salon as Bertram moved toward the cockpit.

His head appeared below and he locked eyes with Evangeline. "What in the hell is it?"

She looked at him but said nothing.

He started up the steps.

"What the fuc—"

The large man picked Bertram up and then slammed him to the deck, cutting Bertram's head. The lawyer struggled, sort of. The other man grabbed Evangeline and wrestled her below. Bertram went to speak, but was quieted as the large man on top of him took out a revolver with a silencer attached, pressed it to Bertram's head, and fired. Blood, skull, brain, and hair sprayed onto the white leather cockpit bench.

The man below came to the steps. "She's subdued. Let's have our fun with her first before we tow the boat in." He wiped sweat from his forehead.

"That body is really something too. We won't get another chance after we turn her over. Guaranteed she'll be big boss's favorite."

The large man leaned his head into the hatch opening. "No. We were given strict orders." The man at the bottom of the steps sulked. The man topside jerked his hand behind him. "Come up here and load him on the boat, drive out a few miles, dump him, and then get back here."

The man below nodded and then turned toward the v-berth where the woman was unconscious and naked on the bed. He paused, and then turned around and headed up the companionway steps.

10

JUNE 1995

It had taken three full summers to restore the boat. The odds had been that it would never make it out of the harbor, let alone sail again. Robin Norris tried to explain the importance to Trist: the opportunity to refinish, refurbish, and restore a wooden boat was the opportunity to *discover* the boat. Trist didn't buy it. He wondered why they just didn't get a fiberglass boat. It was then that Robin had brought in the heavy ammo, "To quote from the greatest novel ever written about sailing, 'Plastic is dead. Wood is alive,'" he had stated.

"What novel is that?" Trist had scoffed.

"*Overboard*, by Hank Searls. A book you need to read before we head out. Plus, you still haven't finished your voyage with Captain Slocum."

Trist had just frowned.

Almost one-quarter of the hull had to be replaced due to rot, neglect, and damage from the grounding on a reef that had almost sunk her off of Florida.

Ralph Shelby had purchased it from a boat yard in Key West where he had worked one summer during college. The yard manager had remembered the young man's enthusiasm for wooden boats and had called Shelby after he couldn't sell it. In a test of trust, Ralph had sent his then fifteen-year-old son Kevin with extra gas, food, and lodging money, a truck, and a trailer to pick up the boat and bring it to Michigan. He estimated two weeks for the round trip as long as his son didn't get pulled over and asked for his non-existent driver's license. Kevin returned with the boat almost a month later with no money left and the truck littered with empty beer cans and McDonald's wrappers.

When the replacement wood for the hull arrived, Robin and Trist unloaded the shipment into their pole barn. As soon as the delivery truck disappeared down the winding driveway, the measuring, cutting, sanding, mixing and applying epoxy, then fitting, more sanding, and more mixing began. At one point, it seemed like he would be having his retirement party in the pole barn while he finished caulking the boat. Nevertheless, the work went on for hours a day until they finally were able to apply the gel coat finish.

The inside of the boat was where the real work had been needed. Everywhere Robin looked was chewed up, splintered, and dominated by rotten, gray-colored wood. The shame was that the majority of it was African mahogany, the best in the world. The rest was Philippine mahogany, and the deck was teak. Day by day and hour by hour, Robin unscrewed, pried, and removed each piece of wood. With the pieces laid in rows on bed sheets on the pole barn floor like soldiers in formation, Robin brought Trist to his workbench. An orbit sander, belt sander, two masks, and two-foot-high stacks of sandpaper—coarse paper with medium grit in one and fine grit in the other—sat on top of the bench. On the floor was a five-gallon bucket that contained new cutting brushes, a box of assorted screws, a bundle of soft cloths, and plastic sheets. Next to the bucket was a perfect cube-shaped stack of 64-quart cans of Marine Spar clear gloss varnish. Ralph Shelby had recommended that he use Sikkens varnish, but Sikkens could run over fifty bucks a gallon.

While Robin sanded the entire hull, Trist worked on the interior pieces. First, he would put a strip of paper on the sander and sand the piece of mahogany or teak down to a bare finish, which took forever since most pieces were old and torn up. Once this was accomplished, he would use one of the cutting brushes to apply the varnish. He would have to wait twenty-four hours, and then he would sand the piece, wipe it with a soft cloth, and apply another coat of varnish. Robin's standard was seven coats.

By the middle of the third summer, every piece glowed on the white bed sheets as Robin inspected them. He patted Trist on the back before sending him to return to the boat's interior. Piece by piece, screw by screw, the salon, v-berth, and galley came alive again. The teak decking now shimmered from Trist's long hours of varnishing. After that, decisions had to be made about how to refit the boat.

Her overall length was thirty-six feet, and Robin had decided to go with simplicity—she'd be comfortable but also practical. He'd economized where he could, but had also pulled money from the raises and bonuses that he had stashed away in a no-load mutual fund for the past dozen years. *Levity* would have what he wanted—even if, now, he would only get her for a short while. The five Great Lakes were known by the acronym "HOMES" (**H**uron, **O**ntario, **M**ichigan, **E**rie, and **S**uperior). His goal had been to complete the 'HOMES Feat'—circumnavigating each Great Lake—by fifty. He'd only bag one leg; Trist would have to tackle the other four.

Instead of a traditional setup in the v-berth, he went with an enormous gear and sail locker where the berth would have gone and one hammock on the starboard side with the mounted Coleman coolers beneath. On the port side were the beer kegs filled with water and their supply locker. Moving aft, there was the head with soft white towels and a new sink and shower on the port side of the passageway and a complete bulkhead of storage compartments on the starboard side. The salon had a long couch with storage underneath to port and across from it was a u-shaped couch around the salon table, which doubled as an additional bunk for two people when the table was lowered. The cushion fabric was navy and the throw pillows were cream colored. Aft of the long couch to port was the navigation station with a cushioned seat behind the mahogany nav table. The bulkhead next to the table had a built-in bookshelf that contained *Chapman Piloting, Bowditch, The U.S. Department of Transportation's Navigational Rules*, and the manuals for every system on the boat. Wiring the entire boat had been beyond his capability, which diminished a bit of his pride as he had wanted to restore the entire boat himself. But after consulting with a boat electrician referred to him by Shelby, he was thankful that he had not tried. His first three suggestions to the electrician were met with: 'That would start a fire—'

Aft of the couches to starboard was the galley with elderberry-colored Corian countertops. The sink, refrigerator, freezer, and gimbaled stove were stainless steel. Aft of the companionway was the owner's suite where Levana had made a burgundy quilt that fit snugly over the double berth. A family picture from a few years back rested on the starboard bulkhead bookshelf along with twenty or so paperbacks wedged in next to a dictionary and atlas. Under the companionway steps was the engine he had overhauled.

Topside, her rigging, lines, and sails were classic. In order to single-hand the boat, he had special modifications made that ran all of the sheets back near the helm console. The wheel was stainless steel, and the helm seat and rail unlocked behind and swung open to give access to the swim step behind the transom. He had teared up when the mast was first raised and the shrouds, forestay, and backstay tightened. The only aspect that, perhaps, dulled the sleek figure the boat cut was the large pulpit he had specially built off the bow that extended beyond where the anchor deployed from—a childhood obsession from watching *Jaws* one too many times. However, it was Trist's favorite place to be when the boat was at sea. He had also installed a new vertical windlass and built a larger chain locker to hold the all-chain rode he had purchased.

"Trist, dinner!" Levana yelled from the kitchen. A moment later she could hear his footsteps going across the floor upstairs. Her eyes traced the sound along the ceiling, down the stairs, and finally into the doorway as he entered from the dining room.

"What are we having?" Trist said.

"Dad is surprising us," she said while placing a stack of napkins on the table, "I'm just setting. Grab a pop from the fridge for yourself and two beers please."

Trist walked toward the refrigerator. Then, the door to the deck opened.

"Here we are, team," Robin said, entering the room with a large plate covered in tin foil.

The smell of barbeque chicken wafted across the room, and Trist's mouth started to water. He pulled the drinks from the fridge and then sat down at the table.

Robin uncovered the chicken and dashed outside where he grabbed another plate full of French fries and a large can of his homemade barbeque sauce—honey, lemons, and sugar mixed in secret amounts with the base sauce. It was so good that friends and family would beg for the recipe, but he would not surrender.

"We haven't had this in ages," Trist said.

"Guess he's trying to give you one last nice meal on dry land before you head out tomorrow morning," Levana said.

Robin brought in the fries and barbeque sauce and sat down. "Thought this would do the trick for tonight. What do you say, Trist?"

No amount of teenage angst could wedge itself into this meal. "Lovin' it. Thanks, Dad."

There were some meals that just made you feel good to be at home. Levana's lasagna was a strong contender in the race, but Robin's barbeque chicken was the ship he was ready to go down with. He gave Levana's hand a squeeze and Trist a loving pat to the shoulder.

Levana's grin was full—of gratitude, of memories, and already full of longing for the remaining dinners that they would be able to have like this. The doctors couldn't predict when his appetite might change, but they all knew it could happen soon. Her eyes welled up, and her mind wandered back as Robin and Trist attacked their plates.

Her husband sat in a hospital gown at the edge of the examination table in a room where normally he was the one taking patients' blood pressure, temperature, and pulse before the doctor arrived. Levana watched him. For the first time in her life, she saw her husband nervous. She inched her chair closer and held his hand, which was warm and sweaty. Whatever news they were about to receive, they would figure it out together. They had already figured out so much—pregnancy in college, loss of parents, loss of a child... She steeled herself: *bring it on, we will survive.*

The door opened, and Doctor Marcus Henry Jacobsen entered with his team of nurses—Betsy Pickford, Karen McManus, and Audrey Knight, all good nurses, all four good friends. From hospital holiday parties and fundraisers and long Saturday night dinners with wine and jazz music, they had become a tight-knit group. It was hard not to in a small town hospital; it was also hard not to because Robin always made everyone feel like he or she was valued.

The hospital team assumed the notifying-a-patient-of-his-condition formation, Doc Jacobsen forward on the level of the patient, the nurses in the wings. If the patient is standing, the doc stands; if the patient is seated, the doc sits. Robin had told her about this procedure a thousand times. It was unusual to experience it, now, from the other side.

She scanned the eyes of the nurses for signs. Karen looked down, Betsy looked at Robin's chart, and Audrey just looked like she might cry. Levana looked at Doc Jacobsen—poker face. How many patients had he calmed down with his baritone voice and easy smile? Robin said that it was like a spell the man cast when he walked into a hospital room—'He even calms me down, and I'm the goddamn nurse.' It was more than that, though. On Jacobsen's first day at work, Robin had noticed how nervous the young doctor was and had pulled him inside a room and steadied him—"I've got your back. No patient wants to be here, Doc. Together, we have to keep him calm." And Robin hadn't told her about this; it had been Jacobsen who confided it years ago as they sat alone at a bonfire on the Norris's beach while Robin went to get more wood.

And here they were now. Jacobsen took her hand, gave it a squeeze, and then looked into Robin's eyes. He sat down next to him on the bed. "Robin, you have pancreatic cancer, and it is very advanced."

Tears started to run down her face.

Jacobsen paused.

Robin nodded. "Give me the rest straight, Marcus."

"We found exocrine tumors—adenocarcinoma—in the ducts of your pancreas." Jacobsen looked to the ceiling for answers. "If they were endocrine tumors and we had found them earlier, then maybe we would have had an outside chance at beating it. But because this type of cancer can form before someone has any symptoms, it's almost always too late to treat when the symptoms do show up." He took a breath, his face a mixture of guilt and bewilderment. "You're thirty-five...it's almost unheard of for someone to have this type of cancer at that age."

know I pride myself on staying in shape," Robin said. "When I naving back pain, I thought I pulled a muscle; I never thought it would be something else." He looked at Levana and then back at Jacobsen. "Surgery?"

"It would have been an option if we had found it early. In fact, it's the only real option to treat this type of cancer—when the tumors are treatable." He paused. "But it has already spread to your liver. Your back pain started when the tumors began to block the ducts from it."

"How long?"

"No way to know for sure. We'll go the pain management route where some pancreatic cancer patients have carried on normally for a few months, but the end is usually quick. It's just difficult to nail down when that transition will take place."

Robin closed his eyes. Then, he leaned over and gave Jacobsen a hug and Jacobsen's eyes let loose. "Dammit, Robin, I'm the one who's supposed to be there for *you* right now."

With a reserve of stoicism unknown even to her, she watched and listened as Robin said into Jacobsen's ear, "I know how difficult that was for you, Doctor." He let go of his old friend.

Jacobsen gathered himself and gave Levana a hug—holding her for a long time.

They released, and he stood up. "We'll talk palliative care when I come back," he said and then exited.

Karen and Audrey sniffled. But the lead nurse—a surrogate mother to every nurse in the hospital, including Robin—seventy-one-year-old Betsy Pickford summoned the courage to carry out the rest of the routine. "Is there anyone I can call for you both?"

Two head shakes 'no.'

"Anything I can do to make you more comfortable before we leave?"

Two head shakes 'no.'

Betsy walked forward and placed one hand on Levana's shoulder and her other on Robin's right knee. "I'll give you some time and then I'll come back and check on you. If you need me there's a call bell and I'll—"

"—come back right away," Robin finished her sentence.

Their eyes met, and suddenly Betsy turned and motioned the nurses out of the room before tears started to stream down her cheeks.

The door opened. Levana heard the sound of a bed being wheeled past the room, an announcement on the intercom system, the murmur of voices in the hallway, a man saying, "Nurse?" before the door closed, leaving them in silence.

Robin leaned back on the bed and rested his head on the pillow. He stared at the ceiling and then closed his eyes. She caressed his head from forehead to hair to ear to cheek and then repeated the movement again, and again, and again.

"Lost my touch?" Robin said to Levana.

She stared down at her full plate and then looked at Trist who was already starting to dish up seconds. "Absolutely not," she said, "just taking it all in before I start." She dipped a piece of chicken in a pool of barbeque sauce and then savored the bite in her mouth before swallowing and washing it down with a sip of ice-cold beer.

"That's more like it," Robin said as he dished up another plate for himself. He turned to Trist. "Figured out our dive plan."

Trist finished his coke in one giant gulp and got up to get another. "Let's hear it."

Robin pulled a piece of paper out of his shirt pocket. "Well, we're putting the boat in at Munising, so I figure we'll hit the *Bermuda* first. Plus, we'll get treated to some of the best scenery the earth has to offer there when we see the different-colored cliffs, fine beaches, sea caves, and the pictured rocks: Chapel

Rock, Indian Head, Miners Castle, and Lovers Leap." He rubbed his neck. "There's just nothing like it."

"I've seen pictures, but the way Uncle Tyee talks, nothing beats seeing it in person," Trist said.

"Your Uncle is right. We used to go fishing up there together."

Levana gave a tortured smile—so many memories erupted with each word—and tried to focus as Robin continued.

"After that I think we can get in five more wrecks as we make our way counter-clockwise around Superior until we end with the most advanced dive on *Mesquite.*"

Trist opened the fridge. "Seven dives huh? I'm game." He grabbed a coke from the top shelf and closed the door. "What makes *Mesquite* the highlight?"

"*Mesquite* is a Coast Guard cutter that grounded off the Keweenaw Peninsula in December of 1989. The crew made it safely away on lifeboats, and the ship was later determined to be unsalvageable. Then, as what happens to some ships that can't be fixed but are still afloat, a bidding war started over who would get to sink her and where."

"Bidding war?" Trist said as he returned to the table, cracked open his coke, and dug back into his food.

"Well, when a ship can't be saved, it usually becomes a shipwreck and part of an underwater preserve. Naturally, specific groups want the ship sunk in their area, where it will attract more scuba divers and drive the tourist economy. After months of haggling, *Mesquite* was scuttled in July of 1990 in 115 feet of water a little over a mile from where she hit the rocks."

Trist nodded.

"Is the depth what makes it an advanced dive?" Levana asked.

"The wreck rests between 80 and 110 feet. So, you've got hypothermia risks, it's dark and we'll need dive lights, but also it is a wreck that can be penetrated—and that's the most dangerous part because of the silt that can be stirred up. It's dangerous to go inside any wreck, but if you penetrate one like the *Mesquite*, take a wrong turn and stir up a lot of silt, then you can be blinded inside the wreck in a few seconds and not be able to find your way out." Robin took a pull on his beer. "We'll have to be careful if we go inside."

Levana looked uneasy. "Uh, *yeah*. No shipwreck is worth losing your life over."

Robin looked at Trist. "We've been inside wrecks before. Just not one this deep."

"What's inside this one?" Trist said.

"All types of stuff. Filing cabinets with files still in them, some clothing, and what's left of the galley supplies after some idiots dove and removed them." Robin set down his beer can. "That's one thing we won't be doing is taking anything off these wrecks."

"Oh, c'mon, Dad. Everyone takes a little something as a souvenir. It's part of the experience."

"Not for us. When a ship goes down, you let her be. It's a sign of respect. I can't stand scuba divers who loot." Robin's eyes locked with his son's. "Even a visit to some shipwrecks like our most famous, the *Edmund Fitzgerald*, doesn't sit well with me. That ship *above all* should be left alone. Take one look at what corporations are doing to the *Titanic*, and you'll see my point."

"What about the stories you used to tell me about the *Griffon*? I thought *that* ship was our most famous shipwreck?"

He had a point. "Perhaps, but *Griffon* hasn't been found yet. Although—"

"What?" Levana said.

"I had a patient the other week whose relatives live in East Tawas. He said that there is an old legend of a wooden ship that is somewhere beneath the water in an inland lake named Lake Solitude that could be the *Griffon*."

"I thought *Griffon* wrecked in either Lake Michigan or Lake Huron," Trist said. "There's no way it could be at the bottom of some inland lake."

"I'd normally agree with you, but this guy said that research of the area has led some to believe that Lake Solitude used to be a part of Lake Huron."

Trist's fork, with a load of chicken and sauce dripping from it, stopped inches from his mouth. "Maybe we could drive down there when we get back."

"We just might have to do that," Robin said.

"Have you thought about making the one port call we discussed earlier?" Levana said to Robin.

"You mean we're getting off the boat at some point?" Trist said.

Robin shrugged. "Well, we've got the camping gear, but your mom heard of a wealthy guy who rents out his place called 'The Funky Beach House' a week at a time over the summer. She thought it might be a nice break from the boat for us, but only for a night or two."

"I checked, and the owner said he would work with us since you wouldn't be staying for the entire week," Levana said.

"Dad?" Trist asked.

"I'm still thinking about it. Might be nice to have a few days on dry land. I mean, we could island hop around Lake Superior, but I'd rather hug Gitche Gumee's coastline."

"Gitche what?" Trist said.

Robin shook his head. "You've got to be kidding me. Have you already forgotten?"

"Forgotten wh—"

Robin kept going. "That Lake Superior's original name was Gitche Gumee? Well, let me back up. The Ojibwe named it kitchi-gami, which means 'Great Lake of the Ojibway'. Longfellow's epic poem *The Song of Hiawatha* uses Gitche Gumee as does Lightfoot in his famous song. When the British took control of the region after the French, they re-named it Superior."

On the rebound, Trist said, "I heard Superior is so large that you can fit all four of the other Great Lakes inside it."

Levana gave Trist a wink, which Robin saw.

"I think you're right," Robin said. *He's so competitive.*

They ate a few bites in silence.

"So, we leave tomorrow morning at six, right?" Levana said.

"Yep. Boat's on the trailer, truck's in the driveway, and Tyee will be here in about an hour to stay over," Robin said.

"How long of a drive is it to Munising?" Trist said.

"Somewhere around 4 to 5 hours depending on the Mackinac Bridge traffic," Robin replied. "We'll hug Lake Huron along 23 on the way up. I don't want to get anywhere near I-75 with the trailer until we absolutely have to." He took another chug of beer. "About an hour to get the supplies loaded and the boat launched. I'm guessing that we'll cast off lines around one o'clock in the afternoon tomorrow."

"I'm glad we're going that way. One of my favorite drives and one of Michigan's great secrets." Levana said.

"What secret?" Trist rolled his eyes. "We get paradise up here for about 4 months a year and then dress like we're in the Iditarod for the other eight months."

"You've been spoiled, my sweetie," Levana said. "What I'm talking about is that most people don't know that, minus the salt, if you are on the beaches of any of the Great Lakes, it feels like you're looking out at an ocean. Plus, there's nothing in them that will eat you!" She poked Trist in the side. "It's incredible, and I'm always bewildered by people who think that the Great Lakes are just regular inland lakes. Tomorrow, we are going to have one of the most scenic drives that you can take on this planet."

"Ah, Mom. You're so loyal," Trist said. "What has Michigan ever given to you?"

"And you, my dear, are a typical cynical and egocentric teenager," she needled while casting a wicked grin. "You Gen Xers. You're all so independent and skeptical."

Robin just sat back and watched, happy to be out of the firing line for once.

Levana looked over to him. "Jump in any time."

"Couldn't," he said.

"And why not?" she shot back.

"Because this Baby Boomer still doesn't give much credibility to any other generation. Pick any topic that's worth anything, and you'll see *us* on the front lines. Except..."

"What?" Levana asked.

Robin frowned. "Don't ever follow my high school class's motto."

Trist became interested. "What motto?"

Robin stood up and spread his arms wide, "We drank the Great Lakes dry; the ocean lies before us."

Levana and Trist laughed, and then Robin joined in, and once he started he couldn't stop. It was one of those laughing fits that didn't start out to be much, but because other emotions were involved and had been locked away for so long, it became a deep-cleansing-eyes-watering laugh.

Holding her side because it hurt so much, Levana got herself under control. "What are your plans for the evening, Trist?"

"Thinkin' about takin' Rachel out to a movie and then meeting up with a few friends for ice cream afterwards," Trist said with a straight face.

Levana could see Robin start to stir. "Enjoy," she said to Trist. A cool breeze blew in through the open window, and Levana adjusted her shawl.

Robin leaned back. *Ice cream my ass.* "Well, don't make it too late. I need you rested."

Trist took his plate to the sink. Robin watched the waves start to crawl further and further up the beach as the wind picked up.

"Did you get the mail earlier?" Levana asked.

Robin shook his head. "I'll walk down and get it now."

"I'm heading out," Trist said.

"I'll walk with you," Robin said.

11

They stepped off the front porch and on to the driveway. Robin was in the lead.

"Just be careful tonight, okay?"

"Dad, I'm just going—"

"I know what you told us in there," he cut in, "but I wasn't born yesterday, Trist. This is your last night at home for over a month."

Trist was quiet as they continued to walk.

"I'll take your silence as at least an acknowledgment that you were thinking of doing something different tonight." He stopped without warning.

Trist almost walked into him but slid to the side and stopped. "Dad—"

"Hey, I'm just looking out for you. If you're seeing Rachel," he pointed at Trist's groin, "you better wrap that rascal. And, whatever you do, stay the hell away from that Shelby kid, okay?"

Trist contemplated. "Okay."

They continued to walk. Near the end of the driveway, Trist peeled off, got in the Suburban, and started it.

Robin reached the mailbox and turned around in time to see his son back up into the street and then drive off. As he watched, unexpectedly, Trist rolled down the driver's side window and gave him a wave. He felt a lump in his throat and waved back. Then the SUV disappeared around a bend.

He opened the mailbox and saw that there were only two items. He pulled them out, and his heart hardened. In his hands were two glossy cards: one from a Democratic Senator running for re-election and one from a Republican Senator trying to unseat the incumbent. Robin looked at the smiling face of the Republican Senator wearing a Carhartt jacket and a John Deere hat. He was seated on a tractor—was that a *bible* on his lap?—in a corn field with ominous skies in the background. The caption said, "Robin (so personal), the working man was born a Republican. We need you in '96, old ally." He wanted to barf. The Democratic card was even worse. On it, the incumbent wore a military uniform—Robin knew that the man had never served—and sat on a front porch swing holding a glass of...beer? apple juice?...the picture was so low quality that he couldn't tell, and looked grave. The caption said, "Robin, it's time to come home. We need all hands on deck in '96, and we've missed you."

"The hell with you clowns." Robin tore the cards to shreds and deposited the remains in the pole barn garbage can as he walked back toward the house. If there was a subject to get out of the way first in his journal to Trist, this was it.

—*From the Journal of Robin Thomas Norris*—
Religion and Politics

Gonna give it to you straight, Tristian, because I don't need to be reserved anymore—not much time left. You already know that you were raised without a specific religion; this was on purpose. We never belonged to a church, we never dissuaded you from going to any church if you wanted to try it, and we also never forced our agnostic worldview on you. I think it would be good to speak with your mother about her religious journey and see where you stand. Here's where I'm at. I've never been given an adequate answer to the question: if God created the heavens and the Earth, then who created God? I am not a believer, but I am also open to the possibility that there could be some sort of being or beings in the universe. Some people call this being spiritual; I call it being open-minded.

If you look at the arrangement of the major world religions, you'll find that they follow the same basic structure. Much of religion is a form of conditioning to try and help maintain social stability. Religion, and praying to some superior being, also fills a physiological need that most human beings require: the realities of life and the uncertainty and pain evident can be eased/explained/let go of if one has a belief that there is a steady hand at the tiller of the universe to ensure that everything will work out the way it is supposed to in the end. You'll hear it in different phrases: the man upstairs has a plan, the Lord works in mysterious ways, God has a plan for my life, I guess it was the way it was meant to be, etc. To me, I can't believe that there was some grand plan at work when plagues decimated the Renaissance populations or when the Nazis exterminated the Jews. Can you believe six million people looking to the sky and asking for God's grace only to choke moments later on gas and die? Somehow, I don't think there was an all-powerful being 'looking' down on the Earth saying, "It's all part of my master plan." You can name about a thousand other disasters that have been explained away in hopeful terms, and this practice should just cease. But there lies the world you will soon enter as an adult. Not trying to preach to you, but when your life is about to be cut decades short, you get to have your say—for whatever it's worth.

Most institutions operate as follows: entice, indoctrinate (mostly through shame, bullying—some overt, mostly covert—groupthink, repetition, withholding of information—lots of people playing 'senior with a secret', etc.), reinforce, train, and pass the torch to the next generation to keep the institutional flame alive through whatever means necessary. Fear and power dynamics are the tools of the trade. Now, have the major religions that have existed on earth for centuries been all bad? Not at all. There are some great guidelines that have done more good than bad. However, like belonging to a political party—which is why I don't— you are not allowed to be a sometime member. Moderation is becoming an obsolete concept in all walks of life. It's only 1995, but our president may be the last moderate we ever have who unites and helps people find common ground. I know, I know, I saw the news the other night with you when he was walking across the tarmac to attend a funeral and was laughing with a dignitary when he thought the cameras weren't on him and then noticed they were on him and we roared because he became solemn and wistful in a microsecond. It's a daily show in the great machine, son.

My advice: don't let religion or politics define who you are—never be owned by a specific denomination or ideology. And don't you ever look down or shame someone who sees the world differently than you do. Life and death is life and death, but the overwhelming majority of your interactions with people will not be. There will be those who act like every topic is. Steer clear of them. Be proud of our heritage, but if anyone ever tries to tell you how you should vote or dictate where your 'natural political home should be', don't just walk away— run! Be your own man. Grow into yourself. Do what you believe is right. Be generous to those who are less fortunate than you, and stand up for those who are marginalized, forgotten, and unable to help themselves. We already have enough kings and queens of the mountain in our world. Remember: Trist, you will always be enough. Whether you travel down the religious path or not, or the political path or not, the most important thing to keep in mind is to be a decent person.

Thanks for waving goodbye to me tonight from the Suburban.

The seaplane's pontoons touched down on the sapphire surface of Lake Superior and cut two straight lines of white wake behind them as the craft glided to a stop. In the main cabin, Grant Livingston sat back in a custom leather recliner and looked out at the vast rocky cliffs that defined the lake's eastern shoreline for miles.

Movement on the water's horizon drew his attention as a large cabin cruiser approached the plane. His eyes lit up at the prospect of seeing the newest addition to the Livingston fleet: a 90-foot Hatteras. Normally, either the 40-foot Carver or 20-foot Bayliner would pick him up, but he had requested a short cruise aboard the new Hatteras. Later in the summer, he would be taking the yacht on its maiden voyage from Lake Superior to the Atlantic Ocean and down to Key West and back.

The co-pilot entered the cabin. "Everything okay back here, sir?" he asked Livingston.

"Give the captain my compliments on a smooth landing," Livingston said.

The co-pilot smiled and disappeared back into the cockpit.

Livingston finished off his dirty martini and turned toward the passenger seated across the aisle from him. Dai Sanders snored, his head bent back and slightly to the left against the seat's headrest.

A newspaper ruffled behind him as Livingston's bodyguard, Eric Bannon, turned the page and continued to read.

"Wake the old man up," Livingston said.

Bannon lowered the paper and reached a strong arm forward and shook Sanders's shoulder. The old man jolted upright, eyes searching for recognition of something. Bannon went back to his paper.

"Good evening," Livingston said to Sanders.

Sanders blinked and then focused on Livingston's hazel eyes. "Good evening."

Livingston pointed out the window. "The Hatteras is on its way."

"Four luxurious staterooms, showers with sitting benches, three bars, a circular staircase from the lowest level to the flying bridge, two whirlpools, and—made just for you—mirrors on the ceiling in the master stateroom," Sanders said as he stretched. "You're never going to want to get off it."

"We'll see," Livingston said. He thought for a moment. "Do you think she'll be aboard?"

Bannon lowered his paper enough so that his eyes broke the top edge.

Sanders sat up straight and then crossed his legs. "I wouldn't be surprised."

Livingston ran a hand through his hair. "You told me she mostly stays in the main house these days."

Sanders momentarily peered past Livingston at the shoreline cliffs in the distance. On top of the cliff, a quarter mile north up the shore, rose a gargantuan house sided in cedar shake with white trim around the windows and a large deck that extended out over the one-hundred-foot drop to the water below.

"Madame should enjoy a change of scenery," Sanders said. "But the lavish lifestyle she is used to will be the same whether it's on the boat or in your mansion on the cliffs above us." Sanders leaned toward him. "Besides, your wife is back home in Vancouver. So no cat and mouse this visit."

Bannon raised his paper back up and resumed reading.

"True, it's always easier when she stays back," Livingston said. "And 'cat and mouse' is a little harsh. It's more about discretion and balance."

Sanders sat back, crossed his legs the other way. "If that's what you want to call it, then fine by me, boss."

"It is." Livingston paused. "Eric has been scouting replacements for Madame as well."

"I—I didn't know, sir," Sanders said.

"It's become...necessary," Livingston replied.

Sanders looked like he was trying to recall who the first five Presidents were. Livingston looked away and out the window again. The Hatteras was perhaps twenty yards away, and a sleek speedboat was being lowered into the water from a davit off the vessel's port quarter. Then, a figure emerged from a sliding glass hatch on the main deck.

Livingston's palms became sweaty and he rubbed them together. At the same time, his breathing took on an uneven pattern; every three or four breaths, his chest would heave on the inhalation and then shudder in tiny spasms on the exhale. His eyes were fixated on the blonde-haired woman now standing on a private balcony wearing a white short sleeve polo dress. Her dark sunglasses glinted in the fading sunlight. She appeared to be staring straight down at him;

then, she raised a champagne flute to her mouth and shifted her gaze to the small boat in the stern where four crew members from the yacht embarked.

One crew member got behind the helm and started the engine while another readied a line in his hands. The other two sat in the stern. After the boat pulled away from the yacht, it made a tight loop to starboard and was soon parallel to the seaplane with only five yards of separation.

Livingston looked back up at the woman.

She took another drink and then headed back inside the yacht.

The co-pilot emerged from the cockpit. "I'll tie us up and then you can board and head over to her, sir," he said to Livingston.

"Did you see her too?" Livingston asked.

The co-pilot stopped on his way to open the main aircraft door and saw Livingston looking up at him with perspiration on his forehead. "I meant *her*," he pointed, "your yacht, sir."

Livingston saw the man's eyes focused on his forehead. Feeling a bead of sweat travel down the center and slip on to the bridge of his nose, he lifted his right hand and wiped. "Of course," Livingston said. "She looks great."

The co-pilot gave a nervous nod and then opened the hatch. A warm breeze blew inside the cabin as he stepped out onto the plane's starboard pontoon. A crew member from the boat stood amidships and threw him a line. The co-pilot then pulled the craft over and secured the line to a cleat on the pontoon.

Bannon and Sanders unbuckled their seat belts and grabbed their duffel bags. Then, Bannon moved past Sanders and picked up Livingston's bag.

The co-pilot stuck his head back inside. "All ready, gentleman."

"So, how does this work?" Trist asked.

Kevin Shelby laughed as he took another puff from his cigarette, exhaled into the cramped cockpit of his Camaro, and then tipped back a fresh can of

Miller High Life. "Relax, buddy. He'll be here soon." Another sip. "Gonna show you how easy this shit is."

Trist sat back in the passenger's seat and cracked open a beer.

"There ya go," Kevin said.

Trist took a drink. "Who are we meeting?"

Kevin grinned and reclined. "You remember Brad Armstrong, right?"

Trist shook his head 'no.'

"Graduated two years ago, football player, dad owns Armstrong Lumber?"

It clicked. "Got it," Trist said.

"Well, you probably didn't know this because you're such a goody two shoes—"

"Hey—"

Kevin punched Trist's shoulder. "C'mon, you know it's true."

Trist took a huge gulp of beer. "Okay, Okay."

Kevin's eyes scanned around outside—driver's side window, front window, Trist's window, then the rearview mirror. He continued. "Well, Brad used to be one of the local dealers. Another guy dealt to adults and Brad's turf was the high school and junior high." Kevin motioned to the tennis courts and parking lot with his hand that held the cigarette and beer can. "This here parking spot is where Brad turned his job over to me right before our sophomore year."

"I remember you riding around with him Freshman year."

Kevin smirked. "Learned the ropes that year. Where the spots were, how to approach kids, and...how to not get caught." Kevin finished the beer and crushed the can. "Got my set of wheels that summer, and Brad passed the torch."

"Why is he still dealing?" Trist asked. "I thought he had a football scholarship."

"Dropped out after the first semester." Kevin squirmed in his seat and turned far enough around to grab a small Igloo cooler from the backseat. He took out two beers. "Finish your beer, puss," he said to Trist and handed him a cold High Life. He put the cooler back, opened his can, and gulped. "Brad's moved up now. Deals out of Detroit. He comes up here every few weeks and delivers the goods to me. I sell it all, take my cut and give the rest of the cash to Brad when he comes back. It's a piece of cake."

"What's your long-term plan?"

Kevin paused and stared at him. "What do you mean?"

"I mean, you staying in the business or passing it on when you go to school?"

"Fuck school, man. I ain't budgin'."

Trist finished off his beer and opened the new can. "Don't you have a replacement?"

"Not right now. Gotta a couple of prospects in this year's freshman class, but I'll have to watch 'em for a little bit."

"But you'll have to pass on the job to someone. You can't hang around school after this year or it would look suspicious."

"So now you're the local drug dealing expert, huh? Just let me worry about it, okay?" He did a surveillance sweep with his eyes again. "Plus, my old man's headed for an early grave anyway. I don't think it's even registered with him how I was able to afford my truck and this beauty. A few more bottles of Smirnoff deposited in his liver and I'll be running the marina. Then I'll talk to Brad about passing the torch. He'll know what to do—guy's a genius."

Headlights appeared in the distance. Kevin was way keyed up, despite the 4 beers, so he noticed them first. As they got closer—traveling at a slow but steady speed—he perked up in his seat. "That's him," Kevin said. He looked at his watch. Ten-thirty, right on the nose. "Goddamnit, he's smooth as silk," Kevin smiled. "In the business, this is what we call professionalism, Trist. You show up on time, every time. You receive the delivery quietly and then drive off like nothing ever happened. Plus, we're small-time here in Hampstead.

From what Brad told me, the regional boss lives somewhere up in Canada." The car's blinker came on. "Get ready to watch and learn."

Trist wiped his sweaty palms on his jeans and observed the car turn into the tennis court parking lot. It was an SUV. "I thought you said Brad always showed up in his old Chrysler Cordoba?"

Kevin tilted his head. "I—" He leaned forward and squinted. The SUV continued to roll toward them. "Trist, how many people do you see?"

Trist's eyes focused on the windshield, but the headlights made it impossible to make out the interior, even shadows. "I can't tell."

Kevin reached under his seat and pulled out a .357 Magnum.

"Whoa. What the hell, Kevin?"

"Shut up," Kevin said. He looked at the oncoming SUV and then his eyes darted to Trist's. "I don't think it's Brad."

"Let's get outta here," Trist said.

"Naw. Too late now." The SUV came to a halt three spots away, parallel to the Camaro's driver's side. "Be ready."

"Ready for *what*?"

The SUV's passenger's side door opened and out stepped a man wearing boots, jeans, and a lightweight jacket. He closed the door and approached the Camaro.

Kevin slid the gun between the seat and center console, barrel down and safety off. He lifted his leg to conceal it and placed his right hand on his knee.

The man smiled as he reached the car and motioned for Kevin to lower the window.

Kevin rolled the handle. As the window came down, the man bent over and his head filled in the open space. "Evenin', boys. Now, don't you get spooked. Everything is fine." He looked at Kevin. "Kevin, right?"

Kevin shook his head.

The man eyed Trist. "And who do we have here?"

Trist cleared his throat. "A friend."

He looked back at Kevin. "That true?"

Kevin looked at the man. Behind him, the sound of a door opening could be heard. "Yeah," Kevin said.

"Well then, you're in business." The scent from Kevin's breath reached him. "You boys been drinkin' tonight?"

Before either of them could answer, a voice behind the man said, "Get 'em out of the car."

Kevin and Trist froze.

The man rose up and stepped away from the Camaro. "You heard him. Let's go, nice and slow."

Kevin started to reach for the Magnum's handle but was met with Trist's hand instead.

Trist squeezed, then he whispered, "No."

Kevin shook his hand free.

"C'mon. Stay cool," Trist said.

"Okay."

They climbed out of the Camaro and met near the trunk where the men were waiting. The second man was enormous, around the size of Uncle Tyee, and had a shaved head with a goatee that looked like steel wool.

"You boys armed?" the large man said.

"No," Kevin said back.

Then, the man who had been by the driver's side window came over and frisked both of them. Satisfied, he gave his partner a nod.

"I like honesty," the giant said. "Now, come over here. Wanna show you boys somethin'."

They followed the men to the back of the SUV. The smaller man motioned for them to step back a few paces. Then, the large man opened the back door.

Trist's stomach started doing cartwheels as he saw the body of Brad Armstrong curled up on the floor of the SUV. His hands and feet were bound with rope, there was blood on his t-shirt, and his face was a mess—bruises and cuts and one eye was swollen shut. Brad moaned, "Help me."

Kevin took a step forward. "What the fuck!"

The giant turned around, put both hands around Kevin's neck and picked him off of the ground. Kevin wheezed, trying to breathe. Trist made a motion to help but then saw that the other man had pulled a gun with a silencer out of his jacket and had it pointed at Trist.

The man shook Kevin side to side and then released him. Kevin hit the pavement and sucked for breath on his hands and knees.

The big man crouched down next to Kevin. "Now, we don't want to speak out of turn again. Understood?"

Kevin could only cough.

The man grabbed a handful of Kevin's hair and jerked the boy's head back in order to make eye contact. "Understood?"

Kevin's eyes twitched in fear, and he nodded.

The man rose back up. "Good. Now, where were we?" He glanced at Brad Armstrong. "Right. *This* shit." He lifted Kevin to his feet with one arm. "Now, I don't know who you brought with you tonight," he said looking at Trist, "but it's good for you to have a witness along." He let go of Kevin's arm and walked over to Brad. "This is what happens when you steal from your supplier." He pulled back and slugged Brad in the stomach.

Brad curled up tighter and sobbed. His one open eye looked straight into Trist's.

The man turned around. "Keep this vision in mind anytime you think of skimming some product or money off the top." The man paused. "Also, don't lie. This asshole told us it was *you*," he pointed at Kevin, "who was ripping us off."

Kevin's sympathy for Brad disappeared, and he straightened up.

The giant closed the trunk and put his hand on the shoulder of the man carrying the gun with the silencer. "Meet your new contact, Kevin. This is Orson."

Orson lowered his gun and shook Kevin's hand.

"What's going to happen to Brad?" Trist asked.

Orson spoke to Kevin. "Better teach your friend here to shut up."

Kevin eyed Trist and then looked back at Orson. "He didn't know about any of this. I just thought it would be a quick pick up from Brad and then we'd be off to a party. He's not involved."

The giant opened a side door and removed a shoe box. "Well, I better never see him again then. And don't bring anyone with you from now on unless it's your replacement." He closed the door. "In the meantime, let's see if he can hold on to something. C'mere," he called to Trist.

Trist walked over and put his hands on the shoe box. The man didn't let go. "Now, the two of you be on your way. Orson will be here next month to collect." He let go of the box. "New meeting place too. You know the scenic overlook a mile north of your old man's marina?"

"Yeah," Kevin said.

"Good. Orson will meet you there, same time."

Trist and Kevin walked over to the Camaro. By the time they got in, the SUV was gone.

Kevin lit a cigarette with a shaky match and then turned on the car.

"Man, you're in over your head," Trist said.

"I'm fine," Kevin said. "And maybe you didn't notice, but I kept your ass out of this."

"Thanks," Trist said. "Are you okay?"

"I'll be fine. Put that box on the back seat and cover it with the blanket."

Trist did, and they took off out of the parking lot.

Kevin turned on the radio and inserted a tape. AC/DC began to thump from the Camaro's speakers. "Need a drink?" Shelby asked.

"Hell yes," Trist said.

"Let's head out to the bonfire at Fogarty's. You need to get sloshed and have sex in the woods with Rachel."

Trist exhaled.

The Camaro roared down the street.

PART II

Cast Off

12

"I think that's it," Robin said as he came up the companionway and entered the cockpit where Tyee and Levana were sitting.

"How is he?" Tyee asked.

"Passed out in the hammock up forward. Still hungover as hell. I ought to leave him here on the dock and make him swim out to me. This cold water could knock some sense into him."

"He'll be okay in a few hours," Levana angled in. "There is nothing left in his insides, I can vouch for that. He spent most of the ride up with his head out window feeding the animals on the side of the road."

"I saw. He tried to drink the Great Lakes dry by himself," Robin said. "I told him last night—"

"Robin," she said. "Let it go right now, or it will gnaw at you for the rest of the trip. He's a kid—our kid—and he made a mistake."

"Let's hope it was only *one* mistake."

"Well, there's nothing we can do about that now. Just let him sleep it off, give him lots of water, and try and let things settle in starting tomorrow morning."

Tyee walked forward and pretended to check the main halyard.

Should he press harder or retreat? He looked at Levana. Damn it. She had that convincing stare—not one that pleaded, one that commanded. He folded. "All right. We'll start over tomorrow."

She walked over and gave him a hug. They separated, and she looked out at the flat water. "Five lakes, one Superior," she said.

"Now where did you get that saying from?" Robin asked.

"You're not the only one who does research in this family," she pointed a finger playfully at his chest.

Tyee wiped his brow, and then returned to the cockpit. "You need anything else?"

Robin looked around. The pain-in-the-ass work was thankfully over: the escort car and permit for trailering the boat, the crane to raise the mast, and getting the boat into the water. "Not that I can think of. Just a hand casting off."

"Not a problem," Tyee said. They shook hands and Tyee stepped onto the pier.

Robin and Levana embraced again. "I know it will go well," she said.

He kissed her and they parted. "It will," he said.

She put on her sunglasses and he helped her onto the dock. She watched him as he took his position behind the helm and started the engine. "Robin?"

He looked up at her.

"Take care of him, and both of you come back to me safe and sound."

"Yes, ma'am," he said. "I'll check in when we hit our first port in two weeks. You can always have someone reach me on VHF Channel 16."

She blew him a kiss and then walked down the dock and grabbed the stern line.

Tyee was already up forward and holding the bow line to check *Levity*'s forward motion.

Robin looked around. Traffic was clear. He addressed his wife and brother-in-law. "Okay, team, normally I would give my first mate below the command to cast off the stern line and then cast off the bow line, but we're going to have to settle for the two of you throwing the lines on my deck."

With a nod, they obliged and *Levity*'s starboard side started to rub against the dock fenders as she surged forward.

Robin throttled up and *Levity* was soon clear of the pier and heading for the navy colored water off the bow. After perhaps thirty yards, he stole a glance back.

Tyee had his arm around Levana, and they waved goodbye to him. He gave them a hearty wave and then turned back around and concentrated on the water ahead.

He brought up the first waypoint in his Loran: the wreck of the *Bermuda*. He looked through the open hatch and into the salon. *He won't be ready to dive until tomorrow.* Parenting. There were some aspects of it he would not miss; dealing with a hungover teenager was at the top of the short list. However, the rest of what he would be missing weighed on him now.

Robin turned the wheel a few degrees to starboard. He'd get deeper then run her a few miles east and anchor—they'd head to the *Bermuda* tomorrow morning. He knew what his journal entry would be about tonight.

The bar was overcrowded as usual. From the middle of a pack of hungry twenty-one-year-old males marched Jill Elizabeth St. John—nearly six feet, sporting blue eyes, shoulder length layered cut silky blonde hair, and an athletic build that proclaimed her campus celebrity status as Lake Superior State University's starting middle hitter. And tonight she was in no mood to deal with the little boys trying to convince themselves that they were men.

"Jiiillllll...c'mere, baby," shouted one of the boys.

She ignored him and kept moving until she joined her fellow volleyball teammate, Missy Prosser, on stools at the bar.

"You made it past the pin-dicks back there, sweetie," Missy said.

"Hoo-fuckin'-ray," Jill said as Missy handed her a tall shot of Jack Daniels.

Jill started, "Call him Jack tonight," and the shot glasses were raised—downed—slammed upside down on the bar, followed by Jill and Missy in unison, "but come mornin', it's *Mister* Daniels!"

The shot warmed Jill's insides like a fire in the hearth back home in Traverse City during a Michigan winter—not some bullshit winter down south, a *real* winter. She gave Missy a mischievous grin while another shot of Jack was placed in front of her. Own it, girl. She tipped it back and smacked her lips.

Some of the amber liquid spilled out the corner of Missy's mouth.

"Foul, MP," Jill said.

Missy laughed and then leaned back, revealing four empty shot glasses next to her purse. "Catch up, bitch," she lovingly fired back.

Jill felt a prickle on her neck, and seconds later one of the boys who had dared to venture beyond the pack appeared over her right shoulder. He wasn't bad to look at, maybe her height, black hair swept across his forehead to his ear, stuck in place by perspiration beading above his eyebrows. A polo shirt neatly tucked into his jeans, deck shoes, and leather belt declared that this frat boy was in full form tonight.

"Hi, I'm Todd," he said and put out the hand for the customary friendship greeting to Jill first and then to Missy, with a wink he intended for Jill not to see, but she did. He jerked his thumb toward the group of similarly dressed boys all working on a fresh pitcher of beer—probably Molson Golden. "Those bastards back there giving you trouble?" he said in a tone that tried to exude both contempt for his dipshit friends and concern for the two girls he was now in between.

Three years ago this might have been fun, but she was twenty-three now and just wanted to cut loose before her final summer semester started in a few days. Her volleyball career was over, and it was time to get serious about law school.

"No, they're just having fun," Jill said, "You should go back and join them."

Thrown off his game, Todd managed a, "Oh, I'm not with them."

Missy enjoyed his misery. "Whatchya up to tonight, *Todd?*"

He enjoyed the reprieve from Jill's direct gaze. "Depends on what you two are doing?"

Missy smirked. "Oh, the *two* of us?"

His confidence roared back to life, "Of course."

"Todd?" Jill said.

He gave Missy another wink and turned to Jill. "Yes?"

She bore her eyes through his own, then gave a quick smile, and said, "Get lost."

He turned to Missy for help, but all he got was a wave goodbye from her as two more shots of Jack arrived on the bar.

The boys at the pitcher table let out a laugh after overhearing Jill's exclamation.

Todd's face looked like a stove burner that someone had turned on high. "Fuck you both," he said.

"Now that's something you'll never do, asshole," Missy snapped back.

Jill sensed danger. Todd took a step away from them and then spun around ready to launch his drink at Missy.

His hand never made it, for it was caught in the grip of a man a few inches taller and about twenty years older than he was. The man squeezed enough to make Todd almost drop to his knees in pain, and then the man let up the pressure. "I think it's time for you to leave," the man said.

Todd hesitated, and the man applied the pressure again.

"Okay, okay. Jesus," Todd said.

The man released his grip, and Todd backed away.

Jill and Missy exchanged glances with each other.

Seeing Todd depart, the man turned toward them. "You both okay?"

When he had turned, Jill had caught a whiff of his cologne, and compared to the cheap fruity shit that boys like Todd wore, this was subtle and strong and...intoxicating. "We're fine," Jill said. "Thank you."

He gave a slight grin and approached the bar where he ordered a glass of scotch with a splash of water. Jill had never heard of 'a splash of water' added to scotch before.

"What's the water for, Mr. Wonderful?" Missy said.

The man looked at her, not in an annoyed way but not in a friendly way either. "To open the bouquet," he said.

She nodded as if she had a deep understanding—a mutual admiration for non-college-student libations.

The drink arrived. He took a sip, let it sit in his mouth, and then swallowed. "My name is Stephen," he said and shook their hands. "From across the bar, it looked like the little frat boy might never go away, and then I would miss my chance to finally meet our star volleyball player."

Jill blushed. "You know who I am?"

Stephen raised his hands as if she had a gun pointed at his chest, "Guilty," he said.

She had a strange phobia about bad teeth, and she squinted ever so slightly as his grin went wide. Thank God, she thought. His teeth were white, perfectly proportioned, and straight with no gaps. She felt a tingle—her phobia could also do an about face on her and become a turn on if the smile was right. His was.

"I've been following you for the past two years, and I must say that I was sad to hear that you were not going to try out for the Olympic team."

"Not quite good enough," she said. "And there's law school."

"That is a matter of opinion," he said and took another drink of his scotch. "And why in the world would you ever want to become a lawyer? With the way this economy is starting to take off, there are about a million better professions out there."

"I think it all comes down to job security," Jill said.

Stephen laughed. "Now that's the most honest answer I've ever heard from a lawyer-to-be. They'll try and beat that out of you in law school, you know?" He grinned. "In fact, I saw a billboard the other day with some greasy lawyer's face on the far left and a quote bubble coming out of his mouth that said something like, 'When a person enters my office, I don't see a client...I see a friend.'"

Jill couldn't help but titter.

"C'mon, are you seriously signing up for that type of life?" Stephen said.

"B-o-r-i-n-g," Missy said. "My girl knows what she's doing."

"I'm sure of that," Stephen said. He drained his scotch and then looked at his watch.

10:45 p.m.

"Well, I should be moving along. It was a pleasure to meet the two of you." He swiveled around and saw that the pack of frat boys had left the bar; he turned back. "Looks like the little boys went home for the night."

Jill smiled. "Don't let us run you off. Stay for at least one more."

Stephen thought. The jukebox started in with Dr. Dre's newest and the dance floor started to shake. "One more, but I need to make a call first."

He excused himself and walked over to a pay phone next to the restrooms.

"Well he's yummy," Missy said.

"I hadn't noticed," Jill said.

"Oh, get out of here. You practically begged him to stay."

"Well, one of us had to. I didn't see you stepping up."

Missy looked over Jill's shoulder and saw Stephen talking into the phone. He was leaning up against the wall and looked like the most relaxed person in the bar. Her glazed eyes wandered over to one of the pool tables where she began to stare at a boy wearing a hoodie who had been lining up a corner shot. He stared back at her.

Jill noticed her gazing and then saw who she was ogling at. "Oh no," she said. "No. No. No."

Missy broke her gaze and took Jill's hands. "I haven't had some in a while, lady."

"Uh, but with *him*?" Jill sighed. "Are you two ever over?"

Missy lit up and hopped off her stool. "Mostly," she said. Then she laid down a fifty on the bar. "This takes care of our tab and should get you another round with Mr. Cologne—don't think I didn't notice that heavenly scent too." Missy paused. "Now, according to teammate rules, I shouldn't let you go off with some new guy."

"I'll be fine," Jill said. "The guy we had to worry about was toddler Todd, and he's long gone."

"You sure?" Missy said.

"Go enjoy your booty call."

They hugged, and Missy slithered over to the pool table to reel in her prey.

Jill watched in agony as the boy wearing the hoodie gave Missy a familiar hug and then poured her a beer. *College days.* Jill turned back toward the bar and picked up the fifty, but was startled as Stephen sat down on the stool beside her.

"Where's your friend?"

Jill nodded at the pool table. "Old habits die hard."

Stephen nodded then leaned toward her. "Hey, since it's just us two, let's head down the street to Flannigan's. This place is fun, but I don't last long in places where I can't hear myself think. If you come, I'm buyin'. You've heard of their wine list, right?"

She surveyed the bar. Suddenly, it felt cheap. What in the hell was she doing here? It was time to put these days in the past and start focusing on the future. In a few years, she'd be dining at expensive restaurants like Flannigan's every weekend. "You're on," she said.

He reached for his wallet.

She shook her head no and showed him the fifty. "Missy's Good Samaritan moment of the month." She placed the bill on the bar and they headed for the exit. One last look over at the pool table. Missy was laying her head on hoodie's shoulder and swaying her hips. Jesus.

Outside, the night air helped her shake off the buzz. Stephen took the lead, and they headed across the street. She thought they looked like an attractive couple—he was, what, maybe forty, but built to last and she was still in the best shape of her life after her final volleyball season. Where could this lead? She wanted to find out.

They slowed up by a narrow alley two blocks before Flannigan's. Stephen seemed to be looking around.

"I would have thought more people would be out," he said to her.

She looked around. "I know. Maybe Flannigan's will be—"

Two hands came out of the alley and pulled her off the street.

She looked to Stephen for help as she was dragged further into the alley, but instead of fighting her assailant, she watched as he pulled something from his jacket pocket.

Before she had time to process what it was, she felt the full and paralyzing force of the taser. Her body shook and she attempted to scream but nothing came out. Quickly, the man behind her threw her over his shoulder and they sped up the alley.

They stopped, and she heard a car door opening. Then she was inside. She was gagged, tied up, and blindfolded. She felt the seat next to her sink as someone sat down on it. Stephen? Tears started to leave her eyes.

'Stephen' took a final look around and made sure that no one had witnessed the abduction. Satisfied, he opened the driver's side door to the black SUV and climbed in. He started the car and glanced in the rear-view mirror at his employer who was sitting next to the girl and making sure that she wasn't going anywhere. Well, that wasn't true. She *was* going somewhere. But she would never be seen again.

"Well done," Eric Bannon said.

'Stephen' nodded, put the car in gear, and drove for the dock where the boat was waiting.

13

Parenting

I've hemmed and hawed over what to say here, Trist. Right now, you are sawing logs in the v-berth hammock, sleeping off a hangover from partying with your friends the night before we left on our journey. Your mom and Uncle Tyee talked me away from the ledge. We're anchored, and the water is so calm I can't even feel us move. We might not have another night like this during our entire trip, so I'm enjoying a beer and trying to impart some wisdom to you. You know I'm a fan of brevity, but the joys of parenting and passing on what one has learned in life are anything but brief. As far as being a parent—if you are blessed with a child one day—I think you'll find it as mysterious, mind-boggling, wonderful, terrifying, and rewarding as this deeply-flawed man has. But, there is nothing that prepares you for the burden of raising a child, and it's not something you approach in a half-measure way. For instance, right now I want to travel back in time to when you were three and spend an afternoon playing Tonka Trucks with you. At the same time, I could beat you within an inch of your life for driving home intoxicated last night. This is how parenting goes if you decide to do it. As far as getting to be a grandparent, well, that's a phase of life I'm sure I would have looked forward to, but it wasn't in the cards. I must keep my thoughts focused on you. Mom will be an unbelievable grandmother; she has been the anchor in our family, and I can't imagine a better future grandma than her.

In terms of words of advice, I think I'll settle on a surprise. <u>Hamlet</u>. I don't think we've had a single conversation about Shakespeare in our time together, and I'm embarrassed. Embarrassed because you know how much I think of books and the wisdom that can come from within even a single volume. Embarrassed because I know that you have studied Shakespeare during the past couple of years and I haven't engaged you in any conversation. Too busy—horrible excuse—too worried about you leaving our home and now it's gone by so fast I never even told you half of what I thought I would. I'm down to my last few months, and I feel the weight of trying to capture it in this journal. I set out to be different with you than my father was with me. For the most part, I think I was. I'll leave you with Polonius's advice to Laertes. They are still good words to live by and should help you keep life in center field, which is what your old man has always tried to do. The rest of life's lessons, I hope they have been passed on by my good examples to follow and my bad examples for you to not follow. I could try to paraphrase and summarize, but it would take away the beauty and power of the bard's passage. So, here I am at 1:32 a.m. copying down word for word from our family copy of <u>The Complete Works of William Shakespeare</u> that I brought onboard—I don't even know if you were aware that we have one at the house (it's usually on the top shelf in the living room bookcase). Here we go: <u>Hamlet,</u> Act I Scene 3, Lines 59-82

And these few precepts in thy memory
Look thou character. Give thy thoughts no tongue,
Nor any unproportioned thought his act.
Be thou familiar but by no means vulgar.
Those friends thou hast, and their adoption tried,
Grapple them unto thy soul with hoops of steel,
But do not dull thy palm with entertainment
Of each new-hatched, unfledged comrade. Beware
Of entrance to a quarrel, but being in,
Bear 't that th' opposèd may beware of thee.

Give every man thy ear but few thy voice.

Take each man's censure but reserve thy judgment.

Costly thy habit as thy purse can buy,

But not expressed in fancy—rich, not gaudy,

For the apparel oft proclaims the man,

And they in France of the best rank and station

Are of a most select and generous chief in that.

Neither a borrower nor a lender be,

For loan oft loses both itself and friend,

And borrowing dulls the edge of husbandry.

This above all: to thine own self be true,

And it must follow, as the night the day,

Thou canst not then be false to any man.

Farewell. My blessing season this in thee.

Grant Livingston exited the shower and grabbed a towel that the yacht's staff had warmed in the vessel's dryer. The shower light automatically dimmed as he toweled off and closed the door. His footing was solid and he made his way to the double sink with ease. So far, the yacht made way through the water like a dream; he couldn't even tell that they were making, what—he looked at a control panel mounted on the bulkhead next to the shower—ten knots right now. Calm seas were one thing, but so far the Hatteras was everything it had been billed to be. The wider beam and overall design had the boat gliding through the water. What an experience it was going to be on the trip down to the Keys in this heaven-sent machine. Tomorrow, they would return to his main house and get the yacht loaded up. In a few weeks, he'd be swimming in turquoise water and sipping margaritas in palm tree paradise.

At the double sink, with the towel now around his waist, he made a few swipes under each arm with his deodorant stick, combed his thick wet hair back, applied lotion to his face and hands, and then splashed on a small amount of cologne.

Behind him and outside the head, he heard the hatch to the master stateroom open and then close, followed by the sound of someone sitting on the king-sized mattress. The lights in the master stateroom went out. He looked at his profile in the mirror—acceptable—and exited.

A terrycloth robe hung over the back of a chair at the stateroom's vanity. He could smell her perfume already. Small running lights had been placed around the perimeter of the island berth a few inches above the deck, which made the berth look like a floating stage. Livingston's eyes made their way from the lights up to the gorgeous nude body spread out on top of the covers. His breathing became labored as he met eyes with Madame.

"This is later than usual," she said. "Losing my appeal?"

"No," Livingston said. "Had to inspect the yacht."

"That's not an excuse worthy of you," she said.

She was right. But how could he break the news to her that she would be replaced soon by a much younger version of herself? She still could not be trusted. No doubt before she entered the stateroom she had been searched for any steak knives concealed in her robe; it had been years since she had tried that stunt, but he wasn't taking any chances—especially now.

As he marveled at her trim torso and worked his eyes up to her huge breasts, he felt something unknown. She had lasted far longer than any of the others—and she wasn't even supposed to be his. He could never forget seeing her for the first time. He had stood next to his father and witnessed her being presented to a cartel underboss as a gift. She had been the most beautiful woman he had ever seen, and the boss had rejected her. There were no hard feelings between his father and the boss; his father had been misinformed that tall blondes were the boss's type.

Livingston exhaled and looked out through a small porthole window beyond the berth. Somewhere out there was a brunette who didn't know just how close she came to never seeing anyone she knew again. Madame had taken her place. He looked back down at her. Madame. What was her real name again? Eve? Evelynn? He couldn't remember. The last name had started with a 'B' though because when she had been left with them, his father had called the dilemma 'Plan B'. Did she even remember her real name? She hadn't said it in years. Regardless, the man who had provided the incorrect information had been reassigned to the bottom of Lake Superior after the cartel underboss had departed for New York.

They couldn't just let her go. Her husband was dead and the sailboat had been sunk in over five hundred feet of water. The underboss had left the decision up to Livingston's father: either kill her or keep her. Livingston, and for some reason Sanders, lobbied his father to keep her. So, a hypnotist had been brought in for regular sessions, and Madame had been given a combination of sedatives and small amounts of cocaine for a year. She had also undergone plastic surgery to alter her look just enough to never be recognized again. During recovery, she had been isolated, with Livingston providing the only positive human contact—long talks, monitored walks through the woods, healthy dinners, and eventually brandy by the fire. She was given access to books, music, but no television—nothing of popular culture or world affairs. Then, her privileges grew as he visited more often. Designer clothes, a large suite in the estate on top of the cliff, a private workout and meditation coach, and accompanying Livingston on overseas business trips where she was introduced to an even more lavish lifestyle. Winter weekends in a Swiss lodge on Lake Geneva, dinner parties in Paris, summers in Rome, and month-long cruises in the Caribbean. The sexual aspect of their relationship had started during the first trip, and for the past nine years had included every variation known and thought up by him. Last year, it had reverted to just the two of them—necessitated by her attempt to throw a woman they had included in a tryst over the balcony railing...and over the cliff to the water a hundred feet below. A few nights later she had come after him with a knife while they slept next to each other, and his shoulder had required surgery. That had started the increasing doses of drugs and sedatives again, the beginning of the end. Now, the cycle would start all over with someone new and Madame would soon be gone.

"Well?" Madame said.

Livingston opened the drawer of his night stand and took out a black box that fit in his palm. After seeing *Belle de Jour* in his late teens, he had become obsessed with what was in the mystery box. His search had led him to what he now took out.

Madame's eyes sparkled at the sight of it.

Livingston slid off his towel.

Twenty minutes later it was over, and he rolled onto his back and panted. Was the room soundproof? If not, then they had just woken up the entire population of the Upper Peninsula. His eyes were wide open and he observed her from the mirror mounted on the overhead. She placed the object back in the box and passed it to him. He took a final look, closed the box, and leaned over, placing it on the nightstand. His head rested back on the pillow and he watched in the mirror as she parted her thighs and then brought the soles of her feet together making a diamond with her legs. She slid her right hand down and pleased herself once more.

When she was finished, she rose from the bed, walked over to the vanity, and put on her robe.

"Tomorrow," she said and exited the room before he could reply.

The strange feeling returned. What was it? He would see her tomorrow—they had built a relationship. *What was her name?* His breathing picked up instead of slowing down. His entire body began to feel like it was being heated on a stove top. Sweat soaked the sheets and his stomach tightened. He felt bile rise into his throat. He knew he would be unable to stop it, and so he swung his legs over the edge of the berth and darted for the head.

Reaching the commode, he dropped to his knees and then, as if someone had two arms around his waist and was pulling the closed fists upward in violent thrusts to push his insides up through his mouth, he vomited.

His head hung down and started to bob while tears left his eyes. As someone who was always in control, these episodes bothered him. The doctors had found nothing wrong. *Why was this happening?* He flushed and then watched as the dark colored liquid was sucked down the vacuum hole. The bowl refilled with water. He sniffled and blew his nose into a wad of toilet paper. His body relaxed for a moment and he breathed in and out, in and out. *What does her name matter?* A second attack came on and his stomach muscles clenched. He moaned as his body shook in agony, and he vomited again.

He cried; it was getting worse.

14

The blood red sun was over the horizon and warming the surface of the boat when Robin Norris emerged from the cabin with a steaming cup of coffee. The water was still calm—a sheen of cobalt blue that stretched endlessly to the northern horizon.

He wore a long-sleeved Henley t-shirt—the morning air was chilly—and his trusty cut-off jean shorts, the uneven frayed ends tickling his thighs. He cringed at the thought of clothing stores that now made jean shorts like this *on purpose*. Hell no. The only way you should get jean shorts was because you had worn out a pair of jeans to the point of having to cut them off—and only when you could no longer patch up the knees. A country that had retailers who made clothing to look worn—and people bought this garbage—was headed in the wrong direction. *Fashionable my ass.*

He sat down with his back against the stern rail and put his feet up on the port gunwale. The first sip of coffee was heaven on earth as the cream softened the blow to his stomach while the sugar and caffeine ignited his motor. How many days would he still feel normal? Hopefully throughout the cruise. He had nightmares of becoming weak as they traveled along the northern shore, heading west. He saw himself fading fast, having to pull the boat into Isle Royale, and dying in a cabin waiting for Levana and Tyee to arrive.

He shook the thought off. Trist should be up soon and then they would head for the dive site. Hydration shouldn't be a problem; an hour ago, Robin had started an IV of saline solution for his son. He frowned. Should he have just let him suffer some more? Probably. But would it teach his son a lesson? He was less sure of that. No, better to get him up and going. A flock of seagulls flew by off the stern and Robin took another pull from his coffee mug.

"Don't even think of landing on this boat and shitting all over it," he said to the flock as he watched the birds dip low over the water and then peel off toward the shore.

He heard the creek of deck boards up forward, below deck.

Tristian eased his legs out of the v-berth hammock and lowered them until his bare feet touched the cool deck. His head no longer throbbed, but his throat was still sore from upchucking all over US-23 and I-75. Man. What had he been thinking that night? He wanted water now and food. Lots of greasy, deep fried food. McDonald's was his usual post-hangover stop; what was onboard that could come close? His vision was blurry and as he went to rub his eyes, he noticed the IV in his right hand, attached to the bag of saline hanging from a hook on the overhead. The bag was nearly finished.

He rubbed his eyes with his other hand and took in a few breaths. He hated needles—almost passed out every time he had to give blood—but right now, he didn't care. Once, right before a sports physical, he fainted and awoke to an ice pack on his neck and a cold washcloth on his forehead. A nurse leaned over him and placed a cup filled with coke and ice into his hands. He chugged it, smiled, and then threw up all over the nurse. During the entire fiasco, his dad had sat in a chair reading a paperback about some Vietnam battle and shook his head in disappointment at his son.

Carefully, he removed the IV from his hand and used his other hand to apply pressure to the tiny hole that the IV's needle had left. He went to stand up but felt lightheaded and laid back down.

Thankful that the room was not spinning, he closed his eyes for a moment. A vision of the Hampstead community tennis courts came into focus from the current mist in his brain. Damn. *I am never doing that again.*

He heard steps in the boat's salon and opened his eyes. The door to the v-berth opened, and in stepped his father.

"Feeling any better?" Robin asked.

"Yeah," Trist said.

Robin leaned up against the scuba tanks on the port bulkhead. "I'll make you some breakfast, and then we'll head for our dive site."

"Okay." Trist sat up, and the boat's motion went to work on his head. "Whoa..." He laid back down. "I don't know if I'm up for diving today."

Robin took three measured breaths...

He sprang and picked Trist up out of the hammock.

"Dad! What the hell?"

With one hand wrapped around Trist's neck and the other hand squeezing Trist's left arm, Robin dragged him through the salon, up the companionway steps, and through the cockpit until they were at the stern rail. "Let's see if you can fly, Batman." With one final heave, he pushed Trist overboard.

He watched as Trist disappeared into the water. Then, he went to the mast and quickly lowered the main sail.

When he returned to the rail, he could see Trist treading water twenty yards off the stern.

"Damnit!" Trist yelled.

"You awake now?" Robin said. "You've already wasted one day. You're not wastin' two." He unlatched the section of stern railing and swung it open. Then, he stepped down onto the swim platform and kicked the swim ladder into the water. "Now, get your skinny ass up here and get some coffee. I'm going below to get you breakfast."

Trist continued to tread water as he watched Robin go below. Then he began a painful crawl stroke toward the swim ladder.

Robin stood behind the gimbaled stove and stared into the frying pan. He cracked an egg and watched the yoke fizzle as it hit the oil in the pan. *Let's see if you can fly, Batman.* Where had that come from?

Then, he remembered.

15

HAMPSTEAD, DECEMBER 1989

"I want a divorce," Levana Norris said as she stood up from her seat on the couch.

Robin's eyes opened wide in disbelief. She had never said the 'D' word before. "Now, hold on just a goddamn minute, Levana!" Robin shouted.

"No, I've made up my mind. I can't argue with you every night anymore."

It wasn't every night—it was every hour. He reached for her hand and she swatted it aside.

She started to walk away but paused when she heard his voice shaking with uncertainty in a way that she had not heard since they lived in her parents' house.

"Please stay and talk with me," Robin said. "I'm begging you."

Hands on her hips, she turned around, scowled, and then walked back to the couch and sat down hard.

He breathed a momentary sigh of relief. He was going to get one shot at this. He covered his face, exhaled into his hands, and then slid his fingers down along his nose and crossed them in front of his face. "Look, I know I've hit a rough patch since turning three zero in August."

She snorted. "That's a start."

She's mad but still not leaving—good. He continued, "Look I haven't stopped working or worrying since we had Trist."

"And you think I have?" she snapped.

"No, but you haven't been the easiest to live with lately either," he said.

"I'm a teacher, Robin. And that blood bath in Tiananmen Square was awful. I tried to talk with you about it when it happened this summer, but I didn't feel heard at all. You just sat there."

"You've been holding that in since then?"

"Look who's talking."

"The Chinese are goddamned communists," Robin said. "What did you think was going to happen when a bunch of students tried to protest? Those totalitarian assholes crush that stuff immediately over there."

"You can be so cold sometimes," she said. "It was *horrible.*"

"I agree, okay? But what we saw on television was the reality of that way of life." He put his hand on her shoulder. "Look, I'm sorry, and I'm just speaking for me right now. I'm worn out, Levana. I've put everything into trying to make it work with us so we could get away from your parents and create our own life. I didn't walk out when you almost had that fling with Principal Shithead, and I sure as hell held it together when we lost our second boy."

She stared at him, but some of the anger seemed to have given way to shock.

"I heard something the other day. Men have mid-life crises in their forties because they realize that they have sacrificed building relationships in the

125

pursuit of climbing the achievement ladder. Well, I had to start early because of our situation. So, four months ago when I hit thirty, it shook me up, okay?"

She leaned back, listening.

"I don't share my personal feelings, and you know that. I'm not wired that way. But something is happening inside of me, and I don't know what to call it...acting out, or something like that. I've got anger and resentment about the life I didn't get to live because I got you pregnant."

She leaned forward and went to speak.

"Just let me finish."

She sat back.

"I stuck around, and I don't regret it. But I have had to watch all of my other friends get to mosey on through life, enjoying college, enjoying being single after college, pursuing their careers, while I've been stuck in some hospital when I could have been an athletic trainer traveling the world. I don't know what else to say except that I'm struggling, and I need your help to get through this. If I don't, then I feel like I'm going to self-destruct, which I prefer not to do. You know me," he said, "better than anyone else." He took a hold of her hands. "I haven't been reading. I haven't been working out. I am in one abyss of a funk." Tears started to well in his eyes. He fought them back in. "Don't give up on me."

She rubbed his hand back. Silence filled the room except for the steady ticking of the grandfather clock in the corner of the living room. She licked her dry lips. "That is more than you've said to me about your feelings in ten years."

He rubbed his eyes. "I've got too much of my dad in me. I—I can't articulate what I'm feeling. I just ignore it. But it has been different this time. I feel..."

"Older?" she said.

"Yeah."

126

"You know, you're not as bad as you think you are at communicating. But—"

"What?" he cut in.

"Bringing up my former principal. That was out of bounds."

"I hate that fucker."

"Robin *Norris!*"

He gave a wicked grin. "If I ever see him again—"

"Okay, relax."

"Bringing up the 'D' word, now *that* was out of bounds."

She thought for a moment. "I know."

"Did you mean it?"

"No. It just came out."

He exhaled. "Okay."

She started to warm. "There may be hope for you yet."

"Don't count on it. This may be my one and only Oscar-worthy clip," he said.

"I heard Billy Crystal is going to host this year," she said.

"No kidding? I like him."

"Agree. Good to get some new blood in there and mix things up."

He shook his head. "Jesus, we're all over the place tonight. We just went from an all-out argument to the Oscars."

"That's us, babe."

A creak in the floorboards directed their attention to the hallway where an eleven-year old Trist wearing sweatpants and a Batman t-shirt walked into the room.

"I can hear you both fighting again," he said, rubbing his tired eyes.

Robin and Levana looked at each other. Their joint expression said: we are horrible parents.

Robin took the unexpected lead. "Hey buddy. We're sorry. I know this has been going on a lot lately, but your mom and I are going to do better, okay?"

Trist was still half-awake. "Okay," he said. "You're not getting divorced or anything are you?"

Levana jumped in. "No, that word doesn't exist in this family, remember?"

Robin shot her a look—one that Trist missed, thankfully.

Trist nodded. "I'm heading back up."

"Got your favorite movie t-shirt on again I see."

Trist looked down at the giant bat symbol and smiled.

"Get some sleep, T. I'll see you in the morning before I leave for work."

"I love you, baby," Levana said. "I'll pop my head in and check on you when I head up."

"Okay," Trist said and headed back down the hallway.

After his steps could no longer be heard on the stairs, Levana turned to Robin. "I don't know where the D-word came from tonight. I'm sorry."

"I'm not worried now, but I admit you scared me a little," he said.

She shrugged.

"I'm going to try and be more open about what's going on with me from now on. If anything, these past few months have taught me that I can't keep shoving this stuff deep down, pretending that it doesn't exist."

"Well, you're lucky because by the numbers you've got at least fifty years left to get better," she grinned.

Robin laughed a sigh of relief. "Yes I do, ma'am."

"If the Berlin Wall can come down, then we can learn to communicate better."

16

JUNE 1995

Trist lowered the main sail as they approached the waypoint Robin had programmed into their Loran.

Robin turned on the engine. "We're almost to the wreck," he said to Trist. "Go up forward and get ready to drop the hook." Trist gave a pathetic salute and headed toward the anchor locker near the bow. *At least he's moving.* Robin peered down at the display in front of the helm and adjusted course to starboard.

They were now on the southern side of Grand Island and not far from where they had put in at Munising. It had almost been an embarrassment to anchor last night without traveling very far. His son had made a mistake, but he had made mistakes at that age too. The Loran beeped as they approached the waypoint.

Bermuda was in thirty feet of water and still looked like the nineteenth century schooner that it was. At one hundred and thirty-six feet long, there was

129

plenty to explore, and the ship was one of the most visited wrecks in the Great Lakes. It was also one of the safest to explore. *Bermuda* sat perfectly on the bottom with the deck only twelve feet from the surface. There were three open hatches that lead into the hull where he and Trist could explore, and the only dangers were the normal ones associated with penetrating a wreck, mostly silting. On the surface, there was a fair amount of tourist boating traffic—the only way to dive the *Bermuda* was to take a boat out to her—so they'd have to be careful when they surfaced.

Just off the bow, Robin spotted a Boston Whaler bobbing at anchor near the wreck site. He pulled the binoculars hanging around his neck up to his eyes and scanned. There was no one onboard. They'd have company beneath the surface. He lowered the binoculars and checked the Loran one more time.

Robin brought *Levity*'s engine to idle and pointed the sloop into the wind. "Drop the hook, Trist!" Robin shouted.

Manning the anchor windlass up forward, Trist let go the anchor, and it entered the water with a familiar *sploosh*. He watched as the chain payed out and the anchor disappeared.

When the desired 5:1 scope of chain was let out, Trist set the brake. He tied a piece of line around the chain and then tied it off to a cleat, transferring some of the load from the windlass. "Go ahead and back down," Trist said.

Robin throttled astern at around 1500 rpms for a moment to let the flukes set in. When the boat would not move aft at 1500 rpms, then Robin was confident that the anchor was set, and he cut the engine.

The cloudless sky allowed the sun to warm everything from the deck beneath Trist's bare feet to the shirt sticking to his back. There was no hint of a breeze and the water looked like a never-ending mirror. Satisfied that the anchor was secure, he headed aft.

Robin emerged from the companionway with two scuba tanks.

"Need a hand?" Trist said.

"Nope," Robin replied.

"Should I even be diving?" Trist said.

"Yesterday? No. Today? You're fine," Robin stated.

Trist watched him lift the tanks through the hatch and set them on the cockpit deck. He made it look so easy. The one exception to the 'no television rule' in their house had been his father's favorite show, *Magnum P.I.*, and though many people weren't quite sure that Robin was not Harrison Ford, Trist knew that his real alter ego was Magnum's best friend, T.C. His mom had a different take. She claimed that Robin had Ford's ruggedly handsome good looks, T.C.'s arms and shoulders, and Magnum's sense of humor. Whatever. He didn't understand why *Magnum* had been appointment television for his mom and dad in the '80s. He'd much rather watch *Friends*, which he had to sneak over to Kevin's to watch under the cover of *a big homework project*. Well, he wasn't sure if he'd be spending much time with Kevin anymore after the other night. And he preferred *Frasier* to *Friends*, but Kevin always had a packed house—that included Rachel—to watch. A clank from another tank brought his attention back to his dad. He'd been lifting for two years now and still couldn't come close to Robin's pipes—his arms more like tiny knots than bundles of kettle bells like his father's.

Robin came back up on deck with two sets of mask, fins, snorkel, weight belt, and regulator. "C'mon, let's get our wetsuits on," he said to Trist.

Trist followed him down below.

Jill St. John awoke to darkness. She gasped when she tried to open her eyes as her eyelids felt like a thousand tiny needles had decided to prick them all at once. She closed her eyes to let the pain subside while she took stock with her other senses. Wherever she was smelled like a hospital room, and her face felt cold. Her eyes still felt like they had been branded with a hot iron. Her head was on a soft pillow and she was covered with crisp sheets and a fluffy comforter, lying in a small bed. Her arms, resting next to each side of her body, had only inches to spare from the left and right edge of the bed; when she curled her toes, they extended past the foot.

The room was silent except for a soft hum, like an air conditioner on low power. Where was she? How much time had passed? What was the last thing she remembered? Her right forearm began to throb. A needle? She had been abducted; absolutely, she was sure of that. By the man who was driving the vehicle...she was in the back seat unable to move because...because...yes, because she had been tased. Then, the vehicle had started to move and she rode for some time. How long? An hour? Two? In any event, she had just started to regain feeling in her fingers when the man beside her had stuck a needle into her arm and injected her with something. "You're going to be fine, sweet baby," he had said. That was the last thing she remembered.

Jill placed her left hand on the inside of her right wrist and slid it up toward her elbow. She touched a gauze pad held against her skin with medical tape that wound around her forearm. She took a deep breath, held it, and let it out. She opened her eyes slowly. One, Two, Three walls. A dresser. Is that a door? Ouch!

The pain was too much and she closed her eyes. Her vision became an inferno at first. Then the edges cooled to black and the center became a twisting kaleidoscope, spiraling her mind over an edge and into an infinite void. She drifted back asleep.

Robin and Trist stood next to each other on *Levity*'s swim platform. They were in full wetsuits including hoods. It might be June, but the lake felt like it was still thawing from winter. They each had a tank strapped on, wore a weight belt, had a dive knife strapped to the right calf, and wore a pair of fins. They both had a dive light as well. Robin took a breath from his regulator and then removed it from his mouth. Trist followed suit.

"Okay, we've got perfect conditions but that doesn't give you a blank check to scoot off and try something dangerous," Robin said.

"Dad, lighten up. I'm still not feeling a hundred percent."

"That's the first honest thing you've said all morning."

Trist paused.

He's gonna come back with some smart-ass remark, and I'm gonna crush him.

"I'm following you, okay?"

Nope, can't predict children—even my own. Robin nodded. "Okay." He pointed to the Boston Whaler. "We'll have some company down there, so stay safe. Whoever it is, he or she was here early." He swiveled his head to the right and then to the left, surveying the surface of the water. "I don't see any other boats right now, but that doesn't mean that there won't be any when we surface later. Safety, safety, safety."

"Dad, I got it."

Robin put the regulator in his mouth. *Stop overthinking everything and trust him.* He gave Trist a thumbs up sign and they both jumped into the water.

Robin's body shivered. Goddamn Lake Superior. This arctic soup could freeze your bones. He shook it off and saw Trist next to him, eyes behind his son's mask saying, "What in the hell are we doing in water this cold?" Robin checked his depth. Nine feet. He motioned for Trist to follow him and they swam up under *Levity's* hull and inspected it. God, the boat rested pretty in the water. He ran his hand along the hull as he moved from the stern to the bow. Trist turned on his light and swept the beam across the hull as he followed.

At the bow, Robin grasped the anchor line, made eye contact with Trist, and then started to follow the line down. At thirty-two feet, they reached the anchor. Robin motioned for Trist to aim his light at it. Once it was illuminated, he inspected the connection between the line and the stock: it was secure. The flukes had dug in; unless weather came out of nowhere, *Levity* was staying put. Robin checked his underwater compass and oriented himself in order to head toward the *Bermuda*; he had anchored far enough away to not risk fouling his anchor on the wreck, which could damage the underwater preserve and royally screw up a day's dive. Untangling an anchor—no matter what it was fouled on—was one of life's events one would rather never experience. Snag a fishing line? Cut it and move on. Lose an anchor...

When Trist asked if it was that big of a deal, he had replied, "Would you ever volunteer to get a flat tire and have to change it on the side of the road?"

Robin steadied up on the course to the wreck and began to move, Trist beside him. After a few dozen kicks, the Boston Whaler's anchor and line came into view. Then, *Bermuda* emerged out of the shadows. The masts and rigging were long gone, but some of the railing was still intact. The aged wood was beautiful and preserved by the cold fresh water of Lake Superior. Had *Bermuda* wrecked in saltwater, there would be little to nothing left of her.

They followed the hull up and over the railing where they could see the entire length of the schooner. Bubbles rose from one of the hatches amidships. Robin and Trist stopped aft to examine the rudder stock that rose up from the deck a few feet. They exchanged a look of satisfaction at the superb craftsmanship and preservation. Robin motioned to a hatch just past the cabin trunk and they paused above it. He turned on his dive light and entered the hatch. Trist followed and they were soon below deck.

Further forward, they could now see a light trained on the bottom with bubbles rising nearby; it looked like just one diver. Robin was about to give the go ahead to explore when he heard a clanging noise made by the unknown diver. He motioned Trist to follow him.

They approached the diver, and Robin could now see what had made the noise. The man had rigged a light on a stand to aim directly at the deck and he was using a crowbar, trying to pry some of the decking up. Robin grabbed

Trist's arm with authority and his son snapped his head around to look into Robin's mask. *Gonna straighten this out.* Robin let go of Trist and motioned for him to stay back. Trist signaled okay.

The man dug the crowbar into the wood with a crunch that made Robin's stomach turn. The effort had also stirred up a small cloud of silt making visibility worse. However, the diver saw Robin's light and stopped working on the deck. Robin gave him a look that said: *No! Get the hell out of here.*

The man now saw Trist as well. He flipped Robin the middle finger and reached for something on the deck that was hidden by the cloud of silt. Robin maintained his position a few yards away.

Out from the cloud of silt, the man leveled a spear gun...at Trist. Then, he looked back at Robin and raised his eyebrows.

Robin brought his dive light up and aimed it right into the man's eyes, blinding him. Then, he kicked directly at the man, dropped his light, put his hands around the man's neck and squeezed. The man spit out his regulator in his panic and dropped the spear gun. With powerful strokes, Robin kicked with the diver in his grasp up through the hatch. The man struggled but was soon out of breath and kicked with Robin rather than against him. In a few seconds, their heads broke the surface. The man started coughing, and Robin changed his grip from the man's neck to his air hose. Trist surfaced a few yards away and took out his regulator.

"What the hell!" The man finally got out.

"We don't damage and steal from underwater preserves, asshole," Robin said.

"You could have killed me," he said.

Robin grabbed the man's neck and pushed him underwater for a few seconds. Then pulled him back up. He was too mad to think about the fact he was half-drowning a complete stranger. If his fellow nurses could see him now.

The man had swallowed water and was hacking away.

"And you pointed a gun at my kid. Now, get your ass outta here, before I report this," Robin ordered.

"Man, you're crazy," he replied and tried to swim away, but Robin yanked on his air hose.

"You got it?" Robin said.

"Okay, okay," he said. "But what about my gear?"

Robin looked at Trist. "Swim down and bring up his stuff—except for the crowbar. Drop *that* on the lake floor away from the wreck."

Trist put in his regulator and submerged.

He turned back toward the man, pulled his air hose so that their faces were inches away from each other. "Don't come back here."

The man could feel Robin's hot breath in his face like a victim about to be eaten by a grizzly bear. He nodded, and Robin released his grip. The man started to swim toward the Whaler, looking back at Robin every third or fourth kick, and then continuing on.

Trist rose next to him. "Here," he said handing Robin the tripod and dive light.

"You got the spear gun?"

Trist raised it out of the water.

"Good, let's get this guy out of here and then leave. I think we've seen enough of the *Bermuda* for today."

They headed toward the Whaler.

"Never mind us reporting him," Trist said. "What about him reporting *us*?"

Robin stood behind the helm and eased off the wind to port. Both the mainsail and jib were raised, and the morning calm had turned into an afternoon full of wind—*Levity* was on a beam reach and dancing through the water. He looked down at Trist who was seated on the starboard cockpit bench sipping on a can of Vernors. "He won't report us." The sun peeked around a cloud and hit Robin's face. He squinted and raised his sunglasses from the cord that hung around his neck. "Fool knows he was in the wrong." He paused. "Only thing is..."

"What?"

"He'll be back. Maybe not tomorrow or next week, but some day. We scared him, but guys like that operate by a different code."

Trist took a swig from his can. "What code, Indy?"

Robin grinned and looked up at the wind vane on top of the mast. "No code," he said. "Those guys have zero respect for history." He motioned for Trist to get him a pop from the cooler underneath the port bench.

Trist lifted the cushion and dug into the ice-filled chest, pulling out a can of Canada Dry. Robin looked at the can. "That's the stuff."

"Traitor," Trist said and threw the can to him.

Robin grinned and cracked open the lid. "It's just better, T. Sort of like how *Star Trek* is better than *Star Wars*."

"Like hell it is," Trist said.

"Trek is literature. Star Wars is pulp."

"You're never going to convince me. You Trekkies are so loyal and stubborn. Isn't there enough room in space for both franchises?"

Robin took a long pull. "Nope. Anyway, back to the *Bermuda*. Three lives were lost when she wrecked in Munising Bay. Doesn't sound grandiose, I know, but those are three people who didn't get to come home. And for that reason alone, you don't *touch* a wreck that is at its final resting place underwater. Idiots like Mr. Crowbar don't get it and never will. Our society is so enamored with collecting stuff and displaying it that we forget to consider *what* we're displaying."

Trist sat and studied the bearded gnome on his can of Vernors. He looked up at his dad, "For once, I agree wi—"

Robin swayed to the right, lost his grip on the wheel, and fainted.

Levity heeled over hard, and Robin and Trist were thrown up against the rail. The boat continued to tip and Trist grabbed Robin's shirt to keep him from going overboard. Then, the boat righted itself and the sails began to luff. Trist went for the wheel, but there was too much momentum and *Levity* jibed—the boom shot through the air and crashed to a halt on the other side of the boat. Now, the sloop heeled to port and Robin's body slid across the cockpit and landed on the port bench.

Trist made it to the wheel and turned until *Levity* was pointed directly into the wind. Both sails luffed and he released the jib sheet. With nimble feet, he raced forward and lowered the jib. Then, he sped back to the mast and worked the halyard until the main sail was hauled all the way down.

With the sails now lowered, he centerlined the boom. Satisfied that the boat was secure as possible for the moment, he jumped down into the cockpit and held Robin in his arms. "Dad?"

Robin made no movement. His eyes seemed welded shut.

"Dad!" Trist put his hand on Robin's neck and felt a strong pulse. Next, he lowered his ear to just above Robin's nose and mouth...and both heard and felt his father's breathing. "C'mon, Dad," he said.

Robin's eyelids started to flutter and his eyes finally opened. Trist could barely focus on his face for the tears now pouring out. "What happened?"

17

The Hatteras cut through the water with precision and grace, the wake leaving a line of white foam that divided the deep blue surface. It was just past noon and Grant Livingston took a seat across from Madame at the well-appointed table aft of the flying bridge. A waiter meandered over with a stainless-steel push cart and replaced Madame's finished espresso with a new one.

She paid him no attention.

He placed a second bowl of fresh fruit on the table between her and Livingston and then handed a folded newspaper to Madame. Before shuffling off, he placed a cup of espresso in front of Livingston.

"Last night was...extraordinary," Livingston said, reaching for the espresso.

Madame opened "The Arts" section of *The New York Times*. "You're a bit out of practice," she said.

"Now where did he get you a copy of *The Times*?" he said.

She lowered the paper. "*Last* Sunday's edition."

"I see," said Livingston. He went to grab a section for himself but she moved the paper from the table to the chair next to her.

139

She raised "The Arts" back up. "Am I still cut off from pop culture?"

He yawned and reached for his espresso, "I need to get up earlier, and, no, I think you can handle *The Times*."

The paper did not move.

Livingston sipped the revitalizing liquid and felt his body twitch as the caffeine went to work. He wished for the simple, charming conversations that used to start his days with Madame.

Dai Sanders entered the flying bridge from the forward ladder. He took a final puff from his cigarette and threw the butt over the side as he approached the table.

Ah! A distraction... "Dai," Livingston said. "Please, join us."

She lowered her paper and scowled at Sanders. What a waste of a human being. Wasn't he supposed to be retired? Why was he on the boat? How many times had Livingston told her Sanders would be replaced only to have to live with his presence in the main house for another miserable year? He had never touched her—the only positive thing she could say. She pointed at the old man. "What's *he* doing here?" she said.

Sanders looked to Livingston for help.

The same waiter as before seemed to materialize out of the air—he was so quiet—and put a large cup of coffee and an ashtray in front of Sanders. He gave a polite smile and then dissolved away.

"No," Madame said, looking at Sanders's ashtray.

Sanders frowned and grabbed his mug of coffee.

Livingston sat back and crossed his legs. "Mr. Sanders is here to oversee a transition, my dear."

She folded "The Arts" and placed it on the stack of newspaper. "It's about time Keach took over," she said. Mason Keach was someone she *had* allowed to touch her during the past five years. Post intercourse had led to late night talks and confessions. Sanders was so inebriated during the winter months that he never realized Keach would enter the main house many nights to be with her. And neither man at the table knew that he had promised to help her escape when Sanders was gone. It was her last rung of hope.

"I thought you had told her," Livingston said to Sanders.

What did this mean?

"Mr. Sanders *is* retiring, but his replacement will be Eric Bannon not Keach. In fact, Keach won't be spending much more time up here. His services are needed in other places."

Keep your composure. Don't let them know. She tipped back her espresso. "Interesting," she said. "No, he has not told me that."

Sanders raised his hands in a quick *it had never occurred to me* motion.

She wanted to kill him.

Livingston spoke again. "Actually, he's not the only one retiring."

Her eyes narrowed, and she aimed them directly into Livingston's. "Oh?"

Livingston exhaled and looked beyond her at the calm surface of the lake. "I've been giving it some thought, Madame, and think that it is time for you to enjoy some time off."

Time off?! *I've woken up each day not knowing if it would be my last. I've been your sex servant for ten years and now you are telling me I'm retiring? Retiring to where? Retiring to what? If Keach could have gotten me out then I would have either disappeared forever or come back with the entire might of the United States Government and destroyed you, this place, and the entire operation.* But now? There was no way she would ever be allowed to leave. Or, worse yet: there was no way she would be allowed to live once she was replaced. She had to buy some time. Was Sanders grinning?

"Nothing to say?" Livingston said.

She smiled. "It would be nice to start slowing down." She moved her gaze to Sanders. "Since he gets to meet his replacement, do I get to meet mine?"

Sanders grin was replaced by his more familiar nervous tic of biting his thumbnail. How awful it must taste.

"I think it is essential," said Livingston, "that you meet her and explain how things are."

Go with the flow. You need time. You have to find a way to talk with Keach. "It could work," she said and gave Livingston a seductive stare—one she knew he liked. "When do I get to meet the new Madame?"

"Oh, there could never be another *Madame*," he replied. "But you will be meeting her tomorrow."

Shit! She'd have to work fast. She rose from the table. "Well, I better get some rest before then," she said, grabbing the stack of newspaper.

"We'll be pulling in tomorrow morning," he said looking at his watch. "See you tonight, usual time?"

She waved and walked away toward the aft ladder that led below. What to do?

After she disappeared down the ladder, Livingston finished his espresso and studied Sanders. "Well, that went better than we thought."

Sanders continued to bite his thumbnail. "There's something about it I don't like," he said.

"Relax," Livingston said. "She's not going anywhere but the bottom of Lake Superior in a few days. In fact," he picked up a toothpick from beside his plate, "that will probably be the last part of your turnover. There's someone else who will be going with her."

Sanders started to sweat, and his innocuous nail biting became nail gnawing. "I—I thought we were fine," he said.

Jesus, he thinks it's him. "Of course we are, Dai. It's not you, my old friend!"

Sanders exhaled and gave the sky his thanks. "Sorry, Mr. Livingston. I just—"

"It's Keach."

"Keach?! I don't understand."

Because you're blind, old man. "Yes. Keach." Livingston stretched out his legs. "He and Madame have been *together* for some time now."

Sanders looked shaken, then confused, and then offended. "Are you sure?"

"Yes. The way they look at each other...something's up."

"What do you think it is?"

The old fool loved gossip—especially when it involved something he should already know. "It doesn't matter." Livingston leaned toward him. "Just make sure that they think everything is going as planned." Or you'll be with them.

Sanders composed himself. "Absolutely." He fumbled with his pack of cigarettes and finally shook one cancer stick out. The waiter appeared again and lit it for him. Sanders's hand shook while he brought the cigarette to his mouth. Once there, he closed his lips around it and inhaled deeply. He blew the smoke out of his nose. "There won't be any problems."

Livingston stood up. "Good. We'll talk later. Until then, enjoy this view. I imagine the eastern Florida coastline will top this, but to me it's a toss-up."

Sanders took another drag and then grinned as he exhaled three smoke rings that rose into the sky.

Robin Norris sat at the salon table and put another forkful of spaghetti into his mouth. Then, he washed it down with a sip of red wine. Trist sat across from him and continued to work on his own plate.

"So, how long do you have, Dad?" Trist asked.

Robin put down his fork and sank back into the bench's cushion. "Don't know for sure. Probably less than a year."

"I still don't understand," Trist said. "Why can't you have surgery or radiation treatment?"

"Not the way it works with this kind of cancer, T." He picked his fork back up and twirled it in the noodles and meat sauce. "Your mom met with every specialist in the state, even some big shot in Boston. There's nothing we can do."

Trist stopped eating. "Then why the trip with just the two of us?"

Robin chewed his bite and took another sip of wine. "Yeah, about that. I tried to convince mom to come, but she wouldn't budge."

"Why not?"

"She knows things haven't been good between you and me for a while and thought this trip could help shore some things up while I'm still feeling okay."

Trist took a drink of water.

"You have to admit, we haven't seen eye to eye much during the past year. Now, I know that it is just a part of you growing up and becoming independent and that most likely in a few years we'd come back together, but we don't have that kind of time, Tristian."

"I'm ticked that you both didn't tell me sooner," Trist said. He held up a hand when Robin started to speak. "And I have every right to be," he said and bit into a piece of garlic bread. He chewed and said, "Finding out after you faint and nearly go overboard was not the way to go on this one, Dad."

Robin finished his wine. "You've got me there." There had been tears and questions and anger, but it had finally come out. They should have told Trist earlier, but Robin was surprisingly relieved. Everything was out in the open, which was not where his comfort zone was. However, the question eating at him was: would his body hold up? Was the fainting spell the start of the final unraveling or was it just an isolated incident? There was only one way to find out; they had decided to press on.

Seeing his empty glass, Trist said, "Want me to grab the bottle?"

Robin shook his head, "No, I'm good. Still surprised that you can make spaghetti this tasty."

Trist smirked. "It's not that difficult."

"Well, it was for me when I was starting out. You pick up on things easily. You always have."

"Feeling better?"

"I can't remember the last time I took a thirteen-hour snooze." He took the pitcher of water on the table and filled up a glass. Through the salon porthole he could see that the sun was still out. The boat had a steady list to starboard. "But more so than the late lunch, I'm impressed that you sailed her on your own while I rested." He paused. "And shocked that you continued through the night without waking me."

"I thought about flying the spinnaker—"

"You didn't?!" Robin cut him off.

"I chickened out, but I wore my harness and clipped in," Trist said with pride. "I set the autopilot and slept topside...well, I rested on the cockpit bench but I don't think I got much sleep."

Robin felt his temper flare up. He squeezed his glass of water and waited for it to pass. How could he have explained it to Levana if Trist had gone over the side in the middle of the night? How could he have lived with it? Then, he realized that he was not angry; he was embarrassed. He felt weak, diminished, and not in control. He eased his stranglehold on the water glass and took a sip. He looked at his son who had not averted his eyes. *He's expecting a lecture. Well, we're past lecture time—he proved himself last night. Let's go with it.*

Robin pointed to the digital readouts above the navigation station. "Well, we're already northeast of Whitefish Point. Unless you want to turn around, let's skip diving on the *Myron* and head north of Gargantua Harbor."

It could be the waning amount of adrenaline left in his son's body, but he could see a fire behind Trist's eyes that had never come to the surface before. "I'm game," Trist said.

He motioned back to the readouts. "Look at what we're *making* through the water. This is the beam reach to beat all beam reaches. We're movin' like *Sassy* in the Port Huron to Mackinac race. If this keeps up, we'll be within range of the eastern shore by tonight."

"Think the wind will change?"

"Not as far as any of the weather reports say. This may be the most epic run this sloop ever has. Let's ride the line as long as we can."

Trist nodded.

"Okay, I'm going to take a shower, put on some fresh clothes, and join you topside. Think you can handle her a while longer? The automatic steering system seems to be worth what I paid for, but I'll feel better if you're up there."

Trist started to clear the table, but Robin waved him off.

"I've got it. Get up there and make sure we're true. I'll be up to relieve you when I'm done down here, and you can get some sleep."

Trist put on his deck shoes and walked toward the hatch.

A few steps up the companionway ladder, Robin stopped him. "Thanks for taking care of me and," his eyes did a survey of the cabin, "the boat."

Trist gave him a pat on the shoulder and headed up through the hatch.

As he turned away to get the rest of the dishes, Robin Norris felt hot tears run down his cheeks.

18

—From the Journal of Robin Thomas Norris—

Love and Marriage

There is no perfect path for everyone to follow. No playbook to be purchased, no 'if this happens, then you do this' set of rules to follow that are guaranteed to work, and no judgment to be passed in regard to who another person should love or be with. What I can say, T, is that it's harder going it alone. Should you get married? If you're in it for the long-haul, yes: partnership, stability, tax advantages, etc. Our society is structured that way—gotta ensure that we have a next generation of workers and that we consistently produce enough human beings to replace ourselves. Were we built for monogamy? Shit, probably not. Is marriage necessary for love? No. Can it help make human beings think twice before acting on their wandering eyes? Maybe. I haven't seen anything else work. We already have too many young men dipping their wicks and then exiting their responsibilities; your old man was at this crossroads when it happened to your mother and me. I could have walked, but that's not who I am. There are many who do. Just make sure that whenever you go all the way, you're willing to go all the way on the other side of your orgasm. I won't rehash the episode with you and Rachel last year; you confirmed to me that night that you know your equipment works.

What we need are stable partnerships that lead to stable families. I can't imagine that inside every couple there aren't doubts, regrets, uncertainties, and bafflement. There is also probably a lot of support, caring, devotion, and loyalty. Whichever wins out usually determines the relationships that survive or pack it in. I've found that your mother and I made it because we were able to communicate about competing issues, and we either adapted and overcame or just accepted that they existed.

I hope you find someone with whom you can grow and overcome the obstacles that will come up—and they will come up—and I hope you enjoy the company of someone who loves you and accepts you for who you are. Don't get involved with someone to change them or for them to change you. This happens anyways, by the way, but if it is the prime mover for why you're getting involved, it's headed off the cliff from day one, T. Lastly, if you and your significant other are ever up against it and thinking about calling it quits: give counseling a shot. No, it's not an instant fix. But, it can help you see something that you can't on your own. I think it's a good idea to stay away from family or friend advice; most people only have their own relationships to use as examples, and, unfortunately, most of them won't have any advice that will help because what works for them might not work for your relationship. If people really wanted to be helpful, they would pass on their lessons learned to someone before that person got married. But people are too vulnerable to do that. This is why you get so many 'after the fact' self-help book referrals and advice—makes one want to say, "Well, why in the hell didn't you tell me that before?" This question is usually met with the reply, "You had to learn that on your own," (which, in life really means: I had to suffer and so should you). There are no guarantees when it comes to love and marriage, but I will admire you from the grave if you put yourself out there and give commitment a chance.

Finally: light. Jill St. John's eyes no longer hurt as she opened them at the sound...the sound of a door being unlocked. She quickly looked around at her surroundings. The lights on the ceiling had been turned on and she could see it was a small room with the bed she was in against one wall and a toilet, sink, mirror, and corner shower against the opposite wall. There was a nightstand, dresser, chair, and ottoman against the wall adjacent to her, and the final wall across from the dresser contained a closet next to an imposing steel door. Except for the tile and drain in the shower's corner, the room was carpeted in a deep crimson color. This was no guest suite.

This was a cell.

The door opened and Jill tried to sit up but found her body wouldn't respond. What had they given her? And who *were* they?

"Good afternoon, sweetie," a woman said. The door shut behind her and she approached the bed in a stately fashion. Her sweet-smelling perfume—Estee Lauder?—reached Jill as the woman knelt down beside the bed. She was beautiful—tall, golden blonde hair, magnetic blue eyes, tanned skin, and not an ounce of fat on her toned arms. If she looked like this in—twenty? thirty?—years she'd have zero complaints.

"Where am I?" Jill asked.

The woman brushed a strand of hair off Jill's forehead then looked into her eyes and smiled—perfect, glistening white teeth. "You're on vacation, hun."

"*Where* am I?"

"Shhh," the woman said and started folding down the covers in neat one-foot sections from Jill's neck until she stopped at Jill's ankles. The woman studied her figure from head to where the covers now were. She leaned back for a moment. "Yes, I can see the attraction," she said. "I'm going to check you over, okay?"

"Get me the *hell* out of here!" Jill said.

The woman leaned over and kissed her on the forehead and then moved her mouth over Jill's right ear. She whispered, "They're watching. Let me do what I have to do, and then I will try and help you. When I come close to your left ear, smile up at the ceiling and then rub your tongue over your lips. This will distract them while I talk."

149

Jill looked above the bed and saw the small video camera on the ceiling. She searched the rest of the room with her eyes...

...there was another one in the far corner of the room, just below the ceiling.

"Who are you?" Jill whispered back.

The woman brought her body on top of Jill's and straddled her waist, her knees barely staying on both sides of the bed. "You may call me Madame." Her eyes narrowed at Jill's saying *do not resist, this is an act.*

Madame placed her hands on Jill's shoulders and ran them up and down Jill's arms while breathing in, holding the breath, and exhaling loudly. This cycle went on for at least a minute, and then her lips were inches over Jill's, and their chests were touching. The woman smiled and moved her mouth over Jill's left ear.

Jill forced a smile at the camera.

"Nothing will happen today, but if you don't leave tonight, then it will start tomorrow and never stop," she said. "C'mon, sell it. Lick those lips and look seductive."

Jill obliged—her body shaking invisibly.

Madame continued. "You are going to be brought dinner soon. You will eat and drink everything. You'll also shower in the corner and put on the shorts and shirt I leave behind." Madame raised herself up and started to grind against Jill's hips. She put her hands down on Jill's breasts and squeezed them softly. Then, she was down over her other ear, which she kissed and continued whispering. "After you are dressed, you will come back over here and lie down again. The lights will go down and you should rest. I'll be back here a few hours after that. When I show up, we'll only have a few minutes to talk and then you're getting out of here. Now, start to cry and try and push me off of you. Yell: 'I won't!'."

Jill started to cry—there was no pretending needed—and she attempted to push Madame off of her. "I won't!"

Madame pinned her arms down and started to grind faster, her head thrown back. She started to moan as if she were about to climax...

She stopped. "Tomorrow," she said and climbed off. She looked at the crying girl, nodded up at the ceiling camera, and then covered Jill back up.

Madame walked toward the door and it opened. Jill wiped her eyes and watched as the freak took a tray with food and a large bottle of water off the floor—when she knelt down, Jill could see a small hallway with a stone wall behind her—and brought them over to the dresser. Madame walked back over to the door opening and returned with a bundle of clothing, a towel, and a shower caddy filled with soap, shampoo, and lotion, which she also set on the dresser next to the tray.

She met eyes with Jill for a second and then gave a smirk up to the corner camera as she walked across the room, exited, and closed the door behind her.

The lights dimmed, and Jill began to ease out of bed. *I've got one chance at this.* She willed herself to the dresser and started to eat.

"What was she saying to her?" Sanders asked.

"Who knows," Livingston said. "Hopefully, the program and her role." He reclined in his leather office chair. "Whatever it was, it worked for a little while. Did you see her lick those soft lips?" He popped a cough drop in his mouth. After a few sucks, he swallowed and felt some relief in his throat, which was sore from vomiting again after last night's session with Madame. He sucked again—not working fast enough. He bit into it, chewed fast, and swallowed the small bits.

They were seated behind a desk looking at two television monitors in a private den accessible only through a hidden door in the main residence's master closet.

"I don't trust her," Sanders said.

He's been in the game too long. Probably should have let him go years before. He put a reassuring hand on Sanders's arm. "After tomorrow, we won't have to worry about her anymore. And after your boat trip with her and Keach, you'll be headed for the oasis down south." He looked at the monitor and watched as the girl finished eating the food that had been provided.

Sanders relaxed and then leaned forward as the girl undressed and walked toward the shower. Using a joystick on the desk, he moved the camera into a better position to view—and then zoomed in.

The door behind them beeped and then opened. Eric Bannon entered the room with a man who could have been his twin. They walked over to Livingston, who was also watching the monitor.

"Madame is back in her room," Bannon said.

Livingston swiveled around, acknowledged Bannon's report, and then looked up at the other man. "Mr. Keach."

Sanders broke his gaze from the screen.

"Mr. Livingston," Keach said.

"I wanted to tell you both how pleased I am that the turnover is going well."

Eric Bannon and Mason Keach eyed each other.

"It surprised me too, Mason. You were my choice to keep on here as head of operations, and I hate to see you go, but there are needs down south. When *they* say they need new personnel...well, we know how that conversation flows."

"One way!" Sanders said while pointing with his arm like a football official saying *first down*. This was followed by his nervous laugh, which was beyond irritating. Sanders then started to hack. He pulled a handkerchief out of his pants' pocket and spit up into it.

Keach raised an eyebrow at Sanders.

"Excuse me," Sanders said to the group. He put the handkerchief back in his pocket and resumed watching the screen.

"What is our current staff right now?" Livingston asked Bannon.

"Beyond the yacht crew, we're at our usual summer house staff level: cook, waiter, maid, groundskeeper, and front gate security guard. For narcotics," he paused. "you've got me, Keach, Mr. Sanders, two security guards in the cave harbor, one outside of—" he looked at the monitor "—our guest's suite, and four more who man the Bayliner for product transfer."

Livingston tapped Sanders's shoulder and gave him a questioning look that said: *is he right?*

Sanders nodded once, "That's my count."

Livingston searched Mason Keach's eyes.

Keach replied, "Mine too."

"Fine," Livingston said, rubbing his hand on Sanders's neck and smiling at the two men standing. "I told him the turnover would be seamless."

Keach and Bannon glared at Sanders, who bit his nail and then said, "I knew it would be."

Livingston unwrapped another cough drop and put it in his mouth. "The next shipment doesn't arrive for another few weeks. I don't plan on being here. I'm heading to Key West on the Hatteras and might even be taking my—" he pointed to the screen "—*guest* onboard with me depending on how she acclimates."

No one said a word.

Then, Eric stepped forward. "Will you be needing anything else, sir?" he said.

"Not at this moment," said Livingston. "I won't keep you both from your turnover checklist any longer. Probably some odds and ends to still go over?"

Bannon and Keach nodded their heads in agreement and then departed.

After the door closed, Sanders said, "Are you sure you have to get rid of him?"

Livingston's attention was on the screen. The girl toweled off and then put on the new pair of panties, shorts, and t-shirt that he had bought for her. She took a final swig of water from the water bottle on the dresser and then climbed into bed and covered up.

"Sir?" Sanders said and started coughing again.

"Yes," Livingston said. "Don't ask about it again."

Sanders spit up into his handkerchief.

19

The burnt orange sun hung on the horizon off *Levity*'s stern as Robin Norris steered the boat toward the gigantic cliffs lining the Eastern shore of Lake Superior, north of Gargantua Harbor. Trist was still asleep below. Robin had taken down the jib an hour ago and the mainsail twenty minutes after that. The wind had lessened and he motored the sloop near idle through the water.

The weather had cooled and he now had on a sweater. Every ten minutes or so he would do ten squats to keep his legs warm as he stood behind the helm console. He looked over the binnacle at the depth finder and saw that he was now in 30 feet of water. It wasn't the ideal place to anchor, but he wanted no part of testing Superior's rocky shoreline. No, better to anchor here and enjoy a quiet evening with Trist. There was so much he wanted to say even though he had now completed a total of four journal entries. How many would he have by the time he passed away?

A final check of the depth finder revealed that *Levity* was in 33 feet of water. He carried 300 feet of chain rode aboard, so he figured at 5:1 he'd pay out approximately 165 feet of rode. He brought the engine to idle and pointed the sailboat into the little wind that there was. Dashing forward, he released the brake on the windlass, and the anchor began to drop. As the chain rode continued to pay out, he went back to the helm and checked his depth. 60 feet?! He fiddled with the depth finder's buttons, then hit the display. The reading didn't change. Were they near a drop off? He didn't remember seeing one this close on the chart. He sprinted back to the windlass and set the brake, checking the rode at around 45 feet. He pushed the up button on the windlass. The chain moved a few inches and then stopped as the windlass strained. He let go of the up button and then pressed the down button, paying out a foot of rode to take the strain off. Fouled on something? He tried to raise the anchor again but got the same result.

To remove more load off the windlass, he tied a short piece of line around the chain and then tied it off to a cleat. He walked out onto the pulpit and stared down. All he could see was the chain disappear after a few feet.

He returned to the cockpit and looked at his fish finder that gave him a pixelated arcade-like view of the bottom. There seemed to be a mass of something rising up unevenly below them. What in the hell? He checked his current latitude and longitude and went below to the nav table to check their position on the chart. There were no *charted* wrecks, underwater obstructions, or reefs, but the depth *did* change—and fast—where he was currently at. In one direction, they were close to over two-hundred feet of water. It was then that he noticed that he was off just a bit from where he thought he had anchored. He'd been distracted, thinking about yesterday.

Shit.

He mentally reviewed the options. On the long salon bench, Trist snored away. Robin went topside.

In the cockpit, he lifted up the starboard bench. Inside was his harness for going aloft. He grabbed it and closed the bench. The sun cast a warm glow on the hundred-foot cliffs off the bow. There were no signs of civilization, just towering trees on top of the cliff heights. He faced the sun. It continued to slip below the horizon—maybe half-an-hour of daylight left.

He went below and put on a pot of coffee.

Robin nudged Trist's shoulder and Trist's eyes popped open.

"We may be fouled, T. I'm going aloft to see what I can make of it. Bring up the dive gear," he paused, "and that new compressor and Desco equipment. Might be time to use it."

Trist rubbed his eyes. "Why?"

"Longer bottom time and two free hands to work on the anchor. Plus, if we're both down there, I can yell instructions to you if you get close enough to me since the Desco mask covers my entire face."

Trist pulled the blanket off of himself and sat up. "Okay. Sure you don't need me to winch you up?"

"No, the block and tackle system I've got rigged gives me a four to one advantage; I'll be fine." He pointed to the coffee pot. "I've got the coffee started. Bring up two mugs after you've got the dive gear up."

Robin pulled on the 7/16-inch line as he continued to ascend. The top of the mast was over fifty-five feet above the water, which put the spreader over thirty feet above. He'd ditched his bosun's chair last year after falling out of it at, thankfully, five feet above the deck. "You don't fall out of a proper climbing harness," the manager of West Marine had told him. He had ponied up the cash for one.

He reached the spreader and continued to pull until he was a few feet above it. This was another requirement he had when the mast was constructed: "Don't tell me I can't stand on the Goddamn spreader." Holding the mast, he placed his feet squarely on top of the spreader, his toes and heels hanging over, and stood up.

Far below, he saw Trist come up the companionway steps with a scuba tank, which he set on the cockpit's teak decking.

"You okay?" Trist yelled up to him.

"Yep!" Robin said back.

Trist vanished below and Robin looked down at the lake. The combination of calm water, a cloudless sky, and sun still gave him enough visibility to search the depths for what they might be tangled on. However, he knew the chances of a visual were almost non-existent because of the depth. His only chance was if there was something coming up from the bottom whose top was closer to the surface. He scanned the water in all directions.

No outline. No shadow. Nothing he could make out. He'd have to dive.

While he was up here, he might as well check on the antenna connection and wind vane mounting at the top of the mast. He looked down at the cockpit. Trist was putting another tank on deck along with two wetsuits that had been hanging over his shoulder.

"Anything?" Trist said.

"No," said Robin. "Gonna check the top of the mast."

Trist gave a thumbs up and headed below once again.

Robin heaved on the line and soon his hands reached the top of the mast. He inched up as far as he could and examined the antenna connection. It was secure. But when he checked the wind vane mount, there were two screws loose. Reaching down, he pulled out his Swiss Army knife and extended the Phillips head screwdriver. Using one hand as a guide, he fitted the grooves to the screw and guided the hand holding the screwdriver until the head sunk back into the slots. When he could no longer twist it, he repeated the procedure for the second loose screw.

He folded the knife and put it back in his pocket. What had been a warm glow on the cliff face above the shore had now faded to a cool gray as the sun began to disappear. He pulled the binoculars up from around his neck and traced the shoreline south and then north. Far away he thought he could make out a break in the trees at the top of the cliff. A house? Probably not. They were now on the Canadian side of the border and this area had not been lived in for almost fifty years. He remembered Gary Hawthorne telling him about how the sea lamprey had wiped out most commercial fishing in the community at Gargantua Harbor by the 1950s. Some lamprey control measures had been put in place, but in all likelihood the number of herring and lake trout would never return. All that remained of the fishing community were a handful of abandoned structures and the foundations of buildings long since collapsed. If the Great Lakes had a ghost town, Gargantua Harbor was it. He swept the binoculars south again. The empty feeling hit his stomach as he realized that this was yet another sight he would never witness again. Englishmen who had fought in World War II had said that they knew the war would be over when they saw the white cliffs of Dover again on their return trip home. These cliffs on Lake Superior seemed to mark an end too. He let his body swing side to side against the mast for a long moment as he looked out over the water and to the horizon beyond. The wind had completely died. He dropped the binoculars and began his descent.

After setting the compressor on the cockpit deck, Trist slid below and entered the galley where he filled two mugs with coffee. When he returned to the cockpit, Robin was back on deck amidships stepping out of his harness.

"Rig up a tank, T," Robin said.

Trist took a mug to Robin and then headed aft.

Robin took a heavenly chug and set the mug on the deck. Free of the harness, he coiled the remainder of the 7/16-inch line and tied it off. It was getting darker out by the minute. He picked up the mug and joined Trist in the stern.

Trist had the tank ready to go and held out a wetsuit for Robin to put on.

"Keep it," Robin said. "I'll swim down with just mask, fins, knife, and a dive light to take a quick peek at what we're dealing with. I might even be able to untangle it. There's no wind and almost no current."

Trist looked pissy. "Then why all the gear?"

Robin snickered. "Because we can get to work quicker if the anchor is mangled on something. Or, if I'm able to free it up, we can do a night dive and work up an appetite for some mammoth steaks your mom packed. I'm still full from the spaghetti. How about you?"

Trist nodded. "But the anchor is fouled on something in over thirty feet of water. Can you go that deep and make it back on one breath?"

"Son, if I don't have the lungs to do that, I shouldn't own a boat."

Trist's annoyance turned to concern. "But, what about yester—"

Robin was firm. "I'm fine."

"Okay, but I'm watching from the pulpit. If I don't see you in one minute, I'm coming down to drag you up."

"You're as stubborn as your old man."

They shared a laugh and then sucked down the rest of their coffee.

Robin took off his sweater and t-shirt and pulled his mask on; the rubber surrounding the faceplate took suction against his forehead. Trist grabbed the dive light and fins while Robin strapped a dive knife to his right calf. They walked up to the bow.

"I'm giving you a minute," Trist said.

Robin put on the fins and jumped overboard.

He surfaced a few yards to starboard away from the pulpit where he took off his mask, spit into it, and rubbed the saliva all over the inside of the faceplate while treading water. He submerged the mask and then put it on.

Trist walked to the end of the pulpit where he could see the anchor chain disappear into the deep. Robin kicked over and grasped the chain with one hand and held up his long arm to receive the dive light. Trist leaned over the pulpit railing and dropped it down into Robin's hand.

"Cold?" Trist said.

"I'm in no danger of falling asleep," he said and turned the light on and started taking in deep breaths, hyperventilating.

"Be careful," Trist said.

Robin took in one more breath, gave a thumbs up, and then dove for the bottom.

The water's color went from a shade of blue-green to blue to navy to black as his light cut through the cold darkness that surrounded him. He paused a few times to equalize the pressure in his ears and then continued to follow the anchor chain down. The water's temperature dropped as he went deeper.

He reached the end of the chain, no anchor. Below him, was—he kicked up a few feet and swept his light across the bottom—the crumpled wreckage of...not a boat, but a plane of some sort. The fuselage was a twisted mess with the entire tail section either missing or unrecognizable. He focused the light on the end of the anchor chain once more. There was the problem: the anchor had broken through the remains of the cockpit window and was stuck on something inside.

His lungs began to ache—a warm feeling in his chest against the cold water that threatened to freeze him in a block of ice. He used the chain to pull himself down to the point where it entered the plane. He shined his light inside.

The chain continued below, perhaps ten feet deeper? It was hard to tell because the plane was resting on an angle. He could not make out the stock or flukes—there was too much wreckage. He changed his grip on the chain and then yanked it upward.

No movement.

He shook the chain side to side and then at weird random angles trying to pry it loose or at least get a look at what the anchor was stuck on. All he did was stir up silt. At least the plane wasn't moving; the calm conditions above and lack of current were keeping the sailboat from exerting more strain on the chain and anchor. He shined the light into the cockpit and to the right.

A skeletal hand hung down suspended behind one of the seats. He searched with his light for the rest of the body but to no avail. His chest was now on fire. He aimed his light above and kicked—the temperature warming as he rose.

His head broke through the surface and he gasped for air.

"You okay?" Trist said from the pulpit.

Robin took in a few more breaths and then managed a "Yeah."

"Anchor untangled?"

"No. You're not gonna believe what it's tangled on."

PART III

Berthed

20

Robin slid his hand over the stacked air tanks coupled to the compressor. "I think I can get inside if I just have my free flow mask on and weight belt. We'll station you at the opening to guide the air hose down so that it doesn't get tangled. And, to be safe, we'll leave a rigged tank down there just in case with a mask tied to the tank straps."

"So, you think it's an old seaplane?" Trist said.

"I think it was a floatplane," Robin said.

"What's the difference?"

"Not much. A floatplane is just a type of seaplane. You take a land-based aircraft and mount fixed floats—pontoons—underneath the fuselage, which means the fuselage doesn't have to be watertight since it doesn't come in contact with the water. In a traditional seaplane, the fuselage is designed to land in the water—one massive pontoon if you will. Anyways, when we're down there, we can poke around for the pontoons and see if I'm right."

"Wouldn't those have floated to the surface when the plane went down?"

"That's what I'm thinking, but if they hit the water and got any type of a hole in them, then they'd sink."

"Sounds like the pilot is still down there."

"Somebody is. You okay seeing it?"

"I think so."

They both had on wetsuits now along with neoprene booties and hoods. Trist wore a buoyancy compression device. It was dark enough outside to spot any source of light on shore or on the water, but they saw nothing.

Trist did a slow 360-degree scan of the horizon.

"Something else got you bugged?" Robin asked.

"I was just thinking about what Uncle Tyee told me before we headed up here."

"What'd he say?"

"That for most of our trip we wouldn't be near anyone who could help if we got into trouble. It's almost too quiet around here, dad." He bent over and strapped on his dive knife. "You don't think anyone will board our boat and rip us off while we're down there do you? I mean, they could cut off your air supply by turning off the compressor and then you'd be up shit creek without a paddle."

Robin laughed. *He got that phrase from me.* "I'm not worried about it," he said. "However, we don't need to announce our presence to the world either. Let's keep the anchor lights off while we're down below. The compressor will make some noise, but out here it would be difficult to know where the sound was coming from."

"Isn't that against the nautical rules? What if someone rammed us because they didn't see us?"

"C'mon, Trist. We're in the middle of nowhere. You want the lights on or off?"

Trist put his hands through his tank straps and buckled in. "Off."

"I already locked the cabin, so we should be good."

"So you say."

"When did you become Mr. Cautious?"

"Okay, okay. Let's go."

"Cards after dinner?"

Trist paused. "Revenge."

Robin grinned. Before locking up the cabin, he had set out the playing cards on the salon table. *Gonna kick his hind end in Euchre later.* Usually, it was he and Tyee versus Trist and Levana, but when you play with just two people and take out the 9s and 10s, it was still *the* card game in Michigan. *If more people gathered around the kitchen table and played cards instead of zoning out to electronics, the world would be a better place.* He hoped that Trist would keep the family card parties alive.

They put their fins on over their booties and grabbed their dive lights. It was still cloudless. The moon would provide plenty of natural light when they surfaced later.

Robin fired up the compressor and the steady chug vibrated the decking below their fins. Next, he made the appropriate adjustments and put on the face mask, making sure that air was flowing in. He gave the 'okay' sign. "Ready?" he shouted from behind the mask's faceplate.

Trist could hear him and immediately grasped the advantage they would have underwater because his dad could direct him as necessary. If Trist needed to communicate, he could use his dive slate to write down a message.

Robin took off the Desco mask and handed it to Trist. Then, he entered the water from the swim step and swam over to the starboard rail. Trist passed him the mask and hose underneath the railing so that the hose rested on the gunwale. Treading water, Robin secured the mask and then turned on his smaller dive light which was attached to a cord around his wrist. Trist had the larger light to aim where Robin needed it.

Trist stepped down from the cockpit onto the swim step, closing the section of railing behind him. Robin arrived and took a coil of nylon line and the extra tank, regulator, and mask from the platform and started swimming toward the bow. He was definitely warmer with the wetsuit on, but the water still chilled his skin. Trist held the regulator to his mouth and jumped in. He caught up to Robin and they kicked along the surface until they reached the anchor line.

"Ready?" Robin said into his mask.

Trist gave the 'okay' sign.

"Turn on your light, and let's go," Robin said.

Trist flipped the switch on his light, which illuminated a cone of water below. They dove.

The descent was slower than his free dive earlier. Trist finned beside him and searched the depths with his light. *He's anxious to see the wreck. This will more than make up for the one we skipped.* He cracked a grin. *He sailed the boat alone off Whitefish Point, the area with the most unpredictable weather in the entire Great Lakes.* With the tank strap through his left arm, he held his dive light in his right hand and aimed it below, waiting for the wreckage to come into view.

Trist's light found it first, and they slowed their descent.

"Okay, buddy," Robin said.

Trist began to shine his beam on the area around the plane in order to find a suitable location to place the emergency tank. They could now see that the left-hand portion of the wing was still intact, extending out from on top of the fuselage and resting on the bottom; they couldn't see the right-hand part of the wing. Robin watched as Trist moved his light forward of the wing across the sandy bottom. He followed with his own light.

"Stop." Robin said.

Trist's beam was on a flat area of sand between two rocks the size of basketballs a few yards to the left of the plane's cockpit.

"Hold your light right there," Robin said and then swam over and placed the tank, regulator, and mask carefully on the bottom between the rocks—a foot to spare on either side of the tank. Other rocks littered the lake bed but none as big as these two for at least another ten yards away from the plane. He gave Trist the okay sign and then swam up to him so that they were face to face. "Okay, we get into trouble, locate the anchor chain and follow it down to the cockpit. Facing the fuselage, trace the cockpit down to the right until you find the bottom. Stop, put your back to the plane and in one kick you'll be at the rocks where the tank, regulator, and mask are. If you reach the wing, you're too far aft. Got it?"

Trist gave the okay sign.

Robin held the nylon line in his hand and said, "Follow me."

They swam back up to the point where the anchor chain disappeared into the cockpit and hovered over it. Here, the depth was around thirty feet.

"I'm going to shine my beam inside and show you the part of the skeleton that we can see, okay?"

Trist nodded and moved back a few feet in order to see better.

"Then we'll do our survey before I try to enter the plane and free up the anchor."

A strong okay sign from Trist.

Robin turned and shined his underwater light down into the cockpit. The light seemed to bring the dangling arm to life, the palm facing them and the fingers spread out as if the hand was poised to reach out at any moment and pull one of them down into the deep. Robin looked over at Trist whose gaze was transfixed on the bony appendage. After waiting a few seconds, he aimed his light away from the cockpit. "You good?"

Trist gave a slow nod.

"All right, let's get a look at the rest of it."

Robin motioned to the left and they started to swim over the cockpit in the opposite direction of the emergency tank. They reached the edge of the plane, but where they anticipated seeing the lake bottom, they only saw darkness.

They aimed their beams down and still couldn't find the floor. Trist followed him perhaps ten yards out into open water and they turned around to look at the plane.

It was on the edge of a rocky cliff that plummeted almost straight down into the black abyss. The right portion of the wing was gone, which almost certainly would have tipped the balance and sent the plane down the cliffside. Even as it rested now, if it slid just a few more feet toward them it would be history. They'd be hard pressed to find a greater example of one of Lake Superior's textbook drop offs. He'd have to be extra careful inside the wreck—one disruption could send them down.

Trist tapped him on his shoulder and he turned toward his son. On the dive slate, Trist had written:

FOLLOW CLIFFSIDE DOWN...TRY TO FIND BOTTOM?

Robin got his mask close to Trist's.

"No more than thirty feet directly below the plane. I've got more air hose available, but sixty feet is the max depth I want to mess around with, especially if I have to swim down and reach you if you get into trouble."

Trist wrote:

GOT IT. BE RIGHT BACK.

Robin watched as Trist's light started to follow the cliffside down.

Trist kept his eye on his depth gauge as he descended. Forty feet...forty-five feet...fifty-five feet. He started to tread, which stopped his drop at just over sixty feet. Nothing but a rocky cliff face. Above, he could see his father's light aimed down at him. He aimed his own light down below and could not locate the bottom. For his ascent, he decided to swim on a diagonal line toward where the plane's tail would be. He lined up and started to kick.

At fifty feet, the cliff face angled out to a small shelf and he made out one of the plane's pontoons—resting almost vertically with a massive gash that had split open most of the end that was pointed toward the surface. He swam up and reached the back of the fuselage—the tail was nowhere to be seen. It must have broken off on impact, but there was something not right with the fuselage's skin. He swam to within a foot of the structure and shined his light on the surface. The upper portion that wasn't bent was still smooth, but as he moved his light toward the bottom, he saw that some of it was disfigured—melted. Perhaps the fuel tank had exploded and the tremendous heat had caused this. He couldn't think of anything else that could have. Motion to his right caught his attention, and he saw his dad's light approaching.

Robin reached his son and watched as Trist showed him what looked like a melted portion of the fuselage plating. Then, Trist wrote on his slate:

1 PONTOON BELOW. NO BOTTOM IN SIGHT AT 60FT. NO MORE WRECKAGE.

"Anything else?" Robin said.

Trist wrote again:

AIRPLANE SKIN MELTED. FIRE?

"Probably," Robin said. "You sure there was no more wreckage?"

Trist shook his head yes.

"Okay, let's swim aft, go up the left side and then try and work on the anchor."

Making sure his air hose would not get tangled, Robin swam a few yards above Trist and they kicked over to a position directly aft of the fuselage, where the tail would have been. The opening was large enough for one person to squeeze through. Trist aimed his light inside.

The seatback to the aft bench was still upright so they could see nothing except for the water between the top of the seatback and the ceiling. Robin got closer and aimed his light toward the cockpit. The back of the co-pilot's seat was mostly a metal frame, the material covering it gone. Burned off in a fire?

Possibly. He could see the anchor chain disappear out of sight between the front seats. He swept his light behind the pilot's seat. There, he saw the owner of the hand reaching into the cockpit, but he could only see the top third of the body. It was as if the person had died giving the pilot's seat a hug from behind. Trist was now beside him and aiming his light at the skeleton. What had happened? He could probably squeeze in over the back bench if going through the cockpit didn't work. Either way, it would be hard to get out if the plane slipped off the edge.

They backed out and swam along the left-hand side of the plane. The portion of the wing resting on the bottom was in fine condition. In fact, the only damage they could see was a foot-long crack where it connected to the top of the fuselage. Seeing that there was no debris on the lake bed near the plane, they finned over the emergency tank and returned to their original position outside the cockpit.

Robin positioned Trist so that the boy's light would give him the maximum visibility but also be on an angle so that Robin wouldn't be blinded on his way out. He used his own light to examine the frame for any glass that might remain from the cockpit windshield. A few jagged pieces jutted out on the left, but they wouldn't be a problem. He gave Trist the coil of nylon line and then moved back a few yards. Trist got his attention and raised a crooked index finger in the shape of a question mark.

Robin pointed to his fins and then got close to Trist. "I'm going to take them off to give me more room inside. It's going to be cramped in there, and I don't want to stir up a bunch of silt if I don't have to."

Trist held out a fist, the signal for danger.

"I know," Robin said. "Let's take it slow." He took off his fins and placed them under Trist's knees who put his weight on them against the plane's nose.

Trist trained his light inside, and Robin entered the cockpit head first and carefully pulled himself in past the two front seats. To his right, he now saw the full skeleton. The legs had been crushed under the weight of the caved in section of the fuselage. He took a moment to honor the poor passenger.

He moved his light across the back bench and over to the anchor li—wait a minute. He moved his light back to the bench. There was a piece of rope coming out from underneath the seat where the side of the cabin had been bent inward. He took hold of it cautiously. The outside was slimy at first, but as he tightened his grip, he realized that it was not so much a rope as it was a handle. He released his grip and followed it below the seat. There he felt fabric—the handle was still attached to something.

He slid his legs in, making his body into a ball, then turned to rest his knees on the cabin floor. Crouching down, he twisted his neck to avoid touching the skeleton's pelvis and aimed his light underneath the seat where the rope led.

There was a small duffel bag jammed in there. Using his free hand, he felt around and made out the zipper and then the bag's edges. He started to pull on the handle and a small cloud of slit rolled out from underneath the seat. He stopped and watched the particles float in his light's beam and then start to settle back down. Better look at the anchor.

He moved over to the left and followed the line down past the back bench. There it was. The flukes were caught on a bent portion of the aft fuselage, and the stock was wedged below the aft bench's seat. He would have never been able to pull it free from above. He slid around the side of the bench and grasped the stock with both hands, letting the underwater light dangle from the band around his wrist. With a few powerful jerks, he freed the stock first, and then twisted it to pry the flukes out from under the fuselage wreckage. The anchor was now free, and Robin pulled it up over the back bench. The wreckage shifted, making a sick moan, but then settled again.

Trist watched as his father spun around. He kept the light away from Robin's line of sight and soon saw the anchor coming up out of the cockpit guided by his father's arms, muscles straining under the wetsuit fabric. Trist pulled on the chain to help, and together they lifted the anchor up past where the windshield once was and set it on the plane's nose beside him. There, Robin quickly tied the end of the nylon line to the anchor stock and handed the other end of the coil to Trist. His dad smiled behind his mask and got close.

"You've got about a hundred feet of line. Hold on to this so we don't lose our lifeline up to the boat. If the line runs out, hang on and follow it and I'll catch up to you." Trist gave him the okay sign. "I'll be right back," Robin said and then re-entered the plane. As he did, the anchor slid slowly off the nose.

He moved into his former position with his knees on the cabin floor facing the skeleton. Instead of pulling on the handle this time, he slid his hand below the bag, and, through a combination of lifting and pulling, freed the bag. Gently, he set it on the back bench. *Probably this guy's overnight bag.* He found the zipper again and followed the treads until he reached the zipper handle. *Just a peek.*

He started to pull.

21

A small cloud of silt rose up. He stopped. Maybe he should follow his rule and leave this unfortunate grave site undisturbed. He looked at the skeleton. But what if there was something inside the bag that could help identify who this poor bastard was? It was a good bet that the family never found out where he disappeared to. He pulled on the handle again and ran it down the entire length of the zipper. Then, he pulled the bag open and shined his light inside.

His eyes opened as if his eyeballs were being pulled out. Resting on the bottom of the bag was a handful of jewels. The mixture of scarlet, diamond, green, and light blue colors sparkled in his light. Sweet Jesus, how much was this lot worth? And what in the *hell* was it doing here? He zipped the bag shut and his instincts took over as he bent down and looked under the seat for any more bags. He moved his light from left to right and found what looked like another bag, but this one was wedged even further behind the crumpled section of fuselage. With his body on the floor, he moved his arm under the seat and reached. Nothing. He slid closer, positioning his shoulder directly under the seat edge. He reached again.

This time, his fingers felt the bag's fabric. He stretched to the point where he could hold a section of the bag in his fingers and pulled. The bag started to move. This one was heavier. He pulled harder.

Suddenly, he lost his grip and the momentum of his pull threw his body back against the co-pilot's seat. The plane shuddered and a sick creaking sound began to grow in intensity. He could hear banging up near the nose. Trist was signaling him. Trouble. Robin grabbed the bag on the bench and started to head out as the plane started heeling over toward the chasm. He pulled on the cockpit controls and shot out though the open windshield. Trist thrust his fist out repeatedly, and Robin could see the fear in his son's eyes.

The plane tipped over even more and Trist's knees came up off the plane. Robin's fins began to float away. He grabbed one, but before he could go for the other Trist seized his arm and kicked to get them away from the plane. As the plane began to go over the edge, the left-hand side of the wing headed straight for them.

Trist kicked harder, and the wing sliced through the water, missing them by inches. Clear of the danger, they rested on the edge of the drop off and watched as the plane tumbled into darkness.

Robin put his one fin on and showed Trist the bag he had in his hand. He got closer. Trist's eyes were on fire. "Sorry, T. Your old man just about royally screwed up. Let's head up and I'll make it up to you when I show you what's inside this bag."

Trist handed him the nylon rope and then wrote on his dive slate:

I AM SO. He crossed it out and wrote instead: WHATEVER! WHAT ABOUT THE TANK?

Robin looked over at the rocks where the tank was. Then, he looked at his watch. "You're almost out of air. We can get the tank tomorrow before we leave. I'll untie the nylon line and we'll follow the anchor chain up. Then, let's re-anchor with the forward *and* aft anchors to position us straight over this site."

Trist reluctantly gave him the okay sign, and, after Robin had untied the nylon line from the anchor, started to kick for the surface. Robin watched as his son's light moved further and further above. He gave a thought to bringing the tank up now, but with one fin as his propeller, he decided against it. He lifted off the bottom and took a few awkward kicks, barely moving. Forget it. He pulled the quick release lever on his weight belt and it sank to the bottom. He held on to the bag with one hand and the anchor chain with the other as he pulled and kicked his way up.

"How are you feeling?" Trist said.

"A little tired," he admitted. "After this meal, I see a good night of sleep ahead of us." He felt a cool breeze come down the companionway. "The temperature drops fast up here."

When they had surfaced after the dive, they found themselves enveloped in darkness, as if the waterline was the bottom of the sea and the moon was an eternal dive light casting a beam down on them. He'd briefly shown Trist what was in the bag and said they would discuss it over dinner. After anchoring over the site, they'd stowed the dive gear, turned on the anchor lights, and headed below to clean up. Trist had taken a hot shower while Robin went topside and set up the grill on the aft railing. When Trist was done, they had switched.

"How much do you think all those jewels are worth?" Trist asked.

They were now seated at the salon table working on the largest steaks Trist had ever seen his father make—twenty ounces each, at least. The bread, salads and huge basket of fries were already long gone.

"No idea," Robin said. "If they're genuine, and we have no reason to think they're not, a lot." He sat back, and a thought came to him. "I might be able to make an estimate though."

"How? You just said you had no idea," said Trist.

"Sometimes I should..." No use holding back now "...think before I speak," Robin said. "It's an old Norris family curse."

Trist sat speechless.

"You know our local jeweler, Justin Ford, right?"

Trist continued to stare.

"Trist?"

"Uh, yeah. Justin the Jeweler. His ads blanket the local paper."

"Since when do you read the paper?"

"Only the sports, but Justin is everywhere."

Robin snorted, "Yeah, he can be annoying, but he's local so I support him." Robin took a sip. "Anyway, when I was in there late in March picking up your mom's wedding ring from a cleaning, he was quieter than usual. So I asked him what was up, and he said that he just received the Jewelers' Security Alliance Annual Crime Report. If I remember right, he said that something like 55 million dollars' worth of jewelry had been stolen the year before. Now, I'm not sure when that plane went down, but it's been there a while." He looked over at the dry bag resting on the salon bench.

Right before dinner, he had carefully wiped each gem with a soft cloth and placed them in a Ziploc bag and then in a dry bag with a float attached. *Levity* could disappear beneath the waves, but the stones wouldn't be joining her.

"I'm guessing the jewels in that bag are worth at least a couple million dollars."

Trist's eyes sparkled under the salon table light.

"And even more in the second bag that went down with the plane." He motioned to the bench again. "Make sure you put the dry bag and float in the V-berth after dinner."

Trist nodded in agreement. "I don't know if I can finish this beast," Trist said as he sliced a piece of steak, stabbed it along with a mushroom and two onions, and then dipped the combination in Heinz 57 sauce.

"Three more bites and you're there," Robin said and then let out a laugh.

"What?" Trist said putting the forkful in his mouth.

"I used to use that trick when you were a toddler."

Trist shook his head and swallowed. He took a cleansing breath and sliced another piece off.

"Atta boy," Robin said and took another bite of his own steak.

"One thing seems certain though," Robin said. "Those jewels weren't being transported legally. Who knows how many bags were even on that plane?"

Trist gave a wry grin. "Whatever happened to *respecting the wreck and leaving everything in its place?*"

Nothing like having your words tossed back at you. "I always make an exception for jewels in duffel bags."

Trist put down his fork. "I can't win."

Robin chuckled. "Well, there is something to be said for the phrase that old age and treachery will defeat youth and energy."

He picked his fork back up. "I wonder how deep the plane went."

"You said that around eighty feet the bottom was nowhere in sight, right?"

Trist nodded.

Robin swirled the wine in his glass as he thought. "I could go down tomorrow morning and retrieve the extra tank," he said. "After that, we could pull up the anchor and I could run the boat over the drop off to check the depth. I'm comfortable with us diving to 150 feet, but no deeper." He and Tyee rarely went below 100 feet. "All pitch black down there," Tyee had said.

"You want that other bag, don't you?"

Robin's eyes sparkled. "We'll see. Even if we can reach the plane, there may be no way to get inside it now."

"I wonder why no one had found the plane yet. We're not that far offshore."

"Yeah, it's interesting. But I am reminded that we landed on the moon about a decade and a half before finding the *Titanic*. It's humbling to know we'll never discover all the stuff buried beneath the waves or even know exactly *what* is underneath them."

"Where do you think the jewels were headed when they went down?"

"Maybe Canada." Robin rubbed his chin. "Maybe Detroit or even New York."

"Do you think there was anyone else in the plane with that guy?"

"Possibly, but it could have just been him." He paused. "Although, that doesn't sit right with me."

"Why not?"

"Because of the way he was trapped behind the pilot's seat. I think the crash caused him to get pinned back there, so he must have been in the back when the plane hit the water. Therefore, it couldn't have been the pilot."

"Where do you think the pilot went then?"

"He could have been ejected out the front windshield, or thrown all the way to the back and went down with the missing tail section."

"Or he escaped through the windshield," Trist said.

The realist in him had ruled out this option, but he couldn't deny that there was a small chance. Good to know that Trist has some optimism left in him. "You never know."

"If he died and wasn't trapped inside, wouldn't the body have floated to the surface or eventually washed ashore?"

"Not necessarily," said Robin. "The freezing water can keep bacteria from forming gases, and so the body stays submerged. Remember my Gordon Lightfoot record?"

"I know where you're headed, dad. *The Wreck of the Edmund Fitzgerald.* Yes, still got it memorized."

"Memorized? You forgot what Gitche Gumee even stood for before we left. Remember?"

Trist playfully lowered his head and held his hands up in defeat.

"Anyways, it's one of the best ballads ever written. Period."

"I surrender. But what you're trying to tell me is that there are people who go into Superior that never come out."

"We saw one tonight."

Trist chewed his last piece of steak. "What do we do with the jewels?"

"When we get back, we'll talk to Justin first. Have him out for dinner and show him the goodies. See what he thinks."

"Are we rich?"

"Considerin' retiring before you've even graduated high school?"

Trist's face reddened. "No, just wonderin'..."

"Yeah, right. I know what you're thinking, and the answer is, yes, if we get any of this money then some of it will go to you one day, but that changes nothing about you going to school and getting an education first."

"I know, all right?"

"Look on the bright side: We might not get to keep any of it," Robin said and finished off the wine in his glass. "Mom will be shocked though."

Trist broke a smile. "She will be."

"Now that we've got that settled, let's go topside for a surprise."

"What? Cards?"

"Change of plans. Head up and I'll join you in a minute."

Trist swung his legs out from underneath the table and grabbed a hooded sweatshirt off the salon bench before heading topside.

After clearing the table, Robin unlatched a cabinet above the stove. Inside was a deep well on one side and a crisscrossed wooden wine rack on the other. From one of the bottom slots, he took out a 21-year-old bottle of The Macallan. From the deep well he pulled out two cigars, a cutter, and a lighter.

He set it all on the counter and latched the cabinet back up. Bending down, he slid open a drawer and pulled out a box. Celebrating and yet apprehensive about what was inside, he set it on the counter and opened it.

Under the box top were two old fashioned glasses with the Detroit & Mackinac Railroad logo on them. They had been passed down from his grandfather to his father and eventually to him. In addition to his father and grandfather, his two uncles and one great-uncle had worked at the D & M for over seventy-five years. Robin had been saving these glasses for Trist's and— he exhaled and said the name of his deceased son inside his head—*Jonathan's* wedding nights. Knowing that he would never see them, he had decided to bring the glasses on the trip and give them to Trist when he felt the moment was right.

He arrived topside with two fingers of scotch poured into each glass and the cigars in the front pocket of his sailing sweater. The night breeze had cooled the temperature even more, and the moonlight on the water's surface made that part of the lake look like a slice of obsidian.

He handed a glass to Trist.

"You have got to be kidding me," Trist said.

They sat down across from each other in the cockpit.

"You know I'm no fan of underage drinking, but this is different. We're only having this one, but I wanted to do it while I still could, and, well, I won't be around when I wanted to have this take place." Robin explained the history, and the original plan.

Trist looked at the glass in his hand.

"These glasses belong to you now. Take good care of them and pass on the tradition. Deal?"

"Deal," Trist said.

Robin raised his glass. He was already fighting back the emotion. "To my son," he said.

Trist raised his glass.

They clinked glasses, and then took a sip.

Robin pulled the cigars out, cut the ends off, and handed one to Trist. He lit his own and then passed the lighter to Trist.

Both ends glowed red as they inhaled, blew the smoke out, and then took another sip of scotch.

A breeze came up off the water and then died down. Robin watched as his son looked out over the water. He wasn't sure if he could see tears going down Trist's face, but he left him alone. It wasn't the wedding night, and never would be, but he couldn't imagine a more perfect night with his only remaining son.

Trist snored on the cockpit bench as Robin finished up his latest journal entry—his shortest yet.

—From the Journal of Robin Thomas Norris—

Leaving the World in Better Shape than You Found It In

So easy to say—harder to do. It's all about balance, T. You'll have your job, perhaps a family and the demands that involves, your hobbies—the things that keep you alive inside (we all need them; hopefully, your interests don't hurt anyone else), and then your responsibility as a citizen. Try to carve out some time every day to make the world better. It could be volunteering, it could be in how you raise your kids, it could also be as simple as being a good neighbor. Whatever you do, keep in mind that you're trying to leave the world in better shape than you found it in. If you can accomplish this, then I think you'll steer a true course. Remember, human beings are inherently selfish, but if they all tried to do at least one thing every day that benefited another person, then I think we'd be better off. I won't waste your time waxing your brain with utopian visions. There is no nirvana. Most activists go home to pretty comfortable lives, and watch out when unearned bitterness takes control of the steering wheel. You can only control yourself, Trist. Try your best to make a positive impact, but don't let the effort paralyze you. And, at a minimum for your sake, steer clear of the drug scene. Alcohol is dangerous enough, believe me, but if you want the quick and easy path to derail your effort to make a difference, then start smoking tree. One day, that roach won't be enough, and then you're fucked. Unfortunately, not a lot will be done until upper-class kids start getting hooked on bad shit and are dying in large numbers—and you don't have time to wait for that—so just don't start.

He closed the book. Trist turned on his other side and the blanket fell off him onto the deck. Robin walked over and covered him back up, then turned off the cabin light and climbed into his aft berth. He thought about closing the companionway hatch, but the air felt too good and the sound of the water lapping against the hull was like a lullaby.

He drifted off to sleep.

At 1 a.m., he felt the boat rock. Then, he heard wet footsteps going across the cockpit deck.

22

Robin sat up and eased Tyee's shotgun out from the compartment underneath his berth. He loaded two shells and slipped down the short passageway to where he could see the companionway steps. A few drops of water hit the top step before a foot touched down on it. *One more step.* The other foot landed on the next step down, and he could see slender yet muscular bare legs.

"Don't move," he said.

The legs froze.

Trist awoke and rolled over, disoriented. He sat up in time to see the barrel of his father's shotgun silhouetted against the broken moonlight streaming down through the companionway hatch, which was blocked by the figure of...his dad moved in front of the steps and he could only see Robin's backside.

"Dad, who is it?"

Robin looked up the companionway ladder at a tall young woman. Her t-shirt and shorts were soaked, and her hands were shaking as they gripped both sides of the open hatch. Trist was at his side immediately, now staring up at her in disbelief. Seeing that she was unarmed, Robin aimed the shotgun away from her but still maintained a firm grip.

"Are you hurt?" he said. "Is there anyone else with you?"

The girl's legs started to wobble. She was out of breath and her eyes looked dazed. "No," she said. "H-H-H-elp me."

"Take it easy," Robin said. "Back up slowly and we'll talk in the cockpit. We're not going to hurt you. Okay?"

"C-C-C-old," she said.

"Trist, get me—"

"Already on it," Trist said as he went up forward and brought back a towel and blanket from the v-berth.

"Okay, just move back and we'll get you warm," Robin said.

The girl started to back up, and Robin mirrored her movements. As she took a step back, he took a step up until they were both standing in the cockpit. The moonlight came out from behind a cloud and he could see her more clearly. Tall and athletic, she brought her hand up and pulled the wet hair away from her forehead. Around Trist's age, maybe a little older. What was she doing out here?

Trist's head popped up out of the cabin and he threw the towel and blanket on the port bench.

Never taking his eyes off of the girl, he said, "Trist, bring the night vision goggles up and give us a 360-degree scan."

Trist went below and was back up on deck in seconds with the goggles.

"Please, sit down," Robin said to her.

The girl wrapped her legs in the towel and then put the blanket around her back and up over her shoulders. She sank into the cushions on the port bench, the towel shaking as she moved her knees up and down.

Trist stepped up and positioned himself next to the mast where he turned the goggles on and brought them to his face. Turning in a slow circle, he swept the horizon and cliffs before searching the water around the boat. "I don't see anything," he said.

Robin relaxed a bit. "Okay. Get her a bottle of water and a granola bar and then do another sweep."

Trist stepped down into the cabin and got a better look at the girl. He stood for a moment, transfixed.

"Trist?" Robin said.

"Uh, right," said Trist. "On my way." He went below.

"Okay, it appears you're alone," Robin said. "Now, who are you and where did you come from?"

Before she could answer, Trist rejoined them in the cockpit. He made eyes at her and then handed over the granola bar, bottle of water, and a banana. "Looks like you did a lot of swimming," he said. "The banana will keep you from cramping up."

Trist headed back up to the mast to do another sweep.

She tore into the granola bar and banana as if she had not eaten in days. Then, she downed the entire bottle of water. Catching her breath now, she looked around, her eyes frantic. "We have to get out of here."

Robin looked at her, puzzled. "What are you talking about? Who *are* you?"

"Now!" she raised her voice.

He gripped the shotgun tighter. "Calm down. There's no one around here. It's just us."

"Dad?" Trist said.

"Yeah?" Robin replied.

"I think I see a boat headed this way."

The girl screamed. "It's them! We have to leave now."

"What kind of boat?" Robin said, his heart starting to race.

"Powerboat, and it is *moving*."

Robin jumped up on the deck and joined Trist at the mast. "Take this," he said, passing the shotgun to Trist. When his son had positive control of the weapon, Robin removed the night vision goggles from around Trist's neck and looked through them.

The boat was still far off but on a collision course with *Levity*. And Trist was right, it was speeding. He put the goggles around Trist's neck and took the shotgun back. "Keep an eye on it," he said and moved swiftly to the cockpit. The girl had the towel and blanket off and was about to stand up.

"Okay, what in the hell is going on?" Robin said, his eyes reaching an intensity that froze the girl.

She spoke. "I'm Jill St. John. I was kidnapped...two, three, four days ago...I don't know. I was held in a cell in some cave up there," she said pointing north at the cliffs behind the approaching boat. "Some psychotic woman helped me escape tonight. But they must have found out because they're on their way."

"Who?" Robin said.

"I don't know, but she told me that they would do anything to get me back. She said it would be better to be dead than to get brought back there." Jill looked at him and then at Trist up by the mast, scanning. "They will kill you and your son if they get here and I'm with you."

"Tell me more, anything."

"We have to get out of here!"

"Jill, they're on a powerboat. By the time we got our anchors up, they'd be on us."

"Can't we cut the anchor lines and motor to the beach where we could hop off and make a run for it in the woods?"

"We could cut the aft line, but the forward rode is chain. Plus, they'd beat us to the beach."

She looked up at the mast and then around the deck. "Can't we turn off the lights?"

"They've already seen us. Their course was headed straight this way."

She started to cry.

They didn't have much time. How could he protect her and Trist? They couldn't run. He glanced at the water. The boat would be here before he could rig any dive gear. He couldn't radio; they'd be monitoring all channels and get to him well before any help would. No, they'd have to hide below and he could act like he was sailing the boat alone when they arrived. It was the only option he saw.

"Trist, what do you see?" he said.

"They're closing in. It's a big Bayliner. I can make out a few men in the bow."

Shit! "Get down here now!"

Trist obeyed and scurried down into the cockpit.

"Everybody below."

Jill went first, then Trist, then Robin.

"You two are going to hide. Hopefully they don't have any night vision goggles aboard and didn't spot any of us above deck. I'm going to go topside with a bottle of rum and act like I passed out up there and that I'm sailing alone."

"Dad—"

"Listen. No matter what you hear, stay hidden. If something happens to me, you wait until they leave—give it an hour or so. Then you check topside. If there is no sign of them, then you raise anchor and motor south at full speed until you see the first house. You pull in and get help." He grabbed their arms. "Got it?"

"Where are we going to hide?" Jill said.

"Follow me," Robin said.

They arrived at Robin's berth and he reached underneath and unsnapped the cushion at both ends. Then, he raised it up. Underneath was a Jacuzzi tub he had put in for him and Levana. "Get in," he told them. "It's gonna be tight. You're both so damned tall."

Trist got in the tub and turned on his side, putting his back up against one of the long sides. Jill went in right behind him and curled herself into a ball with her back up against Trist's chest. They barely fit.

"Now, if everything goes well, I'll come down and let you know the coast is clear when they're gone. Then, we'll get the hell out of here." He paused, holding the cushion above the tub. Still no sound of the approaching boat. He looked back down at them. "Jill, can you tell me anything else about the people who held you?"

She twisted her neck so that she could make eye contact. "There were the two men who kidnapped me, a guard outside my cell that the woman slipped something to, and a few men down by the dock inside the cave that she distracted while I swam out."

"What was in the cave? How did you swim out?" He took a box of shotgun shells from a cabinet overhead and started loading both pockets of his sailing sweater while listening.

"There was a small powerboat and a larger one. I slipped into the water while she started to talk to the men. She had told me that the cave wall that led out to the open water was a false wall that could be raised to let the boats out and that when the wall was down, she had overheard that there were still a few feet of clearance underneath the middle of it but that it was thirty feet or so underwater. It was so far... I found the center of the wall and it took every part of my breath to get to the bottom, squeeze under the wall, and surface on the other side. Then, I swam as much as I could underwater until I reached the cave entrance. I swam out and saw a huge yacht anchored far offshore to the right and then a house high on the cliffs above. I decided to go the other way. I wanted to get ashore and start running, but it was all rocks and cliffs as far as I could see. So, I started swimming for all I was worth to the south. After an hour, I saw your masthead light—"

Robin held up a hand. "Shhh." He could hear the faint hum now of the boat's engine. He gave Trist's arm a loving squeeze. "Okay. They're almost here. Stay quiet." He lowered the cushion and the cabin looked again like a normal double berth with a set of varnished cabinets that ran along the starboard bulkhead.

He dashed into the salon and grabbed the blanket Trist had been using on the bunk. The sound of the motor was getting louder.

Next, he stowed the night vision goggles in the cabinet above the chart table, then grabbed a bottle of Captain Morgan Black. He poured half of it down the sink, took an enormous swig, and then put the top back on. His sailing knife was still in its case on the chart table and he picked it up and threaded the end of his belt through the case loop and then ran the end through a belt loop and finally buckled it. He headed topside with the shotgun, rum, and blanket.

He crept down and slid over the top companionway step and onto the cockpit deck. Spreading the blanket out, he laid the shotgun next to him and propped the rum bottle up in the corner. That was everything, except...

...Jill's towel and blanket!

He reached up pulled them down from the bench. What to do with them? The boat's motor roared as it approached. He had it. Carefully, he opened the opposite bench up about six inches and pushed the towel and blanket underneath and into the cooler. He set the bench down.

The boat's motor slowed and Robin listened. They were circling the boat. As he heard the boat near the bow, he chanced a look and saw a spotlight searching the water in all directions.

The boat turned again, and Robin laid back down. He waited as it made one more loop in the opposite direction. The sound got farther...and farther away...

Maybe they'd leave?

The sound started getting closer again. He tried to control his breathing and began to sweat.

The engine suddenly cut to idle. Then, he heard the first voice.

"You want us to tie up, Keach?"

He could hear water lapping against both hulls. It was now or never.

Robin stood up.

23

He held the bottle of rum in one hand and attempted to look unsteady, grasping the helm at last. A spotlight blinded him.

"Get that light off me, man," he said taking a drink of rum.

The spotlight moved away, and Robin watched as the cabin cruiser pulled up alongside. There were two men in the stern—both had handguns in holsters on their waists—one at the helm, and two up forward.

The larger of the two men in the stern spoke. "Mornin', my friend."

"Mornin'," Robin said back. "What're ya fellas doin' wakin' my ass up?"

The man laughed. "We do apologize, sir." He pointed at the bottle in Robin's hand. "You been tippin' that back tonight?"

The two men up forward started moving aft.

"Yessir," said Robin. "Just had a pull to steady up. Now what's the deal? I wanna go back to sleep."

"Well, we lost something," he said. "And we were hoping you could help us find it."

The two men hopped down into the stern, which was now only a few yards away from *Levity*'s port quarter. Robin could see that they had their handguns

193

drawn but pointed down at the deck. He could take out those two right away, but he'd have to reload. How fast could he do it? If he had the element of surprise...maybe in time to get shots off on the other two before they drew? That still left the helmsman, who he had to assume was armed too.

"What's with the pistols?" Robin pointed with his bottle of rum, then took another swig.

The helmsman spoke from his position above at the fair-weather console. "Get a load of this guy, Keach. What an idiot."

The larger man's eyes swiveled toward the helmsman and then set back on Robin. "Now, now. Let's not offend our helper," Keach said.

"Helper?" Robin said, sitting down. The shotgun was a quick grab away. "You still haven't told me what you're missing."

Keach took a step forward. "We know you're not alone, fella; we've got night vision goggles—could see your mate when he was standing by the mast. Could see you standing in the stern too. What we couldn't see, however, was if there was anyone else onboard." He clasped his hands together. "So, we're going to board your boat and search it in a minute. It would be smart of you to call your mate topside right now so we don't have to waste time. If we search and find no one else, then we'll be on our way. If we find someone else—well, then you've got a problem." He paused. "Now, the way to *avoid* all of this is to call them both up here right now. We'll collect our wayward little friend and then be off."

They would never let them survive. Looking into the men's eyes across from him, he was sure of that. Whoever these sick fucks were, they would not get Jill or Trist without a fight. He felt the adrenaline spread throughout his body.

"C'mon," the helmsman yelled down. "Waste this loser and let's get on with it."

The boats were now side by side, the aft rails just a few feet apart.

Keach raised his eyebrows. "Well?"

Robin raised his bottle in a toast. "Gotta hand it to you fellas—"

He dropped the bottle and pulled the shotgun off the deck. Both outer men started to raise their weapons, but Robin was faster and he didn't hesitate. Two loud booms sounded as he blasted the two men, blood erupting from their chests, and their bodies fell backward toward the cabin cruiser's deck. Robin grabbed two shells out of his pocket and started to reload. He could do this.

He snapped the barrel closed and went to raise the gun when he felt a body hit him square in the chest.

Keach had jumped over the railing and now wrapped his arms around Robin. The shotgun fell to the deck. Out of the corner of his eye, Robin could see the other man in the stern raising his weapon—and yet another man emerged from the powerboat's cabin. Still four men left. He had only one option.

Robin latched on to Keach's body and with one massive exertion pulled Keach and himself back over the starboard rail and into the water.

They sank a few feet, still locked together. Robin tried to free himself, but Keach was also strong and made it impossible. He wondered if Keach had his lungs though. They surfaced and both men took in a breath.

The other men were now at the rail with their guns aimed down at the water. However, the two men in the water were too close to each other and they would risk hitting Keach if they shot.

Robin pulled Keach back under and kicked down as hard as he could. They didn't get far as Keach knew what Robin was attempting to do, and he began to try and free himself. Robin saw his opportunity. Suddenly, he let go of Keach with his right arm and Keach began to break away. But Robin had already grabbed his sailing knife from its sheath and with one strong kick he grabbed Keach from behind, swept his arm around Keach's torso, and plunged the knife into Keach's stomach. Keach let out a scream of bubbles. Robin pulled the knife toward him with all his strength, and the water around them started to feel warm as Keach's blood poured out.

Keach tried to pry the knife out of his stomach but was unable to. His strength began to weaken and he put all of his energy into surfacing. Feeling this, Robin kicked with him and soon their heads broke the surface. Robin took a huge breath and then dragged Keach back under. A few feet down, he pulled the knife out and then ripped it across Keach's neck. He felt Keach's body twitch and then stop.

Holding on to the dead man's body with one hand, he kicked until they were underneath the hull. Then, he followed it forward and surfaced quietly beneath the pulpit. The two men were still bent over the starboard rail with their guns trained on the water. The searchlight from the powerboat swept the water in front of them. The beam moved to the water off the stern and Robin eased away from under the bow to get a better view.

He saw a body slam into one of the men from behind. It was Trist! He went to kick forward, but before he could let go of Keach's dead body beneath him, he heard a thump. Then, the helmsman's voice:

"That skinny kid dead?"

"No," one of the remaining men replied, "but he's got a nice bump on his noggin now."

"Out cold?" the helmsman said.

"Yeah."

"What about Blake and Jenson?"

"Dead as dead can be," said the helmsman looking down into his own stern. "Christ, what a mess."

Robin could hear the helmsman jump down into the cabin cruiser's stern. "Tie him up," the helmsman said, and Robin watched the man receive a coiled line and then bend over and go to work.

The boat tipped to port and then tilted back to starboard as the helmsman came aboard *Levity* and helped the third man to his feet.

"Little shit jumped me," said the man while rubbing his back in the spot where Trist had slammed into him. He saw Robin's shotgun on the deck next to him, and he picked it up. A sweet Winchester.

The helmsman snatched it out of his hands and threw it into the water.

"What the hell? No finders keepers?"

"Shut up," the helmsman ordered. He arrived at the rail and turned on a hand-held search light. Robin retreated back directly underneath the bow as the man swept his beam in slow arcs away from the boat. "No sign of Keach and that other bastard," the helmsman said.

"They never came up. I'd say they both drowned."

"Shit," the helmsman said. "Well, that's not gonna be good enough for the boss. We better get confirmation. But first, check the boat for the girl."

With Trist down, it was three against one. And they had the high ground. Even if he could climb aboard and get ahold of one of them, they'd shoot him before he could get to anyone else. And they might kill Trist. Right now, they could kill him without any trouble, but they were tying him up instead. Could he live with himself if he got both kids killed right now? His son was injured, but at least he was alive. And the girl...what to do?

The sound of screaming and struggling aboard broke his concentration. He heard, "Get your hands off of me!"

"You'd never believe it," the man who had a hold of Jill said as he brought her up through the companionway. "Guy had a damn hot tub underneath his aft bunk."

Robin saw the girl thrown against the rail and then held down by one of the men while the other began to bind her arms and legs with rope.

"Well, well, well," said the helmsman. "You're not where you're supposed to be are you, honey?"

"Fuck you!" Jill yelled.

The men finished and the helmsman laughed as he gagged her mouth with a handkerchief. "If I didn't have my orders to get you back as soon as possible, you'd be gettin' your wish, darlin'."

Robin watched as the other men loaded Trist aboard the cabin cruiser.

Screw it. Robin let go of Keach and went to reach up for the steel pulpit support when the helmsman returned to the starboard rail.

Robin went under and re-gripped Keach's body. He counted to twenty and then slowly broke the surface until just his eyes were above water.

The men picked up Jill and threw her aboard the powerboat while the helmsman studied the water.

A few moments later, they rejoined him at the rail.

"Gould, you're our scuba guy now that Blake and Jenson are dead. Gear up and search the water for the bodies." He turned to the other man. "Kory, you stay topside while he dives. I'll take the two kids back, dispose of Blake and Jenson, then be back to get you."

"How long?" Kory asked.

The helmsman smirked. "I'll try to buy you both some time."

"What in the hell does that mean?" Gould said.

"You know what that means. The boss lost one of his best men. We all just don't show up without the bodies. I'll come back and get you in a few hours. However, if you find them earlier than that, radio us on channel seven with either 'found one fish' or 'found two fish'."

Gould looked at the water. "What if I can't find them?"

The helmsman pulled him up and looked into his eyes. "Find them." He released his grip and departed. It was silent for a minute and then Robin heard gear being passed over from the cabin cruiser to Gould.

He heard the helmsman say, "What a goddamn mess. Sweetheart we're gonna put you right between these two dead colleagues of mine. Keep you company on your ride back home." There was shuffling and grunting and then he could hear Jill begin to sob. A minute later, the Bayliner's engine came to life, and the boat started to move. *I'll be there to get you both out soon*, he said to himself as he watched the boat speed away.

The sound of the motor faded and was replaced by the sound of Gould gearing up to dive.

"I'm heading below to get some food," Kory said. "Then, I'll sit up here and wait for you."

Robin didn't hesitate. Grabbing the anchor chain in one hand and Keach's body in the other, he submerged and began kicking and pulling himself deeper along with the body. Perhaps ten feet down, he took the sleeve of Keach's shirt and tied it off to the chain. He waited a few seconds to make sure Keach's body was staying put, and then rose to the surface. He started to hyperventilate and then took one last huge breath and dove straight down toward the bottom.

As he kicked with all of his might, his lungs started to ache, but he pressed on, a determination like he had never felt before. He had killed and had answered the question that had run through his mind ever since he was old enough to ask it: "When faced with survival or death, could I take another human life?" He had no military training, but he was an athlete and a nurse who knew the human body. He had seen death up close for his entire career; to save Trist and Jill, he would be willing to kill again.

He reached the bottom and felt around for the rocks. At first, he felt just sand. He kept searching, thinking that he would have to surface and dive again. Then, his hand touched one of the boulders! He moved over it and located the tank. Finding the tank valves and regulator, he turned on the air and put the regulator in his mouth. The air filled his lungs as he took a few deep breaths. He ran his hand along the tank straps until he found the mask. Taking his sailing knife out, he cut the rope attaching it and put the mask on and cleared it. Lastly, he strapped the tank on.

He sheathed his sailing knife again and looked up. Darkness surrounded him. Without any fins, he had no mobility. He would have to surprise the diver. He started to ascend.

Trist awoke. His head throbbed and hurt even more as his body bounced up and down. Where was he? He tried to move his hands but found them tied behind his back. He tried his feet, but they were bound together by rope around his ankles. He blinked and looked up as the sky shot by overhead. He felt nauseous and turned on his side. And then he saw Jill wedged between two men with crimson caverns in their chests and their necks littered with tiny red holes.

Jill's eyes were wide open and staring at him. Water sprayed over the rails and showered them as the boat raced through the water. Like a snake, Trist slithered across the deck until he reached Jill's feet. She motioned with her eyes for him to put his head on her feet and he slid over into position. With one heave, she lifted him up and he now sat on the deck.

He got his head near her right ear. "What happened?" he said.

Her eyes moved up to the fair-weather console. Trist followed her gaze and saw the helmsman driving the boat and talking on the radio, which they could not hear over the roar of the engine and the water spraying them. He tried to loosen the ropes behind his back, but they were so tight he was afraid they were cutting off the circulation to his hands. Dipping his shoulder, he started to squeeze between Jill and one of the dead men. She used her knees to help him push.

The body fell over, and the man's head thumped against the deck. They both looked up, but the helmsman continued to face forward and speak into the radio. Trist leaned over and then straightened up with his back against the stern, now side by side with Jill.

He spoke into her ear once again. "We've got to hang together. Keep thinking of how we can get out of this." He paused. "Did you see my Dad?"

She shook her head side to side. Trist put his head down for a moment. She put her head on his shoulder.

Then, the boat began to slow.

On the way up, Robin found the anchor chain with Keach's body still secured to it. He untied the body, and, holding it along with the chain, descended perhaps another fifteen feet. The night water was freezing. He looked for the diver's light. What he couldn't see was that a small gathering of fish had started to probe Keach's chest wound. If this had been the ocean, the sharks might have already started ripping him to pieces.

A light appeared under *Levity*'s hull and swept back and forth heading away from the boat. Then, the light turned his way but was still aimed about ten feet above him. Quickly, he put Keach's body in front of his and started to swim toward the diver. Robin pulled out his sailing knife.

Gould finned ahead with lazy kicks. He'd make one more pass by the sailboat and then go deeper. This whole night had been a blur. First, he had been woken up from his dream-laced sleep by Keach telling him to get dressed and board the boat. He had looked at his watch. 12:35 a.m. Seriously? Had he misread the delivery schedule? No, he had been told. Someone had escaped. Escaped? He didn't even know someone was being held there—and didn't wanna know. Merchant vessel shows up, he dives and gets the product to the cave. That's it. Professional. Clean delivery every time. His shit was in one sock, and he don't want nobody messin' with it. Sanders said he had leadership potential. Damn straight. And he ain't gonna let no one get in his way of runnin' the joint in a few years. Then he had seen the girl on the sailboat. Jesus H. Christ, what a bod. He shook off the thought. None of his business.

About to turn around, he steered the light one more time to the left and then back to the rig...what was *that*? Rising up toward him was the body of Mason Keach, and, what was rising behind his head? Bubbles? Was Keach still alive? He blinked his eyes. Shit, was he getting nitrogen narcosis? Keach kept coming at him, his eyes open. Gould kicked toward him.

The diver approached, moving his light up and down the body. When he was only a few yards away, Robin pushed the body at him. The diver freaked out and dropped his light. Robin swam around behind him, and, holding the man's hood in one hand, thrust his knife into the diver's neck. Savagely, Robin sawed. The regulator popped out of the man's mouth and soon his body went lifeless.

Robin had no time. He ripped off the man's mask and hood. Then, he took off his own mask, pulled the hood on, and put his mask back on and cleared it. Next, he took the man's fins off and put them on along with the man's weight belt. Taking Keach's arm once again, he swam toward the starboard side of *Levity* until he was twenty yards off the beam. He surfaced with the body and positioned himself behind it. Then, trying his best to mimic Gould's voice, said, "Kory! I found Keach. Meet me in the stern."

He watched as Kory came over to the rail and looked out through the darkness at the body and him. "Sonofabitch, pal. Good work." He turned around and walked to the stern gate and swung it open.

Robin paddled behind the body, and when he was even with the stern he watched Kory step down onto the swim step.

The body approached with only Robin's hooded head out of the water behind it. "One down, one to go," Kory said as he knelt down and reached for the body.

Robin Norris's hand shot out of the water and grabbed Kory's t-shirt, pulling him in.

Beneath the surface, Robin wrapped his hand around Kory's neck and strangled him. Kory stopped kicking and tried to remove Robin's hands from his neck. Meanwhile, Robin kicked down taking Kory deeper and deeper. Kory yelled, sending a shower of bubbles up into Robin's mask. Robin squeezed and kicked harder. In a last desperate effort, Kory flailed wildly, sucking in more water. Robin didn't stop and soon the man's body stopped moving.

He stopped kicking and looked into the man's dead eyes. He checked his depth: forty feet. He let go of Kory and watched his body float away. Then, he swam for the surface.

24

J ill told Trist they were in the same cell that she had been held captive in before. At gunpoint, they had been forced to shower and dress in a pair of shorts and a t-shirt each. They had just taken a seat on the bed when the cell door opened and the lights dimmed.

Jill recognized Madame, wearing an evening gown, followed by a tall 40-something gentleman wearing loafers, chinos, a webbed belt, and a short-sleeved polo shirt. Behind them, a younger man wearing a gun in a shoulder harness and holding a nightstick entered and stood by the door.

As Madame got closer, Jill looked at the right side of her face. It was red and swollen behind the make-up attempting to cover it up. Her eyes looked glazed. She was on something for sure. Cocaine? Heroin?

The older man stood behind her and put his hands on her shoulders. His eyes measured Trist first and he nodded in an approving fashion. Then, he looked over at Jill and smiled. "My, my. Quite the night so far." He kissed Madame's ear and then whispered into it, "Wouldn't you say, Madame?"

Madame grinned and said, "Quite a night, my love." She stared seductively at both Trist and Jill. "I'm ready to go to work on these two."

The man said, "I thought you might. It's been a while since we had a young man down here."

She leaned her head back and said, "I know," then began to tongue his neck.

He tapped her shoulder and she stopped. With his right hand, he reached up and started massaging the back of her head. She breathed in. His face became serious as he addressed Trist and Jill. "Madame has been naughty tonight." His hand snatched hold of her hair and jerked her head back—her eyes showing no fear. "But I am going to give her a second chance. Which is to say I'm going to give you both one chance." He paused. "In twenty minutes, I am going to come back here with a chair and watch as you three have at it. If you participate, then you'll see tomorrow morning. As you've heard, Madame has already agreed to join in. If either one of you chooses not to, then this gentleman over here," he said, motioning to the man stationed by the door, "will kill all three of you, one by one, as the others watch." He let go of Madame's hair and took a step back. "I'll let the three of you get acquainted and then we'll be back." He turned around and started to walk toward the door.

"You sick motherfucker," Trist said.

The man stopped and turned back around. "Now, that's the kind of spirit I like. If you can harness it and put it into action that is *positive*, then this could get exciting." He paused and looked at Jill. "But I'm afraid if you don't change your attitude, this is not going to end well for you and the ladies here."

"Okay, okay. Just hold on," Trist said. "Look, you've got your thing going on with this woman. That's between you two. I just lost my dad tonight, forever." He paused. "And Jill, she has nothing to do with any of this operation either. Just take us away in some van, blindfold us, whatever, man, and let us go. We don't want any part of this."

The man grinned. "I like this kid, Madame. He doesn't break easily."

"So what do you say?" Trist said. "C'mon. Let us go."

"But he's not very smart." He took a step toward Trist. "You don't get it, do you?"

"Get what?"

He stopped in front of Trist and put a hand on his shoulder. The man with the nightstick was now at his side, ready in case Trist tried anything. "You're never leaving here," the man said. "And after tonight...you won't want to." He started to run his hand down the side of Trist's face and Trist moved his head away.

"You just wait until *tomorrow* night, my young friend." The man said as he turned around and left.

The man with the nightstick followed.

Outside the cell, Livingston and Bannon were met by Sanders.

"Everything else back under control?" Livingston said.

"Yes," Sanders reported.

"Good," Livingston said back. "Since we're short a few bodies, we'll need you in the cave harbor tonight. I want the boat cleaned, the corpses taken care of, and the sailboat sunk. Understood?"

Sanders's face showed a tiny hint of disappointment. "Yes, sir."

Livingston knew Sanders wanted to watch from the closet control room, but his men had made a mess of tonight and Sanders needed to make it right. At least Keach was dead. One less problem to worry about. "Wonderful. Maybe you shouldn't retire yet," Livingston joked. "You and Eric seem to be the only ones I can trust around here."

Sanders gave a painful smile and then headed down the stone hallway toward the cave harbor.

Livingston turned to Eric and put a hand on his shoulder. "Okay, let's get ready for the show. Bring me a bottle of brandy."

* * *

Robin cut *Levity*'s engine, and the boat was motionless with no lights on. He sprinted up forward and dropped the anchor.

The boat was in a cove hidden by a section of a cliff that jutted out into Lake Superior that he had spotted with the night vision goggles while standing aloft on *Levity*'s spreaders minutes before. He could have gone further up the coast, but didn't dare for fear of being spotted. When the anchored yacht Jill had mentioned—a Hatteras—had come into view, he had dropped down from the mast and swung the boat into the cove. There were no boats coming his way now, so he felt optimistic that he was still undetected.

He set the anchor and headed aft. He was dressed in a full wetsuit and had his dive knife strapped to his leg. A spear gun sat on the starboard bench along with his mask, fins, dive light, and regulator and tank combo. He missed his shotgun—and wondered if he'd ever be able to tell Tyee he'd been saved by that gun. No time. He put the rest of his gear on and entered the water from the swim step.

The suit and adrenaline helped him fight the temperature of the water, and he swam on the surface until he was past the furthest point where the cliff extended out into the water. In the distance to the north, he could see the huge Hatteras at anchor with her lights on. He'd check there if he was unsuccessful at finding the cave. Lining up with the mega-yacht, he dove down to the bottom and navigated by his compass.

"If we all work together, we can take both of those guys," Trist said.

"I agree," Jill said. "Madame, you helped me once, could you do it again?"

Madame looked away.

Trist stood and walked over to her. "C'mon. Do you want to stay in this place forever?"

She turned around and slapped him across the face. "You have no idea—"

Jill broke in. "I think we do—"

"No! You don't!" Madame yelled. "You had your chance tonight. I gave you something I never got, and now we have to survive." She swiveled her intense eyes at both of them. "And neither of you are going to be the reason that I die tonight. So, you both better start thinking differently right now."

"The hell with you," Trist said. "We'll go it alone without you."

"You won't do that," Madame said.

"The fuck we won't," Trist snapped back.

Madame approached carefully and whispered into his ear. "You won't do that because there is a way to get out of here tomorrow."

He started to pull away.

"Get back here." She pulled him close so that her mouth was just outside his ear. "All we have to do is make it to tomorrow," she said and pointed at Jill. "Are you willing to risk her life because you can't put yourself second for one night?"

He backed up. "Don't play mind games with me. You're on something. What is it, coke?"

Madame ignored him and sat down next to Jill. "I tried to help you tonight, and I'm sorry you didn't make it. But if you want to survive then we have to do this. Can't you help me now?" She stood up and walked over to the dresser and fixed her hair in the mirror.

Jill looked over at Trist. He made eye contact and then started pacing again.

Robin turned off his light and surfaced. He was around the cliff protrusion now and could no longer see *Levity*. The Hatteras was like a permanent fixture on the surface of the water far offshore. He turned toward the cliff.

In front of him was a large opening to a deep cave. *This has to be it.* He dove. Ten feet...twenty feet—he turned on his underwater light—thirty feet...forty. He reached the bottom, adjusted course, and then followed his compass heading into the cave opening with his dive light in one hand and his spear gun in the other. The bottom became rocky and began to slope upwards. He checked his depth gauge. Thirty-five feet...thirty-two...then it leveled off at thirty.

His light hit the face of what he assumed was the false back of the cave. He thought about surfacing but didn't want to chance that they might have surveillance cameras above. He knew he had to find the center of wall; that was where Jill had said there was enough clearance to get underneath it and come up on the other side. He kicked to the right, found the side of the cave, and then moved toward the center.

Sure enough, his light found an area where the lake floor dipped a few feet below the false cave back. But would his tank fit under it? He got as close as he could to the bottom and started to move under the wall.

His tank hit the top, and he could go no further.

He backed out and unstrapped himself from the tank. He could push the tank through ahead of himself and strap back in on the other side, but then the bubbles might give away his position. He decided to leave the tank. Moving it to the side, he hit the quick release on his weight belt and it fell off his waist. He took one last deep breath from his regulator and then swam under the false cave wall.

Once clear, he swam to the right, following the wall until he came to the side of the cave again, figuring that he wouldn't be as noticeable surfacing in the corner than in the middle of the water. He kicked up and his head broke the surface enough for him to grab a quick breath and then submerge back down to where his mask and forehead were the only part of him above the waterline. In front of him was perhaps twenty yards of open water between his position and the ends of two docks. Tied up to one dock was a small powerboat, and on the far dock was the cabin cruiser. To the far left of the cave was a tunnel that disappeared into the rock wall.

He could see that there was clearance underneath the docks, so he dove deep and swam along the bottom until he was underneath the dock with the cabin cruiser tied up. He surfaced and listened. Not a sound.

He moved out from under the dock, but then heard voices coming from the tunnel. He swam back under.

"Okay, I'll go pick those two rookies up and we'll get rid of the bodies and sailboat as usual. Pain in my ass, I tell you, Mr. Sanders."

It was the helmsman from earlier. Now, Robin could see him standing in the tunnel entrance with an older man of Korean descent. He watched as the older man lit a cigarette.

"Just make sure everything is clean and finished," Sanders said.

The helmsman nodded. "Okay, okay," he said walking away. He stopped and turned back at the old man. "You know, I'm going to miss you, Mr. Sanders. Only goddamn person who makes any sense around here. Don't tell the boss I said that though."

The old man inhaled on his cigarette and grinned back while he watched the helmsman step foot on the dock. Then, Sanders walked over to the control panel mounted on the cave wall ten yards away from the tunnel opening. There, he pushed a series of buttons, and the false wall started to retract into the ceiling. The helmsman watched, gave a thumbs up, and Sanders disappeared back into the tunnel.

Robin got his spear gun ready.

Step, step, step, step...the helmsman stopped, thinking he heard something in the water.

"Hey," Robin said.

He looked over the side of the dock, and a spear went into his chest. His body swayed on the dock—eyes wide open in disbelief, blood starting to come out of his mouth.

Robin reached up and pulled the helmsman underwater where he finished him off with his dive knife. Searching, he found the cabin cruiser keys and removed them from the helmsman's pocket. He unzipped his wetsuit, tucked them inside, and zipped his suit back up. He searched the man again. No gun. He pulled the spear out of the helmsman's chest and wiped the barb and shaft with the man's shirt. He reloaded it in his gun as the body drifted away.

He surfaced and heard the automatic door mechanism come to a stop. He looked out and could now see the surface of Lake Superior and the sky above it at the end of the cave opening.

He pulled himself up onto the dock and took off his fins. The smaller boat moored to the second dock had two big Evinrude outboard motors—built for speed; if they escaped on the cabin cruiser, this boat would catch them and be more maneuverable. Conversely, if they escaped on the smaller boat, they'd have a good head start, but not much range. And they needed to travel far enough away to reach the authorities.

He ran over to the second dock, boarded the smaller powerboat, and cut the fuel lines to the engines. Standing by the helm, he put his right foot on the starboard gunwale and gripped the throttle with two hands. Pulling back, he ripped the throttle away from its casing and let it hang down—a metal handle with a tangle of wires and shattered plastic. He hopped up on the dock and headed for the tunnel.

Dai Sanders walked past the room where Madame was with the two young people. A few more steps and he was outside of a second room where Livingston and Bannon were reclining in easy chairs and watching a baseball game on television, facing away from the doorway. People and their weird rituals. He'd seen parts of that particular game hundreds of times—he'd been the one to tape it ages ago and had almost every out memorized—but still couldn't get his mind around how it got Livingston in the mood. A bottle of brandy with two filled glasses was on a wooden table between the chairs.

Sanders tiptoed across the entrance and paused to see if he had been noticed. He hadn't. He continued twenty paces to the end of the hallway where he entered an elevator that would take him up to the main house. There were three levels where the elevator made stops. One was in the garage where the product was loaded in vehicles. Two was the master closet. Three was a two-story viewing room, the second floor accessible by circular staircase; it was the highest point on the property with glass windows all the way around, where Livingston and guests could sit and see out in any direction. To reach the master closet and viewing tower levels required a special key, which only Sanders, Bannon, and Livingston had.

He put his key into the designated slot and turned it. The top two buttons now illuminated and he pressed the button for the master closet. There was no way was he missing the show in the cell tonight. After all, the helmsman had things under control in the cave. He was just doing what Livingston wanted anyways, delegating and relinquishing control.

The elevator stopped and he removed his key. The doors opened. He stepped out and then unlocked the secret entrance to the closet. The lights came on as he entered.

"He'll be here any minute now," Madame said to Trist and Jill. "Trust me, if you go with the flow, it will be over soon and we'll live to see tomorrow."

Trist was now seated on the bed next to Jill. They stared at her and said nothing.

"I'll take your silence as a yes. Good choice," she said. "Jill, I'll start with you; follow my lead. Then, we'll get Tristian involved. Got it?"

The sound of a key being placed in the door could be heard. Madame walked toward the entrance. Trist's heart started to thump. He put a hand on Jill's leg—it was shaking.

The door to the room opened, and Grant Livingston entered holding a glass of brandy and wearing a devious smile. Eric Bannon came through the door after him with a simple chair and tray table, which he set up next to the chair.

Livingston sat down and took a sip of his drink then smacked his lips. "Now, where were we?"

Bannon closed the door and then stood next to it, the nightstick in his hand.

Madame made eye contact with Livingston and then turned around and began to drift toward the bed, unzipping her dress.

The stone tunnel reminded Robin of the ancient castle passageways he had read about in books or seen in movies. The lighting was dim and the air was cold. Water dripped from his wetsuit onto the floor as he held his dive knife in one hand and the spear gun in the other.

He heard noise ahead around a portion of the passageway that curved to the right. He moved to the tunnel wall, tucking his body into the shadows. The hallway started to straighten out and he paused. At the far end he could see an elevator. He checked behind him, saw no one coming, and dashed to the other side of the hallway. He could see two doorways: the closest was filled by a metal door and the far one open, where the sound was coming from. He turned his head and concentrated on the sound.

It was a baseball game.

Impossible. It was past 2 a.m., must be a recording. He moved toward the metal door.

25

The door was solid with no window. There was a keyhole and a slot near the bottom. He gently pushed against the door with his fingertips. It didn't move. He scanned the hallway again and saw no one coming from either direction. Leaning his spear gun against the wall, Robin crouched down and lifted the slot cover. He peered inside.

Madame's dress fell to the floor and she stepped out of it, wearing a matching lace bra and thong. She reached Jill and leaned over—her lips were inches away from Jill's. "Relax," she said. "Act like you're having the time of your life, and it will be over even sooner. Trust me."

Trist's right hand became a fist. Three...two...

There was a knock at the door.

Madame stood up and looked back at the door, confused.

"It's Sanders," Livingston said to Bannon, his anger rising. "Get him out of here."

Eric Bannon nodded and turned the key. He cracked the door to quietly slip out.

A powerful force ripped it from his hands and the metal door swung wide open. Bannon saw the figure in the doorway first.

The spear launched from the gun. If Bannon's body had not been spun on an angle when the door was pried out of his hands, the spear would have hit him squarely in the chest; instead, it hit him in the left shoulder.

Robin Norris dropped the spear gun and shifted the dive knife from his left hand to his right. He went after the man whom he had hit with the spear.

"Dad!" Trist yelled. Seeing his father start to grapple with the man holding the nightstick, Trist joined the fight by running toward the seated man.

Livingston pulled out a radio from his pocket and shouted "Code Zero, Cave!" into it before Trist knocked it out of his hand as the chair tipped over and they hit the floor.

With hatred in her eyes, Jill ran toward Trist to help. A few steps from reaching them, she felt her hair pulled back and then fingernails around her throat. Madame dragged her to the ground, got on top of her, and then squeezed Jill's neck with her hands.

"Fuck!" Sanders said, transfixed by the events on screen in the closet den. He ran to the elevator and pushed the garage floor button. He zoomed down, and when the door opened, he saw the armed security guard from the driveway gate sprinting toward him. In a few seconds he was aboard, and they headed for the cave level. Sanders got out his radio. "Hatteras crew status, over."

A voice from the radio replied, "Powerboat at the rail with four-man crew—be there in ten minutes, out."

Ten minutes! Why had Livingston ordered the Hatteras to anchor so far out?

Robin's knife was knocked from his hand as he thrust it at his opponent. The man was in pain from the spear, but Robin sensed that this was someone who was trained to kill as he minimized the disadvantage and fought ferociously with his good arm. Robin saw an opportunity to grab his knife and reached for it. The man hit the floor, and, in a blinding move, swept Robin off of his feet. Robin landed hard on his back and soon the man had Robin's knife in his hand and was on top of him. He swung down and missed Robin's head by inches as Robin twisted his head at the last second. The force of the thrust was so powerful that the knife sunk into the floor, giving Robin enough time to take his right hand and rip down on the man's left ear, almost pulling it off. He yelled in agony before Robin rolled him over, put him in a headlock, and tightened down. The man struggled for breath and his legs pushed off the floor trying to buck and shake Robin off of him. Robin hung on. The man's strength started to give out, and after a few last kicks with his legs, he was still. Robin released his grip. *Not taking any chances.* He took the man's gun out of the shoulder holster and fired two rounds into his chest.

Jill's face was turning blue and she was losing consciousness. Madame's eyes were psychotic. "You ruined everything," she growled.

With her final reserve of strength, she lifted her legs up to Madame's back, rocked to the left and then shot them over to the floor. Madame lost her balance and released her grip as she fell to the floor. Jill gasped for air.

Madame turned over and was on all fours, ready to spring, when she heard, "Stop." She looked up and saw Robin with a gun pointed at her. She paused, looking at Bannon dead on the floor and then over at Trist, who had his knees on Livingston's shoulders. Blood from Livingston's mouth and nose covered Trist's hands as Trist pounded his face over and over.

As if someone had turned off her power switch, Madame crumpled to the floor and began to sob.

Jill got to her feet and stood behind Robin.

"Trist, get off him," Robin said.

Trist stopped, breathing heavily. He spit in Livingston's face and then stood up and moved by Robin.

Robin pointed the gun at Livingston.

He held up a hand. "Please...don't shoot." He spit up blood. "I have money."

Madame's head popped up. She reached over and opened a drawer on the nightstand. From it, she pulled out a pair of handcuffs and a coil of rope. Her eyes were determined and focused on Livingston. She stood up. "He's mine," she said to Robin.

Robin studied her and then looked at Trist and Jill. "Sit him in that chair."

They raised him up and Madame was soon behind the chair handcuffing Livingston's hands together and then binding his feet to the chair legs with the rope.

Even through Livingston's swollen eyes, Robin could see his fear. Madame gave them the sign to leave. Robin picked up his dive knife and slid it back into its sheath.

They ran to the door, and Robin took a quick peek. When he saw that the tunnel was empty, he unzipped his wetsuit and gave Trist the keys to the boat. "Head for the cabin cruiser. If I'm not there in one minute, take off. I'll swim out. Go, now!"

Trist and Jill sprinted down the tunnel and out of sight as the elevator door beeped.

Behind Robin, Madame approached Livingston.

"Madame, calm down. We can still get out of this—"

She cut him off. "My name is...Evangeline...Bertram!"

And she was on him, clawing at his face—Livingston screamed.

The awful pitch turned Robin's attention back toward the sound and he saw Evangeline holding both eyeballs in her hands as blood poured from Livingston's eye sockets. He aimed the gun at Livingston's chest and fired, killing him.

Evangeline turned around in a rage.

He spoke first. "He's dead. You still want to get out of here?"

She threw the eyeballs at Livingston's chest and watched them bounce off and then roll across the fine carpet. Then, she moved toward Robin, getting behind him.

"Follow me," he said, and they took off into the tunnel toward the boat.

The elevator door opened and Sanders, followed by the security guard, entered the tunnel with weapons drawn. They heard the baseball game still playing as they pointed their weapons into the room. Clear.

They continued down the hallway and crept up next to the cell doorway, which was open. On a silent count, they both stormed into the room.

The security guard tripped over Bannon's body and fell forward. When he hit the floor, his weapon discharged and a bullet tore into the dresser. One look at Livingston and Sanders dropped to his knees and vomited; the security guard heard him and then smelled the awful stench. He got to his feet and then saw Livingston. Feeling bile rise in his own throat, he dropped and gave in to the inevitable.

Robin heard the gunshot behind him as they continued to run toward the entrance to the cave harbor. One more turn and they were there. Up ahead, Trist had already started the cabin cruiser's motor and Jill was seated next to him at the fair-weather console. Robin scanned the pier and saw that Trist had already cast off the lines.

The boat was starting to move away from the pier despite Trist's efforts with the throttle and helm to keep it alongside.

"C'mon! Sprint!" Robin yelled to Evangeline.

She caught up to him and they ran down the dock. The starboard rail was no more than two feet away from the dock as they arrived.

"What is *she* doing with you?" Jill yelled down.

"She's coming with us," Robin said.

He helped Evangeline onto the yacht. The sight and stench of the two dead bodies made her queasy and she ran up forward. The boat moved off the dock another foot.

"Dad, come on!" Trist said.

The sound of a single gunshot echoed in the cave; Robin went to leap when a bullet entered his back-right shoulder knocking him to the dock.

At the tunnel's entrance stood the security guard with Sanders behind him. The guard was poised for another shot, when Robin turned over and squeezed off two rounds at them. He missed, but they were close enough to send the two men back into the tunnel for cover.

"Go!" Robin yelled.

"We'll pick you up outside!" Trist yelled down and throttled forward.

A barrage of shots rang out from the tunnel entrance as Sanders and the security guard blasted away at the boat. Bullets tore into the fiberglass on the fair-weather level as Trist increased the throttle, and the cabin cruiser began to slice toward the cave opening.

"Quick, lower the cave wall to stop them," Sanders ordered the security guard. "I'll cover you." He began to shoot at the section of the dock where Robin was—but Robin was no longer there.

While they were shooting at the cabin cruiser, Robin had slipped into the water and swam over to a position with better cover and closer to the tunnel entrance—the cold water helped numb his shoulder. He took aim from his new position against the cave wall to the right of the tunnel opening; he had one bullet left.

"Wait!" Sanders said.

It was too late. The guard was now in the open.

Robin pulled the trigger.

The guard spun around, dropping his gun and holding his chest. He looked at Sanders and then fell over. Robin dove for the water just as Sanders shot wildly at Robin's position, the bullets hitting the stone where Robin had been a moment earlier. Seeing him enter the water, Sanders dashed to the control panel.

The false cave wall started to lower.

"C'mon! C'mon!" he shouted at it.

He watched as the cabin cruiser sped under it and disappeared on the wrong side of the wall as it touched the water and kept lowering.

"Shit!" Sanders yelled. He aimed his gun at the control panel and blasted it. Then, he aimed at the false wall and pulled the trigger repeatedly in anger.

The sound of 'click click click' echoed in the cave.

Suddenly, he saw Robin emerge from the water a few feet away from him.

The hell with this. He turned and ran for the elevator, hacking and wheezing as if his lungs were about to come up his throat and exit through his mouth. He hunched over by the cell room, pulled out his radio, and managed, "Stop the cabin cruiser—they're on it," before ambling the rest of the way to the elevator.

"We see them," came the reply from the radio. "On a course to intercept."

Robin reached the dead guard and picked up his gun. He went to follow the man but could hear him coughing far up into the tunnel. Instead, he ran for the first dock where his mask and fins were.

He put them on and swam for the bottom of the wall.

26

The cabin cruiser reached open water and Trist backed down the throttle to idle. "Take the controls," he said to Jill.

"Where are you going?" she said.

"Below," said Trist. "To see if there are any more weapons onboard." He scooted down the ladder and disappeared.

"Why are we stopping?" Evangeline shouted from the bow.

"We're not leaving his dad," Jill shot back.

Evangeline stood up and pointed toward the Hatteras in the distance. "But what about that boat?"

Jill's head swiveled toward the Hatteras. "What about it? It's not going anywhere."

Evangeline's tone became shaky. "Not *that* boat," she said, and then pointed a few points to the left of the Hatteras. "*That* boat!"

Jill squinted and searched the water. Then, she saw it. A small boat was approaching them at high speed.

"Trist," she yelled down. "We've got to go, now!"

There was no reply.

* * *

Robin surfaced twenty yards aft of the cabin cruiser's stern. A few more kicks and he'd be onboard. Then, he heard the motor of a boat approaching fast. He kicked hard and made it to the cruiser's swim step.

Finally hearing Jill, Trist appeared in the stern and looked up at her. "What?"

"There's a boat coming our way."

"T, over here," Robin said.

Surprised, Trist whipped around and stepped between the dead bodies. He leaned over the transom. "Dad, let's get you onboard. We've got a boat heading this way."

"I heard," Robin said.

"Where's your tank?" Trist said.

"No time, had to leave it. Listen, that boat is faster than we are. They'll shoot us up before we're able to pull away. Our only chance is to draw them in without any shots fired. Go back up to the helm and have your hand on the throttle. I'm headed underwater. When I surprise them, slam the throttle down and get away."

"But what about you?"

"Once I take care of them, I'll catch up to you on their boat and then we'll all leave together."

"Wait a second," Trist said.

"Trist, there's n—"

But Trist had already sprinted back to the cabin.

The sound of the approaching boat's motor was getting louder.

Jill stood up and looked down at Robin. "Get onboard. We have to go."

Trist flew up the cabin steps and was back in the stern, leaning over the transom. Slung over his shoulder was an automatic rifle. "I found these below." In his hands was a nylon belt containing two yellow canisters, each with a pull-ring on top. "Remember *Jaws 3?*"

Robin snickered, "I never watched past the second one, remember? No Roy Scheider."

Trist exhaled, "Should've known. Anyway, I think they're underwater grenades. You just pull the pin," Trist said.

"Makes sense," said Robin. "These guys don't want anyone messing with their business operations." He paused, a new plan forming. "Give me the grenade belt."

Trist handed it over.

"Okay, when they arrive, I'll swim under their boat and either stick this belt to their hull with my knife or wrap the belt around their propeller. Then, I'll come up and pull on the rail, knocking them off balance. When that happens, punch the throttle and get as far away as possible. I'll dive back down and pull the rings, then bust ass out of there. At worst, we disable them so that they can't follow us; at best, the two grenades have enough power to hit the fuel line and explode the boat. Either way, after the grenades go off, look for me on the surface. Then we'll get out of here for good."

Trist looked at the large yacht in the distance. "What about the Hatteras?"

"Nothing to worry about. She's slow compared to us." Robin stared into Trist's eyes. "Okay, now get up there with Jill and be ready. Hide the rifle but use it if it all goes wrong."

"Dad..."

"It'll work. Trust me." He held Trist's hand, gave it a squeeze, and then slipped below the surface.

Trist climbed back up to the console and sat down next to Jill where he explained the plan.

"Think it will work?" Jill asked nervously.

"It's the only chance we've got. That boat can outrun us and outgun us." He looked as the boat got closer and slowed. "And look, there are four of them onboard."

Evangeline worked her way back to the stern. "You are all fools," she said, her voice shrill with panic. "You're letting them get close. Let's go!"

The boat was twenty yards off the starboard beam. The helmsman throttled up a bit, then cut to idle. Throttled up, then cut again. The other three men had their weapons drawn and had them aimed at Trist, Jill, and Evangeline. The boat drifted toward the cruiser. Fifteen yards...Ten yards...

Evangeline turned toward the men on the boat. "Thank God you're here!" She pointed up toward Trist and Jill. "They took me hostage."

"Be quiet, bitch," one of the men said.

Five yards...

Evangeline continued. "You're in danger. There's one in the water!"

The men looked at each other and then down at the water surrounding the boat. Two hands burst out of the lake and grabbed the port rail.

Robin Norris yanked down hard, and the helmsman and another man tumbled overboard while the other two men lost their balance and hit the deck. Robin went back under.

Trist slammed the throttle down and the cabin cruiser launched away.

The helmsman and other man surfaced a few yards away from the boat to see their fellow crew members standing back up onboard.

One of the men onboard said, "We have to go after them."

The helmsman replied back in anger, "No." He looked at the other man in the water. "Let's get the sonofabitch in the water first. He can't be far."

They both dove under.

"They're not following us," Jill shouted to Trist over the sound of the wind blowing against their faces as the cabin cruiser sped through the night water.

Trist looked back. "It should be any second now," he said to Jill. "I'm going to turn us around."

The cruiser slowed, and Trist turned the wheel to port.

Evangeline cried hysterically in the stern but gathered herself enough to shout up, "I'm so sorry. I didn't mean to—why are we going back?!"

"Shut up," Jill said, and then pointed off the bow.

Evangeline ran up forward, and they all focused on the powerboat as Trist eased the throttle forward.

Robin swam to the belt affixed to the powerboat's hull. He reached for the pull rings...

Two arms closed around his legs and his fingers missed the rings. The man held on and tried working his way up to Robin's torso. Robin found the man's eyes and gouged at them. The man let go of his legs and Robin kicked him away.

He went to turn toward the hull when a second person grabbed him from behind. Robin struggled, but the man tightened his arms around Robin's chest and he could not break free with just his good arm. His shoulder wound was getting worse and his lungs ached for air.

He strained to twist his body enough to get a look up at the hull. His effort paid off, and again he could see the grenades hanging from the belt above. He put the remainder of his energy into his legs and kicked.

They rose.

Reaching, he pulled the rings out of the canisters...

...and was brought back down by the man. Then, the second man returned and wrapped his arms around Robin's legs.

Unable to break free, Robin closed his eyes.

Fifty yards out and closing, Trist, Jill, and Evangeline watched as the powerboat exploded.

EPILOGUE

JUNE 1996

—From the Journal of Robin Thomas Norris—

Mom & Family

    This is the most important entry, Trist, but also the one I hoped that I would never have to write. All of my capacities will soon fail me—first the physical, then the mental. Let's get to it. I know the question that has been on your mind for the past few years: Was I the only reason that mom and dad ended up together? At first, yes. Later, no.

    I was part of the generation that still expected a couple to quickly marry and make it work if there was an unexpected pregnancy. Your mom and I fell into line. I can't count the number of times we almost packed it in, but, somehow, we carried on and eventually fell in love with each other. If you look at the statistics, we shouldn't have made it. In fact, most of our friends are getting divorced right now. I could try to list all the reasons we should have failed and all of the reasons we miraculously overcame our shortcomings, but it wouldn't do any good. There is no yellow brick road to follow in marriage. No path. No 'right way.' No answer book to the test. For us—at the root—it came down to only us. However, there are sometimes moments of support from the outside. You're at a disadvantage, and it bothers me; I wanted to be there for you if you ever decided to commit to someone, and I won't be. Your mom will be, though, and that is a good thing. Seek her out. Lean on her experience. Mom has always been the Swiss Army Knife for my life and for our family—resourceful, steady, and founded on one of the things in this world that is never negotiable: quality.

Which brings me to the end of this entry. You and Mom. I know I'm not big on saying things like this in public or in private—just how I'm wired—but I don't want there to be any questions: I love you both, and I will miss this wonderful family. Hence, I have a final Norris Family Standing Order for you, Trist. I know you hate these, and they are laughable at times, but as someone once said, 'Here we are.' The easy part: as a mom, Levana will always be there for you—no matter what. The more challenging part: be there for her as the years go by. Check in with her, let her be a part of your life, help her, love her, and give back. It's hard to see at your age, but don't let this relationship slip.

Trist closed the diary and placed it back on his nightstand. He let the tears come, thinking of his dad. Tomorrow, he was graduating from high school along with one hundred and thirty-one other students ready to take their places in the world machine. He swung his legs over the side of the bed and walked toward his second-story bedroom window.

Tied up smartly to the new dock that he and his Uncle Tyee had put in was the sailboat formerly called *Levity*, which he had re-named *Robin's Nest*. It was past eight p.m., and the sun was almost down on the horizon behind him. The entire beach, dock area, and water were shrouded in blue-gray.

He turned away from the window and headed for the stairs.

"You ready for tomorrow?" his mother said as he entered the kitchen.

"I guess," he said. "I'm going to head out to the boat and check something real quick."

"Everything okay?" she said.

"Yeah, I thought I saw a line coming loose from my bedroom window," he lied. "Just take a minute."

He left out the door and shuffled down the back deck steps. The moon's light was starting to get stronger as the sunset's glow continued to fade behind him.

He stepped onto the dock and bent down to check the aft mooring line just in case his mom was watching him. Then, he boarded the boat and headed below. The salon was tidy; he had removed a portion of the bookshelf, stripped down the wood, and put on fresh coats of varnish a month ago. The mahogany now shined brighter than ever. That wasn't all he had done.

One weekend before that, he and Uncle Tyee had taken Tyee's boat *Magnum* up to Lake Superior and anchored over the plane site. He had watched as Tyee disappeared into the darkness and went down to 200 feet to recover the second bag. His dad had been right about the bag being bulkier: there were twice as many jewels in that bag compared to the first one.

"No one needs to know about these, Tristian," Tyee had said. "Keep them until the time comes to use them."

"I understand what you're saying," Trist had said, "But wouldn't the fair thing be to turn these jewels over too?"

His uncle had been firm. "No. Don't expect life to be fair. Expect ups and downs, triumphs and disappointments, and when you think you've got it figured out, you don't. Your dad more than paid for these that night he saved you. Keep 'em."

When they returned, Tristian had gone to work. On the long side of the bookshelf facing the bulkhead—that couldn't be seen—he had taken special care to carve out a compartment. In the long trough, he placed the jewels. Then, he glued a piece of wood over it and sanded and varnished it until the compartment was unrecognizable. After screwing the section back in, he placed his father's favorite books on the shelf and lined them up tight so that no more could possibly fit.

Sitting at the salon table, he let a wicked grin escape as he gazed at, perhaps, the most expensive bookshelf ever made. His grin died out as he wished that he and his father could have built the shelf together.

The first bag of jewels had been turned over to the authorities along with their stories, especially Evangeline's information regarding the operations up north. Their identities had been protected, and Trist had found it weird to attend school the past year with the knowledge that no one knew what had happened. The Hampstead community thought his father had succumbed to pancreatic cancer in a battle that had been bravely and privately waged. The newspaper announced that Robin Thomas Norris had been cremated and a service was held less than a week after Trist returned home last summer. In fact, the biggest news to come out of Hampstead in the past year was that Gary Hawthorne, owner of The Hawthorne Fish Company, had died suddenly of a heart attack in the fall.

Jill had been taken home by police escort; her parents had immediately looked for someone to sue but found no one. You don't bring suit against the entire narcotics empire (there was a momentary dip in trafficking last summer, but by the fall it had picked back up again). Trist and Jill had been e-mailing each other off and on since the ordeal. She was in law school and couldn't make it for his graduation, but they planned to see each other in another month. Levana was treating them to a week on Nantucket Island.

As far as the cave complex, the Hatteras, and the house on the cliff, the authorities found everything abandoned when they arrived. Granted, it had taken 48 hours to get a team up there, which had given someone enough time to wipe everything clean and escape. They had a description of the man named Sanders, and Trist and Jill had collaborated for the sketch. Even now, he had not been located. The Hatteras had been sold at an auction and was now homeported in Key West. There had been a brief news story about the disappearance of millionaire Grant Livingston—Trist knew better.

As for Evangeline Bertram, Trist knew very little about what had happened after that night. After the horrific and heroic end of his father, Trist had found the sailboat in a hidden cove while traveling south that night. He had rigged *Levity*, and they towed it until they reached the first town. Evangeline had remained quiet, curled up in a bunk below deck, for most of the ride. The last place Trist had seen her was at the small-town police station. At first, they were split up and interviewed separately and then brought together for a grueling 4-hour group interview.

Trist turned out the salon light and went up the companionway steps. He slid the boards into place that covered the aft portion of the entrance and then pulled the hatch cover over until the clasp fit securely over the metal eye coming out of the top board. He ran a padlock through the eye and locked it shut.

Standing up, he closed his eyes and felt the first breeze of a cool Michigan summer night. He inhaled, held the breath, and then exhaled.

He gave *Robin's Nest* a loving pat on the helm as he headed for the dock and then the house to have tea with his mother. Tomorrow was the end of one adventure and the beginning of another.

Beecher Hardware's front door chimed as two customers entered air conditioning, heaven compared to the unusually hot June afternoon. Tyee emerged from the back room behind the register. He was still dressed in a suit after coming back to the store from his nephew's graduation less than an hour ago. There was a small party planned out at his sister's house in another hour, so he had decided to stay dressed up, though he hated it.

"Help you find anything?" Tyee said to the woman. The man had crouched down out of sight a few aisles over.

"No thank you," she said politely and approached. "I'm just here with my husband. New in town."

Tyee went to extend his hand, but it was interrupted by the man's baritone voice.

"Sherry, look at this."

She smiled at Tyee as if to say *I'll be right back* and headed over to the aisle where the man was.

Tyee watched from behind the register as she crouched down. He heard murmuring, and then they both rose up and started walking toward him.

Tyee studied the man. He was a few inches shorter than Tyee, perhaps a few years older but it was hard to tell because the man walked like he had an infinite bundle of energy. He was also dressed and carried himself like a man who was not pretending to be something he was not. His eyes were intense.

The woman extended her hand. "Sherry," she said.

Tyee took it and could tell that the gesture was genuine; he'd had his share of fake handshakes and pleasantries over the years.

She let go of his hand and moved to the side. "And this is my husband—"

"Abner Hutch," the man said and shook Tyee's hand firmly.

"Tyee Beecher," he replied.

"Owner, huh?" Hutch said.

Tyee nodded.

"About time I met a hardware store owner who had his bolts and washers properly labeled and separated." Hutch snickered. "You'll be gettin' my business. Although, I'm not sure about this suit and tie nonsense."

"Nephew's graduation," Tyee said.

"Acceptable answer," Hutch said while rubbing Sherry's back.

She lovingly rolled her eyes. "Don't mind this old salt," she said. "He's got a big heart."

"Hey," Hutch said. "Let's not be sharing the family secrets just yet."

Tyee punched up the washers and bolts on the register. "Secret is safe with me," he said flatly.

Hutch studied Tyee's eyes, then relaxed a bit. "Somehow, I believe you."

AUTHOR'S NOTE

Thank you for reading my book. As an independent author, my success greatly depends on my readers. I know it can be a pain, but I would appreciate it if you could take a moment and leave a quick review (Amazon, BookBub, and/or Goodreads).

If you would like more information on upcoming books, please sign-up for my email list through my website (landonbeachbooks.com) or follow Landon Beach Books on Facebook, Twitter, or Instagram.

If you enjoyed the book, please tell others about it!

As far as *The Sail*...

It's mostly fiction, my friends. However, the *Edmund Fitzgerald* was a real ship with brave men who were lost in a major tragedy. If the *Griffon* is the holy grail of Great Lakes shipwrecks, then the *Edmund Fitzgerald* is the most famous shipwreck, resting in 529 feet of water north of Whitefish Point. Beyond the commemorative and haunting ballad by Gordon Lightfoot, the *Edmund Fitzgerald* will forever be linked to Lake Superior. In fact, whenever I mention Lake Superior to someone, the *Edmund Fitzgerald* is usually one of the first topics that we discuss. Even though the subject occupies only a few pages in this novel, I have tried to recount the tale in a factual and respectful manner. As someone who has been to sea for a living, I know what it is like to put my life in the hands of other capable sailors; I also know what it is like to lose a shipmate. In his book, *The Great Lakes Diving Guide*, author Cris Kohl notes that, "Broken in half, this controversial wreck has been visited by submersibles, but only once by a pair of trimix divers (1995). The wreck victims' families have asked that no further visitations take place to the largest shipwreck in the

Great Lakes" (p.394).   It is this author's hope that these wishes will be respected. A few books that stood out in my research were: *The Great Lakes Diving Guide* and *The 100 Best Great Lakes Shipwrecks, Volume II*, both by Cris Kohl, *Shipwrecks of the Great Lakes*, by Paul Hancock, *Indian Names in Michigan* by Virgil J. Vogel, and, of course, *Hamlet* by William Shakespeare—a play that continues to inform my life with each new reading.

Next up: *The Cabin*.

A Lake Superior-sized thanks to MB, BB, JBx2, EL, and APH who all provided helpful comments on an early draft and to my editor, ED; your perspectives and friendship mean everything to me. To my fans (The Beachreaders), thank you for your support, and I hope *The Sail* delivered. I look forward to entertaining all of you for many years to come. My deepest gratitude to my devoted mom, talented dad, and supportive sister. Finally, I could not have done this without my dedicated wife and two wonderful girls. Your love, emotional sustenance, and encouragement have guided me on this fun journey!

Happy Beach Reading!

L.B.

If you enjoyed *The Sail*, expand your adventure with *The Cabin*, the third book in The Great Lakes series. Here is an excerpt to start the journey.

THE CABIN

Landon Beach

PROLOGUE

BERLIN, DECEMBER 2005 – PART I

The spy was late. CIA Officer Jennifer Lear sat inside a toasty café drinking a cappuccino, *Die Welt* open in front of her. She was at a table for two against the front window and right next to the door. Outside, the snow fell as if there was an unlimited supply, and Berliners wearing dark heavy overcoats and knitted hats made their way along the Kurfürstendamm. She felt a hint of sympathy for her partner who was outside weathering the freezing temperature a block away. A feigned yawn and stretch gave her the opportunity to glance at the clock on the wall above a booth with two loud Germans arguing over a game of chess. 7:02 p.m. Her agent, Sari, had never been late, which would give Lear the grounds to call off the meeting right now. But, Sari would be doing a surveillance detection run, and the weather might be slowing her down. Lear and her partner had decided on a 5-minute window. Sari now had 3.

She moved her toes up and down inside her hiking boots. Her feet were sore from her own hour-long surveillance detection run with her partner, performed to make sure that no one was following them before she entered the café. First, they had driven around for a half an hour to spot anyone tailing their car. Then, she had gotten out and started to walk while he parked the car up the street in front of a bookstore. As soon as he exited the car, a third officer emerged from the store, took the keys from him, and drove the car out of the city. For the next half hour, Lear had strolled the shopping district while her partner followed from a distance.

The door chimed, and Lear took a sip of her cappuccino to see who had entered. Damn. It was a heavyset grandmother with a scarf over her mouth. The woman shut the door behind her and moved toward the café's bar. Lear set her cup down. *Where was her agent?*

CIA Officer Brian Turner shivered beneath his wool coat. The wind whipped against the snow on the ground, dusting it up like a snow blower and then scattering the flakes in a narrow blast pattern. He crossed the street and began to look in store windows. He pondered, he nodded, he abruptly stopped and acted like the deal he saw advertised on the storefront was too good to be true, and he kept watch on his surroundings to make sure that nothing interfered with Officer Lear's meeting. He had last seen their agent at the rendezvous six months ago, and he wondered what information she would have for them this time.

The corner of the awning above the storefront he was currently "browsing" gave way, dumping a pile of snow directly on his neck and coat collar. As he brushed the snow off with his gloved hands, some of it slipped under his shirt and ran down his back—*Jesus, it was cold.* The summer meetings were much more pleasant. Why did he keep getting assigned to winter meetings? Lear only handled one summer meeting and one winter meeting a year; the rest of the time she was probably at her cover job or working as an analyst at Langley. He was stationed in France, which made it easy for him to accompany her to Berlin. They were posing as tourists for a week and were being treated to all Berlin had to offer: the Gendarmenmarkt, the Brandenburg Gate, the Reichstag, the Berlin

Television Tower, the Berlin Cathedral, Museum Island, and the Berlin Wall Memorial and Documentation Centre. Then, on a pre-arranged day and time, they would meet up with their agent. The usual protocol called for Lear to live in Berlin under the cover of some state job at the U.S. Embassy. Once the CIA had an agent for her to run, she would coordinate all of the meetings using classic tradecraft—dead drops, chalk markings, the opening of a window at a certain time, etc. But in the last decade, this had become more difficult to pull off since most foreign countries now watched *every* employee of the embassy. Updated techniques were needed to effectively run agents and gather intelligence. Using officers once or twice a year for the face-to-face meetings had proved effective. The Berlin station personnel would set up the meetings, but when the meetings actually took place, known officers were followed and unknown officers like Lear and Turner were not—allowing them to slide into a café or take a stroll in a park to meet with their agent. They would exchange money and other items for information, forward it to the Berlin office, then go on acting as tourists for a few more days.

Turner entered a store directly across from the café. The warmth inside restored him. He took off his gloves, smiled at a salesperson, and meandered through an aisle of clothes until he was facing the window. He could see Lear sitting at the table. The other chair was empty. Something was wrong.

He turned toward a rack of men's coats and picked up the sleeve of one to study the price tag, which also gave him an opportunity to glance at his watch. 7:04. Four minutes late. If Sari didn't show in one minute, they would leave. A no-show agent was a pain because of the time devoted to the meeting's set up, communication, and surveillance detection run, but it didn't necessarily mean that anything was wrong. Perhaps the agent was being followed and had to abort. Not a problem, they'd set up another meeting. But still...

He let the coat sleeve go and gave the street a quick survey as if to check the conditions outside. The snow continued to pour from the sky as shoppers walked the Kurfürstendamm. The agent was nowhere in sight. Less than a minute left. He felt uneasy.

Officer Lear finished her cappuccino and dabbed a napkin across her lips. Convinced that her agent was not going to show up, she started to slide her chair back away from the table. It had only moved a few inches when the door to the café opened and Sari entered.

Lear bent down and tightened the laces on both of her hiking boots. The floor looked like it hadn't been swept in months, and the snow tracked in had turned the dirt into a wet grime. She sat up. Placing her elbows on the table top, she rested her chin on her hands and stared out the window disinterestedly as if she'd be there to pass another hour.

Sari joined her at the table.

"Guten Abend," Lear said, still looking out the window.

Sari affectionately rubbed Lear's right arm. "Alles klar."

Lear turned her head and released a smile. "Ja, alles klar, danke." She took out a handkerchief and surveyed the café as she wiped her nose. Nothing seemed out of place, and no one was paying attention to them. Lear put the handkerchief back in her pocket.

Sari had spotted the folded newspaper on the table. After a pause, she laid her large purse next to the paper and began to search the middle pocket with her left hand. With precision and timing, she slid her right hand between the folded sections of *Die Welt*, as if to stabilize the purse, and then removed it, joining her other hand in the search of her purse's contents.

Lear pretended to be annoyed with Sari's searching until Sari finally pulled out a pack of gum. Lear's face said: *about time.*

Sari offered her a stick, which was accepted, then took one out for herself.

Lear said, "Danke," and put the green piece of gum into her mouth while Sari placed her purse on the floor. Lear slid the newspaper into her backpack with her right hand. With her left hand, she took a small cookie tin out of her coat pocket and placed it inside Sari's purse. The tin was filled with cash. When they had started exchanging information, Sari had asked for more specific items—an original Michael Jackson Thriller record, two cartons of Treasurer cigarettes, a Gucci scarf—but now she just wanted cash.

"Bitte schön."

Lear relaxed. The Berlin exchanges were always quick, and the signal that everything was fine was communicating in simple German phrases that any tourist would know. If there was anything wrong and they needed to split, Lear was to say a long sentence in English, and, if there was anything wrong on Sari's end, she was to say a lengthy sentence in German. Lear didn't know why Sari was late, but she was convinced that, whatever the reason, all was well. She made eye contact with her agent and then, using her right index finger, rubbed her watch face in two slow circles.

Sari patted Lear's arm. It was time to get going.

Lear rose from the table and pushed in her chair. She said, "Gute Nacht."

"Bis dann," Sari replied.

Lear put on her backpack and headed for the door. The two Germans playing chess had escalated their insults as Lear slid by their booth. She pulled on the door handle and heard, "Wir fahren morgen mit dem Zug nach Hamburg, wenn ich dich wider sehe, lieber Freund." *We'll take the train to Hamburg tomorrow when I see you back here, dear friend.*

Lear looked over at Sari, gave her a nod, and then exited the café.

Outside, she noticed Turner leaning against a lamppost across the street. After tilting her head back and looking at the sky, as if pondering whether to venture out or head back inside, she took a pair of reading glasses out of her right coat pocket, examined them, and then put them in her left pocket.

* * *

Turner's heart started to beat faster, and his situational awareness became even more acute. Lear had just signaled him that something was wrong. But what was it? It appeared that the meeting had gone smoothly; it definitely hadn't been rushed. Surely, Sari would have signaled trouble as soon as she entered the café, but the two had sat down like old friends. Had Lear seen something after the meeting? He put his hand inside his coat and felt the handle of his 9mm. He slid his fingers down the barrel and felt the silencer attached—the pockets were extra-large to accommodate the handgun. At the same time, his eyes swiveled left and right, then up and across the rooftops. Nothing seemed out of place. He looked through the café window. Sari sat, reading a paperback. She seemed in no hurry.

His eyes met Lear's, and she turned left out of the café. This was the direction they had agreed upon if there was danger. He let her get a block ahead and then began to follow. In another block, he would cross the street and—

There. A man wearing a driver's cap and carrying a shopping bag from an upscale clothing store entered the sidewalk from an alley. He took a little too much time searching the crowd of fellow shoppers until he spotted and began to follow Lear. Trouble.

Turner kept his eyes on the man. After a few paces, the man made a second mistake and turned his head to the right, keeping it fixed for a moment in the direction of another man who was across the street. The second man was half-a-block ahead of Turner and walked with a smooth, confident stride. He had on a black overcoat with a scarlet scarf, and his mop of salt and pepper hair blew in the wind.

Then, the second man veered off the sidewalk and entered a store; the other man continued to follow Lear. Turner saw his opportunity and crossed the street, cycling his eyes between Lear, the man following her, and the storefront where the second man had disappeared. As he passed the store, he did not see the man inside, but he only had a second to scan. There was no time to double check, and he could not reveal himself by stopping and looking in the storefront window. He focused his attention solely on Lear.

From a corner inside the store, the man with the overcoat and red scarf watched his fellow agent follow the woman. He waited an entire minute until they were far away down the sidewalk. He approached the window and scanned both sides of the street. Confident that he had not been seen or followed, he exited the store and headed back toward the café.

Turner began to close the distance between himself and the man following Lear. Up ahead was an apartment complex, and if he could walk past both of them like he was in a hurry to get somewhere, then he could warn her. It was his only chance. He sped up.

Lear saw the apartment complex looming two blocks away. Should she dart into the main office, take an elevator up, walk all the way down the hall, take the stairs down, and then exit out the rear entrance? It was a simple evasion technique, and they had discussed it last week when they arrived and again this morning. She wasn't sure if she was being followed, but Turner wouldn't be far behind. He would join her in the building and they would go from there. The one thing she could not do was turn arou—

"Apartment plan," a voice said next to her, and before she could turn her head, she saw Turner running past her. Ten yards ahead, she saw him look at his watch, shake his head, and then swear loudly in German. He continued to run—past the apartment complex, past another store, and across the next intersection.

Now she knew something was wrong. Twenty yards until the entrance of the apartment complex. She maintained discipline, never speeding up or looking around, and her hiking boots continued to crunch though the freshly fallen snow.

Ten yards.

She put her hand inside her coat pocket and fingered her own 9mm with silencer attached—she hadn't fired a gun since the range, right before she left the United States for the mission. She had never fired at a human being before.

She reached the double glass doors and entered the apartment building. Then, she picked up her pace and strode toward the elevator—same luck! The doors were just about to close. She slid her hand between the doors, and they opened. An elderly German couple frowned; she apologized. The doors closed, and she saw the 11th floor's button was lit. The elevator started to climb; she pushed the button for floor 3.

Turner watched as the man followed Lear into the apartment complex. Then, he stepped away from the outdoor restaurant table he had slid behind and scooted around the space heater before heading back toward the apartment complex's back door where he would take the stairs up to meet her.

Lear exited the elevator and made her way swiftly down the long hallway. At the far end was a door with the sign reading "Ausgang" above it that led to the stairwell. Almost clear. She would go down the stairs, out the back door, and head straight for the waiting car, which would be two blocks away. She knew the car would be there because if everything had gone as planned, they would have already been picked up on the other end of the Kurfürstendamm; her team would have switched to the alternate pick-up location immediately when she and Officer Turner hadn't shown up. She continued to hustle toward the door.

* * *

Turner entered the stairwell and was already on the second flight when he heard the door below crash open. He looked down and saw three men with guns drawn enter the building. They saw him and started racing up the stairs. Then, he heard something that made his insides turn: They were shouting at each other—in Russian. He ran up the last flight to the door numbered 3.

Lear grinned as she moved to within ten feet of the stairwell door. *Piece of cake.* Then, the door burst open. It was Turner.

"Run!" He said.

She stopped, confused. "Brian—"

"Now!"

She turned and sprinted away down the hall.

STATE HIGHWAY 250, NEW YORK
THURSDAY, JUNE 29, 2006

"We're almost to our little bungalow, babycakes," Iggi Hilliard said to his wife as he tapped his fingers on the steering wheel. "Gonna seduce your ass before our company arrives."

Maria Hilliard's large sunglasses stayed focused on the *People* magazine she held in her hands. "Keep dreamin'," she said. "Plus, you just got some last night, and you're lucky you got that." She grinned. "Don't you need a few days to recover?"

He started to roll up his window.

"No," Maria said. "I like to feel the breeze while we drive by the lake."

"C'mon. A little AC, please? It's hot out and not even 9am."

"No," came the final answer behind the magazine.

He rolled his window back down and then observed his reflection in the rearview mirror. His brown forehead was dotted with perspiration, and the black hair that rose four inches from his scalp became wet as he wiped the sweat from his forehead through his hair. His thick full beard was helping to hide the tell-tale signs of weight gain on cheeks and neck. Monday nights filled with beer and snacks at the bowling alley followed by all of the goodies each press box included during football weekends hadn't helped. His playing days were long gone, but now he got to do the next best thing: get paid to watch games, get fed free, mostly delicious, food while he watched and took notes, mingle with prime-time coaches and players and sometimes interview them, and then write it all up for the *Democrat and Chronicle*. "So my thirty-three-year-old body doesn't look like Donovan McNabb's anymore," he said. "I recover just fine."

Maria let out a giggle, "You're damn right it doesn't. You've got your own bowling ball starting to form." The wind blew through her black wavy hair. "This air is heaven."

Iggi took his left hand from the steering wheel and began to rub his belly, which, he had to admit, was out over his pants and close to the wheel. He was sitting though; when he stood up, it all evened out. At least that's what he told himself. "Didn't you notice last night, how I used this to my advantage? It kept my rhythm smooth like a pendulum." He pointed to his gut. "This thing is a weapon."

She dismissed his argument with, "Uh huh," and kept flipping through her magazine.

The road curved to the left, and the trees began to thin out as lakeside houses began to sprout up. Beyond the properties, Lake Ontario was a sheen of cobalt. A few triangles of canvas were spread out on the water like signposts on a road that stretched in every direction. *You'd never get me on a sailboat.* Too slow. Too boring. Too much work. Powerboat or nothing. Slam the throttle down and let's go already.

Maria put the magazine back in her tote bag.

Shoot. She's going to start talking about the weekend.

She looked past him at the lake. "I can't wait for you to meet Cal."

"How come I've never met him before?"

"Well, he's been a little busy since 9/11, don't you think?"

Right. He was a cop. A Detroit cop. "I forgot," Iggi said.

"Well, he's my friend," she said. "So be nice."

"I can't promise that," said Iggi. "He's got to prove himself."

"Why?"

"I can't believe you're asking me that."

She took off her glasses and looked out her window at the passing road signs. "I'm sorry," she said. "I promise he's good."

Iggi exhaled. What does *good* even mean? "We'll see."

She gave his right forearm a quick rub and then put her glasses back on. "Haley isn't seeing anyone right now."

Man, she switches topics fast—always has. "The birthday girl is single, huh?"

"Ridiculous, right? But she's so introverted, I don't see how she's ever going to meet anyone," she said. "I mean, I'm her one friend at school, and if I didn't go down to have lunch with her once a week, I think she'd just stay in her physics lab and no one would ever see her."

Iggi rubbed his beard as he thought. He'd been distracted the past few weeks going back and forth with his editor on the phone over the book manuscript. The editor wasn't pleased with what he had called the 'nuclear missiles' Iggi had shot in the opening chapter about the culture of losing in the Detroit Lions's locker room and the irony of a fierce man-eating lion serving as the franchise logo. The editor was also unsure of the title: *Not with a Roar but a*

Whimper: Three Decades of Ineptitude. He wondered why Iggi didn't write a book about the Bills instead—at least they *had gone* to the Super Bowl four times in a row. Iggi had replied, "New York is where I make my living, Robert, but Detroit is where I'm from. I don't shit where I eat." Anyway, he hadn't had time to think of this weekend—let alone the guest list—until they were getting into the car.

Usually, they invited Maria's college roommate and her husband to stay with them over the July Fourth weekend, but the couple was unavailable. Like the professional athletes he covered, Iggi liked routine. Maria liked to say he needed someone to give him a routine. Left to his own devices, without some game or season to prepare for, his daily journey became unpredictable and inefficient. Now, he was being asked to help host two people he didn't know. Of all years, why did the Fourth have to be on a Tuesday this year? That meant that the guests would be arriving on Friday and departing on Wednesday. In sports parlance this was like playing man-on-man defense for the entire season and suddenly being asked to play zone defense in the championship game—and the championship game was going to take three overtime periods to decide. And why *these* two people? Well, he could somewhat understand Maria's invitation to Cal. Some childhood bonds lasted a lifetime. But Haley? The quiet-as-a-mouse math and physics teacher whom he had seen only once? Twice? Anyway, the last time had been at a bar last year during a boring end-of-the-year faculty get together, which he had escaped by inventing a work emergency while using the restroom and then delivering his lines with feigned regret and surprise to the huddled group of worn out teachers.

Great. A Detroit cop and Haley. Wait a minute.

"I know what you're up to," he said, giving the steering wheel a tap like a coach giving a player a pat on the butt for a good play.

"And what is that?" Maria said.

"You're at it again. Trying to play matchmaker with our guests."

Maria picked up her plastic cup of Starbucks iced coffee and took a sip through the straw. "We'll just have to find out about that."

"Jesus," Iggi said. "Is that all this weekend is? Some booty call?" He paused. "Are you sure Steve and Val can't make it?"

"Let it go," she said.

Iggi shook his head in frustration. "I just want it to be like it always is. Besides, you're leaving me in another week to go 'teach for America' for a month. Can't we have one summer where someone else goes and helps the damn kids?"

"Not a chance. I need my time away doing the Lord's work."

"What about when we have kids? Will you leave then?"

She grinned. "So, now you're thinking about us having kids again?"

"Anything to get my mind off this weekend. I really don't wanna hang with new people."

"You know my girl is beautiful, but her life is so damn boring! I've gotta get her out of her funk. Being with us and meeting Cal will be a good thing. And Cal? His divorce was finalized this past fall, so he's back in the game."

Iggi cracked a smile.

She took another sip of her coffee and then set it down. "What?"

"You know you make my ass weak when you use sports to describe life," he said. "This weekend is going to be a disaster."

"It's going to be fine." Maria checked her watch. "Besides, tonight is all ours."

Their SUV climbed up a hill and then started down the other side. At the bottom, the woods thickened around them as the road curved away from the lake.

Maria's family had immigrated to the United States from Cuba over one hundred years ago, initially settling in Tampa, Florida, before moving north.

The towering log cabin had been in her family for three generations, set in the middle of three wooded beachfront lots, and had been constructed by her grandfather Miguel Ernesto Torres in the spring of 1961 after Kennedy's narrow election win, for which Torres had helped get out the vote and was compensated with manila envelopes stuffed with cash. As a fellow World War II veteran and Roman Catholic, Torres had wept tears of joy when it was announced that Kennedy had won, and he had wept tears of sorrow when it was announced that JFK had been shot and killed in Dallas. These were the only times that Maria's father had ever witnessed his father cry, and it had become a family legend—brought up, quietly shared, and then passed down within the log walls of the cabin: "El padre dos veces lloró"—the two times father cried.

Miguel Torres had wanted a home for his family that would serve as its heart—a pulsating center where celebrations would be held, yet also a sanctuary that would sustain them through life's challenges. However, he had warned that the physical structure alone would never sustain them. 'A house on the beach does not solve any of life's problems,' he had said. What would sustain them was gathering at the cabin and drawing strength from each other. This had been his vision, and the house he had built for it was also an architectural masterpiece.

The log home's great room had floor to ceiling windows that allowed for a sublime sight of Lake Ontario, and there were three bedrooms upstairs all with lake views. Besides the great room on the first floor was a den, kitchen, walk-in pantry, and dining room. The addition had been built in 1987 and included a first-floor master suite, entertainment room, wine cellar, and sun room.

Her grandparents were gone, and the house now belonged to her parents. But they lived in Boston and rarely used it, whereas Maria and Iggi lived only an hour away from the cabin and spent almost every weekend there. Some weekends Iggi would be away covering sports, and she would have time to herself. She rarely had company as her younger brother and his family didn't like the water and had no interest in visiting what had been the family's rallying point for forty years. They were in Boston too, and, as much as her two nephews loved Aunt Maria and Uncle Iggi, they had been spoiled—ruined?—by the fast pace of Boston compared to the solitude of the cabin. If her grandfather had still been alive, then he might have cried a third time knowing this. Friends? There had been a few teacher retreats there, but those had tapered off when her colleagues started having children. The advance from Iggi's book had provided them with enough money to buy the house from her parents. Maria suspected they would be willing to part with it because there were good memories there, but too many echoes whenever they visited. Perhaps because she was another generation removed, she didn't have her grandparents' presence haunting her down the hallways, up and down the staircase, or in every doorway. Her father wasn't an emotional man, but she knew it hurt too much for him to be there with his parents gone.

The woods surrounding the cabin extended for fifty yards toward the road and around thirty yards to the right and left. The neighbors had not sold their extra lots. The houses could not be seen; only by sitting on their beach or swimming were they aware that they had neighbors, and that was only if the neighbors emerged from their residences or had company. The closest town was Bay Harbor—five miles away and far enough to make it a pain if an item had been left off the grocery list by accident. While sitting on the back deck looking out at Lake Ontario in complete silence, she often thought that if there was ever a stretch of property for a celebrity to disappear from the spotlight, this was it. She teased Iggi that he needed this place to hide when angry fans read his honest column every week. He joked back that if the Lions fans ever found the cabin, they might burn it down.

Her routine during the past school year had become more of a Friday countdown every week—watching the clock like the students until the final bell rang. After trying to convince young 12th grade minds that books like *Beloved* and *One Hundred Years of Solitude* should be cherished and pondered, she would exit the brick fortress moments after the bell and speed out of the school's back lot. It took fifteen minutes to navigate the city traffic until she hit State Highway 250. Once on 250, it was just under an hour to reach the grocery store in Bay Harbor where she'd stock up for the weekend and then travel the final miles to her getaway. If the weather permitted, she would lower the windows and turn up the radio. She wished a nurse could be sitting in the passenger seat taking her blood pressure at that exact moment.

Iggi parked the car in the handicapped spot closest to the big doors that welcomed shoppers into Danny's Market. From the glovebox, he removed a white and blue press pass encased in plastic with a black lanyard wrapped around it. He unwound the lanyard, found the knot he had tied to shorten the length, and then used it to hang the press pass from his rearview mirror.

"Cha Ching," Iggi said.

"You're ridiculous."

Iggi whistled the theme to Monday Night Football as they exited the vehicle. "If a cop happens to drive by, it looks just like a permit."

Maria adjusted the purse strap on her right shoulder. "How long have you been doing this?"

Iggi patted his round stomach. "Ever since this little guy started to form."

Maria peered around the parking lot, expecting a patrol car to pull up any minute and arrest them. The lot was quiet. "Let's get this done," she said, pushing his hand away as he tried to hold hers.

Iggi shivered as they crossed through the A/C boundary and approached the grocery carts. His hands hovered over a cart's handles.

"Oh, C'mon!" Maria said and grasped the handles.

Iggi pulled his feet back just in time to avoid them getting run over. "Shit's cold in here," he said.

Recently, 'Beer Caves' had started to sprout up in gas stations across the country, and Iggi got a kick out of going in and freezing his ass off for a minute while grabbing cold beer—*nothing* beat cold beer—and watching his breath escape into the atmosphere. But Beer-Cave temperatures in a grocery story? Guy must be paying a fortune to keep the place cool.

"Let's *go*," said Maria, looking back at him.

They made their way down the familiar aisles with Maria maneuvering the cart around other shoppers like a racecar driver. *She's worried about my press pass being used to park in handicapped parking. Such a rule follower. Relax, girl.*

He walked alongside the cart and nodded as items like steak, hamburgers, hotdogs, chicken, and bratwurst got added to the cart. *Hell, yes. Time to grill. Thank God Maria tackled everything else in the kitchen.*

She threw in spaghetti, garlic bread, Caesar salad, potato salad, baked beans, macaroni salad, Ruffles potato chips, pickles, lunch meat, bread, onions, mushrooms, bacon, eggs, ingredients for homemade waffles, a massive bag of Dunkin' Donuts coffee (his favorite), vanilla ice cream, and—his eyes got greedy—ingredients for Maria's special raspberry pie.

They turned the corner and went down the final aisle—drinks.

Non-negotiables first: He lifted two cases of Bud Light and a 12-pack of Pepsi (Coke could go to hell) into the cart, while Maria put in a 12-pack of Diet Pepsi and directed him to load up two cases of bottled water.

They paused. "Now, what wine should we go with?" Maria said.

"Don't tell me they're wine snobs," said Iggi. "This is the Fourth of July; beer is where it's at."

She rolled her eyes and walked past him.

"What? Am I right or am I right?"

She picked up two bottles of merlot and two bottles of chardonnay and put them in the cart. "It's what our *guests* want that is important. Cal will drink beer with you, but the wine will go with dinner."

"There isn't a thing in this cart that beer doesn't go with."

"Waffles?"

"Watch me," Iggi said.

She looked at their full cart. "Let's check out and head next door."

"What's next door?"

"Dorne's Liquor Store. Cal likes Scotch and Haley and I are having Margaritas on the beach." She maneuvered the cart around a young couple arguing over a bottle of wine. 'It doesn't finish well.' 'Not enough body.' 'They've probably never even tasted a Malbec.' *Christ.*

Iggi shook his head. "I thought you said he'd have beer with me."

They reached the end of the aisle. "He will," she said over her shoulder. Seeing the coast was clear, she crossed the main aisle and arrived at the checkout counter. Iggi took a *Sports Illustrated* off the rack and put it in; Maria grabbed *People*, *Bazaar*, and *Redbook*.

"These won't be around too much longer will they?" Iggi said looking down at the magazines.

"I'm afraid not," Maria said.

Iggi started loading items onto the register's conveyor belt. "Want me to go next door while you pay?"

She searched her purse for the checkbook. "No, let's go together."

"What were you thinking for dinner tonight?" He said while hoisting one of the cases of Bud Light out from underneath the cart's basket.

"I was thinking about a spinach smoothie."

Iggi's eyes narrowed. "What?"

She pinched his arm. "Just kidding. How about we pick up pizza and wings from Miss J's?"

He picked up the second case of Bud. "Now you're talkin'."

They exited Dorne's Liquor store and headed for the SUV. The sun was rising higher and the muggy heat was suffocating.

"What was all that shit about single malt versus blend the owner was talking about in there?" Iggi asked, pushing their overflowing cart.

Maria held a side of the cart with one hand and a black plastic bag containing the scotch, tequila, and margarita mix in her other hand. "I don't know," she said. "Just that the single malt was better or something."

"It sure was more expensive," he replied. "What in the hell does that guy know? And since when do people introduce themselves by giving their age and middle name?"

When the towering figure had approached them in the store, Iggi had momentarily slipped into his sports reporter character and asked if he had ever played football.

The man had rubbed his beard—every bit as big as Iggi's—and said, "No. In my forty-seven years of life, I've stayed away."

Maria said, "Great, Mister—" and searched for a nametag.

"Rick Gregory Dorne at your service," he said.

"Okay, Mister Do—"

"Rick," he cut her off.

She nodded. "We're in need of a little help selecting a bottle of scotch for a friend."

With his hands behind his back, the right wrist held by the left hand, Rick thoughtfully nodded and said, "If I'm asked."

Iggi and Maria looked at each other and then back at Rick. "Um, you're asked," she said impatiently. "What should we get?"

This was the wrong question to ask. Rick went on a three-minute-long history of scotch peppered with bar war stories of him drinking particular brands of scotch until closing time at hole-in-the-wall establishments in New Jersey. It was, "I'm an old bar horse myself—grew up in 'em," and "I know my way around a bar stool," followed by, "It was three against one, and I kicked all their asses." His last tale ended in a wide grin and the triumphant declaration, "I *know* how to navigate a bar." Simultaneously, he placed a seventy-five-dollar bottle of The Macallan in Maria's hands. Iggi had watched, mesmerized. Rick had placed his hands behind his back once again and said, "A Detroit cop...Yeah, in my humble opinion, he'll love this, darlin'."

"You have got to be kidding me!" Iggi shouted as they neared the vehicle.

"Uh huh," Maria said. "And *you're* payin' for it."

Underneath the driver side windshield wiper blade was a yellow ticket.

ABOUT THE AUTHOR

Landon Beach lives in the Sunshine State with his wife, two children, and their golden retriever. He previously served as a Naval Officer and is currently an educator by day and an author by night. Find out more at landonbeachbooks.com.

CPSIA information can be obtained
at www.ICGtesting.com
Printed in the USA
LVHW011912190721
693094LV00003B/416